the
girl
and
the
grove

girl
and
the
grove

ERIC SMITH

Mendota Heights, Minnesota

First Edition
First Printing, 2018

Book design by Jake Nordby
Cover design by Jake Nordby
Cover images by dmbaker/iStockphoto; André Cook/Pexels; 123dartist/Shutterstock
Interior images by Christopher Urie (page 189); Mikey Ilagan (page 362)

Flux, an imprint of North Star Editions, Inc.

Library of Congress Cataloging-in-Publication Data
Names: Smith, Eric (Eric A.), author.
Title: The girl and the grove / Eric Smith.
Description: First edition. | Mendota Heights, Minnesota : Flux, 2018. |
    Summary: "Adopted teen Leila discovers that her connection to nature and passion for environmental activism are part of her unique and magical genetic makeup, and a grove of trees that holds a mythical secret"–
    Provided by publisher.
Identifiers: LCCN 2017055585 (print) | LCCN 2018001150 (ebook) | ISBN
    9781635830194 (hosted e-book) | ISBN 9781635830187 (pbk. : alk. paper)
Subjects: | CYAC: Identity–Fiction. | Adoption–Fiction. | Environmental
    protection–Fiction. | Dryads–Fiction. | Magic–Fiction.
Classification: LCC PZ7.1.S633 (ebook) | LCC PZ7.1.S633 Gir 2018 (print) |
    DDC [Fic]–dc23
LC record available at https://lccn.loc.gov/2017055585

Flux
North Star Editions, Inc.
2297 Waters Drive
Mendota Heights, MN 55120
www.fluxnow.com

Printed in the United States of America

For every kid who's been asked
"Where are you from?"
and had a tough time answering.

And as always, for Nena.

I

Lightning split the willow in two, and the voices in Leila's head shattered.

The smell of burnt bark and charred leaves lingered in the air as Leila stepped into her new family's backyard, closing the large, plate-glass patio door behind her. She walked briskly towards the willow tree, gritting her teeth, as the voices screamed with the roaring wind. She stepped over some of the branches and tiny fires on the ground, still smoldering like little candles scattered about the earth. With the ruined tree in front of her, she reached out and brushed her fingers where the lightning had made its cut.

The heat from the crack scorched her fingertips, and she pulled back quickly as the voices, which usually whispered in her head, let out another roaring, anguished cry.

With closed eyes, she shook her head, pressing them to go away. Taking deep breaths, Leila focused on what felt real around her, a routine she'd been running through all her life, one she and Sarika had developed together at the group home when the voices came. Say the words. Get present. Be here.

"Grass," she whispered, pacing her breath as the voices faded. "Rain. Wind. Cold."

As the voices pulled back into the depths of her mind, as they always did, she looked back up at the ruined tree.

Gone was the cool-to-the-touch bark, a dark brown spotted with slightly darker specks. It had a pattern that she saw a little of herself in; her brown skin freckled in the warmer weather just the same way. Patches of the bark were discolored in places where a piece peeled away, revealing the lighter colors underneath. Her freckles came in little bursts on her face, her shoulder, her forearm, and the larger splash of cream on the right side of her face: a birthmark.

What bark wasn't burnt off by the crackling electricity that had ripped through the tree was seared crisp, and bits of black soot came off on her fingers when she ran her hands along the surface. Instead of the welcoming, thick, V-shaped branches that grew close enough to grasp simultaneously, like two fingers waving a peace sign, there was only one branch now. She had spent so many afternoons this summer reading and reflecting on those branches, and now one sprawled out on the ground amidst burned grass and shrubbery. The once-beautiful limb looked as though it had roasted in a campfire pit, the bark like burnt, discarded charcoal, and the end where it once connected with the willow replaced with blackened, splintered wood. She looked up from the split to the rest of the tree, which still bloomed bright green, as though the other half of the old willow was unaware of what had happened.

It broke Leila's heart.

Her willow was dead, but the rest of the tree didn't know it yet.

But maybe there was a way to save it. If she couldn't do it, maybe an arborist, one of those tree doctors she'd seen posting on the Urban Ecovists board she frequented with Sarika, or in articles on various local environmental news sites. She'd read that one had recently gone into Clark Park in West Philadelphia to help save a rare American Chestnut tree, which was definitely news to Leila. Who knew *any* kind of chestnuts were endangered?

She walked over to the half of the tree that was sprawled out on the earth and searched for any remaining bits of green, twigs that were unscathed from the lightning, but quickly turned her attention back to the still-standing section of the willow. She reached up and touched a low-hanging branch, bracing herself for the voices to come. They stayed silent, the bark still cool and wet.

"Okay," Leila said, exhaling. "Let's do this."

She took a few steps back and took a running jump to grip the slick branch, grabbing it hard, her hands slipping a bit but holding firm. She kicked herself up off the broken trunk and wrapped herself around a thick limb.

She climbed up, inching her way quickly despite how wet the surface was. She could feel the rain that the hurricane had brought soaking into her jeans and t-shirt, and the fabric clung to her skin as she shimmied on up. The cold, eye-of-the-storm winds chilled her as she pushed forward, yet she smiled, a girl on a mission.

She was thinking of Sarika and Major Oak.

Back in the group home, she'd worked her way through a heaping majority of the limited library. It consisted mostly of classics donated by well-meaning liberal arts graduates of one of the nearby universities, probably Temple or St. Joseph's, who apparently never spoke to one another about their donations. The result was several stacks of the same exact book again and again, likely from finished English literature courses, which irritated some of the other children and teens who came through the place.

But Leila didn't mind the collections. It gave her an excuse to try and form book clubs with the other kids in the house. Including Sarika. Four years back, when Sarika had arrived at the home on the same day as a massive stack of Jamie Ford's *Hotel on the Corner of Bitter and Sweet* (likely donated from some first-year college English class), they quietly read copies together on the home's way-too-soft couch. Sarika only stopped to cry a little every few chapters.

"So," Sarika had said, closing the book as it grew dark outside. "What else you got here?"

They'd been inseparable ever since.

Leila drew closer to the top of the large willow, where branches burst this way and that, pushing out and then plummeting down under the weight of the long, green leaves. She thought fondly of the first book club she'd put together with Sarika back in the home.

Some students had dropped off a stack of Alexandre Dumas's *Prince of Thieves*, and another failed foster family had left Leila back at the home the same day. Leila found solace in the pages, holed up with Sarika and their books. But when stories of made-up families and their adventures failed, she sought out words about her own family in the only place she could.

The Internet.

With every near miss and failed family came the searching: on Google, adoption message boards, and anywhere else she could think of.

"Why do you do this? What are you hoping to find?" Sarika would ask, flicking back her thick, black hair before crossing her arms, her heavy eyebrows furrowed. "Ambiguously brown couple dies in tragic train derailment, but not before bequeathing millions of dollars to the daughter they put up for adoption so many years ago. Leila Hetter, please come to City Hall to collect your inheritance and the deeds to your four mansions."

"Well," Leila had started with a laugh.

"Here, I'll show you something better to strive for," Sarika had said that day, nudging Leila away from the computer and taking over the search.

"Major Oak," she'd typed.

It turned out Robin Hood's hideout, Major Oak, was in fact a real tree, one still growing in the actual Sherwood Forest. That had begun a tradition of entering the annual lottery to claim a sapling from Major Oak. Each year Sarika and Leila waited in front of the computer at their group home or in the Philadelphia Public Library, watching the clock count down, signing up to win a baby tree during the limited time frame.

They never won, which Leila thought was probably

for the best, considering the cost of the saplings and the fact that a tree wasn't going to thrive in their group home. Hell, the *kids* hardly did. But it did bring the girls closer together.

Leila sat up, her legs holding on tight to the willow's remaining limb, and snapped some smaller twigs and sticks off one of the branches. She checked each one as she pulled them back, making sure the inside still revealed signs of life, bright green over the white wood. Once she'd gathered a small bundle, she let them go and watched them fall to the ground. A few stragglers clicked softly against the tree's branches as they worked their way down, and one or two got stuck in the hanging leaves.

Once back on the ground, she gathered up the twigs and shook them to get the rain off before she brought them into the house.

"Leila!" a familiar voice shouted. She looked up to spot Jon, her foster-parent-now-newly-adoptive-parent, running towards her. The small fires around the yard had since petered out in the soft rain, wisps of smoke barely visible in the growing dawn.

"Careful, there's a lot of branches on the ground!" Leila shouted, holding the small twigs close to her chest.

"*Me* be careful?" Jon scoffed. "You get in here! The storm is going to pick back up any minute! What were you thinking?"

Leila hustled towards the house with Jon, and when they reached the door, he put a supportive hand on her shoulder as she walked inside. Leila shrugged it away and walked right to the sink while Jon closed the door behind her.

"Any chance you're going to explain what you were doing out there?" Jon asked.

Leila placed the twigs and small branches in one of the two large sinks in her new family's kitchen. She turned the faucet on, letting the water run gently over them, filling the dishwashing bin slowly. Satisfied she had enough water, she looked around the kitchen and made her way to the pantry, which hid inside a large closet. She slowly opened the door, wincing at the soft squeak it made as it swung open, and flicked on the light. The soft glow illuminated the colored mason jars that lined every inch of space in there.

"Leila?" Jon asked, concern tinting his voice. "Come on now, what are you doing?"

Red-and-yellow peppers, bright-green pickles and spicy jalapenos, jars of jam and marmalade in hues of orange, pink, and blue—Mrs. Kline's love of the local farmer's market subscription service and Mr. Kline's passion for pickling and jarring made them the perfect pairing. It was taking some getting used to, calling them Liz and Jon, instead of Mr. or Mrs. Kline. They'd insisted, especially if she wasn't ready to use . . . well, those *other* words. Not yet. Leila smiled as she pulled several empty jars from the bottom of Jon's treasure trove. It was endearing and quirky, in a way. No other family ever treated her this way, the two of them so casual and aloof, and so grossly in love with one another.

And they didn't fuss over her like she was someone . . .

different. Asking stupid questions about how to wash her hair, or freaking out every time the seasons changed. The group home was honest about her seasonal affective disorder, and every foster family she had found herself with had pushed and pressed about it.

The sun is awfully bright today. Will you be okay?

We're thinking of going to the beach, but you know, it gets hot out there.

Have you ever tried not being depressed when it's cold out?

It's snowing. How are you feeling?

None of those had anything to do with her depression, and every comment was more infuriating than the last. And although the diagnosis had come quickly from a clearly inexperienced doctor at an understaffed clinic near the group home in Philadelphia, she'd spent years before that reading up every little thing she could about it. As long as it wasn't on the Internet, where reading about a cough could make you think you had some sort of rare incurable disease. She knew her stuff, even if the nervous, quivering young doctor had looked as though he was in dire need of sleep and some studying.

No, it seemed like Jon and Lisabeth had actually done their homework, and not just with her illness. She definitely had Lisabeth to thank for the that stuff. Lisabeth had the right shampoo and conditioner, the sulfate-free kind that could be rather expensive, for Leila's thick hair which she loved to let grow natural. Lisabeth kept hers short with weaved-in, thick braids, but knew all the best products like the back of her hand.

They let her take her meds without any serious helicoptering. And since she was the only child, there weren't any younger kids to ask her dumb questions about her therapeutic light box. The last foster home she was in, one of the kids thought it was a Lite Brite, and shocked himself when he broke it with small plastic pieces.

She found herself back at the group home a week after that incident, a thick bruise blooming on her cheek from "falling down the stairs."

A heaviness swelled in her chest at the thought, threatening to take her out of the moment and away from her mission at hand. She fought against it, closing her eyes to push the darkness away.

"So, uh, brushing up on canning?"

Leila jumped, almost dropping the jars she had bundled in her arms.

"Hah! Easy there," Jon said, a soft smile on his face. "I see you've decided to follow in your ol' man's footsteps, and start pickling. I'm . . . I'm so proud right now." He feigned wiping a tear from his eye, and then crossed his arms and stared at her silently, his mouth still turned in that accusatory grin he was so good at. "Though it's a slightly odd time to start. Storm and all."

"What?" Leila asked, shifting uncomfortably. All that "ol' man" talk that Jon was so fond of always made her feel a bit weird. It'd had only been a few months, here in this new home, even less time since the adoption went through. And while the Klines certainly didn't seem like they'd be going anywhere anytime soon, at least not without her, the mom-and-dad-type talk made her incredibly uneasy. Especially when Jon was so quick to toss it around, goofy as he was.

It wasn't fair to toss words around like that, when they could be taken away just as quickly as they were said.

And they often were.

She'd seen it. She'd felt that sting before.

"What's going on with all the sticks?" he asked, nodding at the sink.

"They're from the willow," Leila said, trying to hide the melancholy in her voice as she made her way over to the sink and looked down at the snapped-off twigs. A bubble of pain blossomed inside her chest and she pushed it back down. She nodded towards the kitchen's large bay window, which showed off a view of the backyard and the now-split tree. "After that, she's probably not going to make it."

"She?" Jon asked, still smiling.

"Yes, like all living things that give life on this planet, the willow is a she," Leila said with a smirk. She reached into the sink and plucked out one of the willow's sticks, examining the end where she'd broken it.

"Ah, my little feminist," Jon said, beaming proudly. "You've got something right here—" Leila felt Jon picking something out of her hair. She shot her head back and gave him a scowl.

"Jon! Come on, man, don't touch my hair!" she shouted, running her hands over her thick curls that took an eternity to get just right. Granted, it was all a mess right now after climbing up the tree, but still. He had to learn. She figured he should know better after all these years with Liz.

"Sorry, sorry! You had some leaves," Jon said, still smiling. "I'm working on that."

"I know. Thanks. I appreciate it," Leila said, returning to look at the sticks. She opened one of the kitchen drawers and plucked out her Leatherman, a multi-tool she used when out fussing in the gardens with Jon or pruning shrubs in front of the house. He'd given it to her a couple of days after she'd gotten settled in the new home, when he caught her staring through the bay window at him and Liz working in the garden. This was one of the many endearing quirks that Jon had, his misguided attempts at being sweet and the "cool" parent, like giving Leila—mostly a complete stranger—a knife less than a week after she arrived. She smiled, thinking of the fight he'd had with Liz about it, as she slid it out of its worn fabric case. Bits of frayed string stuck out this way and that, and she opened the silver-colored gadget to the tucked-away blade inside.

"So—" Jon started.

"Look, I know what happens," Leila said flatly, as she peeled away some of the bark on the ends of the sticks, revealing the green, cutting an inch or so from the bottom of each small branch.

"Happens?" Jon asked while she worked.

"Yes, to the tree." Leila nodded up towards the window without actually looking out it. She started to fill the mason jars up with just a bit with water, a few inches or so. She placed one down in the sink with a satisfying *clink* and looked back up at Jon.

"It's damaged," Leila said, curtly. "And now you and Liz are going to get rid of it."

A confused look washed over Jon's face, a mixture of puzzlement and worry, and he peered out the window, and then back at her.

"Oh, I don't know about that, Leila," he said, his eyes back on the tree. "You know how much your . . . how much Lizzie and I care about, well, stuff like this." He looked down at the jars, and then back at Leila, as she pretended not to notice the almost slip-up. "And we know you're really into the environment. Up all night on those message boards. I hope you're being careful with who you're talking to—"

Leila flashed him an exhausted look and yawned.

"Ha, okay, okay," Jon said, conceding. "Look, we'll remove the dead limb over there on the lawn and prune away the other bits. Half the tree could still be fine! I don't think we'd rip it out just because it's damaged."

"Pronouns. Because *she's* damaged," Leila corrected, smirking.

"*She's* damaged," Jon amended. Leila looked up at him, at his warm smile. Years of late-night corporate lawyering had clearly taken its toll on him, carving deep-set wrinkles around his eyes when he laughed or squinted just a little. His new career as an environmental journalist certainly suited him better, even if he wasn't exactly great at taking care of anything green around him.

The less-stressful gig had come too late, though, as his dark-brown hair now had bits of white and gray peppered through it. There were frequent "should I dye it or shouldn't I?" conversations over dinner, and generally they all ended the same, with Lisabeth's exasperated sighs and sideways glances at Leila.

Leila raised an eyebrow at Jon and returned her attention to the jars.

"Look how deep that lightning hit it. There's no way it didn't kill the roots." She picked up the jars and placed them up on the countertop, checking to make sure enough water was above each trimmed stem.

"Ah. I see what you're up to," he said. "I guess we'll see if any of them *stick*."

Leila smirked.

"Get it? Stick? Because they're sticks and you're putting them in the jars to—"

"Oh my God, yes, Jon, I get it," Leila said, shaking her head. He might make things awkward with his frequent *dad* and *mom* references, but his dad-like jokes were at least amusing in their badness.

He stepped up towards the sink, looked out the window towards the tree, and let out a loud sigh.

"I totally forgot to cover the garden," he muttered, shaking his head. "As if I didn't put those poor plants through enough hell this year, they get decimated by this."

"Aw, Jon," Leila said. She tentatively offered up a consoling hand on his shoulder. It was the kind of gesture that should come naturally, but she forced it out of herself.

"Poor things," he said. "After we finish your project, care to help me out with all of that? Maybe search for survivors before the rest of the storm comes through?"

Leila looked outside towards the garden. In addition to

the vegetables Lisabeth brought home from the CSA, there was also Jon's miniature farm to deal with. Cucumbers, tomatoes, zucchini, squash, peppers. All vegetables that didn't really need a lot of time and care, and could mostly grow on their own with enough sun and rain. The little bit of work they did need, Leila happily provided. In her first week with the Kline family, she had quickly discovered Jon's well-intentioned but disastrous gardening skills, when he poured piping-hot leftover coffee on a head of lettuce.

"They say coffee is good for gardens and the soil, did you know that?" he'd explained, holding the mug in his hand while Leila looked on, horrified.

"Coffee *grounds*, Jon. *Grounds*," Leila said, watching as the lettuce wilted in front of them.

Despite everything Jon managed to throw at the garden, it had been pretty resilient. But not even those tough plants could hold up in this weather, meeting doom in their battle against the tropical storm and the adult caretaker that forgot to cover them.

"Sure," Leila said, smiling. "I'm sure there's some stuff worth saving."

"Maybe," Jon said, disappointed. "We'll probably just have to uproot all of them and toss them out. Might be less wasteful to turn them into mulch, though, or put them in Lizzie's composter by the shed." Something about what he said struck a rough chord with Leila, and she winced, her chest heavy. For a moment, she felt as though she heard another whisper, and shook it off, the ghost of a sound vanishing as quickly as it appeared.

"Yeah, yeah sure," Leila said, wrestling with the feeling. Jon turned back to her, and evidently noticed.

"Something wrong?" he asked. He nodded at the jars. "Besides all this, that is."

"No, no," Leila said, shaking her head and grabbing a jar, studying the end of one of the sticks inside. "It's fine, I'm fine. This one looks like it needs a little more trimming though."

"Hey, fun fact—" Jon started.

"Oh God, not right now, Jon, seriously," Leila groaned. Jon wrote both locally, in the Philadelphia region, and abroad for news outlets such as *Slate*, *Farm & Agriculture*, *The New York Times*, and *Grid*. Back when she was in the group home, Leila regularly read those kinds of websites on her beat-up, donated tablet or on trips to the library. She dreamed of one day making a difference, quite literally, in the outside world. She was pretty sure she'd read an article or two of Jon's in the past few years, but she wasn't about to let him know that. He also taught part-time at St. Joseph's University, in their small environmental studies department.

The result of all his constant research and once-a-week lectures though, was this.

The "fun fact" tidbits.

And while Leila certainly appreciated Jon's wealth of knowledge about nature and all, he always brought them up at the worst time, his poor attempt to neutralize tense and awkward situations.

"*Fun* fact," Jon said again, stressing the fun in the sentence, which should have told him no part of this was actually fun. He picked up one of the mason jars, clinking it with the ring on his finger. "They call this cloning. Technically, these sticks, if they bloom into new trees, are really just the same exact tree."

Leila gave him a look.

"Yeah I should have figured you knew that one," Jon said, shaking his head and placing the jar back down with a light *plink*. "Still, cloning. It's like we're mad scientists in here."

"Sure, Jon," Leila said, shaking her head with a smile. "Sure. Think Liz will be okay with me putting these up along the windowsill? I'd like to make sure they get some sun and have a chance to grow a few roots. They need to take root before—"

"Yes, yes," Jon said. "Before it gets too cold and the trees go to sleep."

"It's called dorman—" Leila started.

"Dormancy," Jon said. "Yes, I know. It's like hibernation, only for trees. Everything slows down. Abscisic acid in deciduous trees signals the leaves to fall, suspends the tree's growth, stops cells from dividing . . ." He grinned as he faded off. Leila stared at him. "You do remember me being a journalist and professor of all this, yes?"

"I do," Leila said with a smirk.

"Let's wrap these up before Lizzie gets down here with *her* questions," Jon said with a wink. Leila shook her head and focused on the jars, moving them from the sink to the window.

But with each small movement the voices came back, and they whispered.

She squinted as they spoke up, trying to focus on them while at the same time wishing they would just go away. The speech was soft and delicate, dancing around her ears like ghosts.

When it came to the voices, every now and again she could make out a word or two, sometimes the broken part of a sentence. The voices had been louder back at the group home, and sometimes they came back stronger when she took the local train into Philadelphia to visit Sarika at the cafe; but out here in the suburbs of the city, they were weak and muttering, pieces that made little sense. Even when they had roared as the tree was struck by lightning, the phrases still came out in hard-to-figure-out bits.

Thi . . . saf . . . whe . . . than . . .

Leila shut her eyes and shook her head, trying to push the voices away, push back the growing darkness brewing in her chest, the swirling mass of anxiety and panic. Not here. Not now, with Jon hovering over her like this, trying to do his way-too-perfect parent thing. *Helicoptering,* she'd heard Lisabeth call it. She didn't need him to ask what was wrong so she'd have to make up lie after lie to cover it up. She didn't need him figuring this out.

Sending her back.

Not after she'd gotten this far.

The voices called, whispering. It was the sound of a number of people talking all at once, quietly, like a crowd muttering in a movie theater before the previews.

She whispered softly to herself, so Jon wouldn't hear.

"Kitchen. Jar. Floor. Sink—"

And then the voices spoke loudly, in one clear sentence, like the roar of the wind in the storm.

Thank you.

Leila's eyes opened wide and she fumbled with one of the jars, catching it before it slipped and crashed onto the hard kitchen floor.

"Whoa there!" Jon laughed, reaching down to pluck the jar from her hands. "Careful now."

"Thanks," Leila said, willing her heart to stop racing, taking deep, long breaths. The voices seldom got a real word or phrase in, and when they occasionally did, it felt like the volume had been turned up to ten. She picked up the last jar to move it to the windowsill, noticing a stick that still needed to be trimmed a bit.

"Tsk." She sucked at her teeth and pulled out the Leatherman again. The knife made gentle *schickt schickt schickt* sounds against the wood. "Can you get some twine or something, to secure the little branches in place, in the jars? With this one I just need to fix the edges so—"

"Jon!" Lisabeth gasped, storming into the kitchen. Leila stopped cutting and looked up at Liz. She was wearing a bathrobe, her dark-black braids curled up around her head, one rebellious red braid tucked behind her ear and peeking out around the rest. Her soft, dark skin glowed as if she hadn't just rolled out of bed, and her effortlessness at being pretty cast a strong contrast with Jon's rugged, practically leather, weathered-skin look. Even though she and Jon were in their early fifties, Liz could easily pass for thirty.

"Oh! Leila, you're awake!" she exclaimed, smiling

brightly, her light-brown eyes sparkling and happy at the sight of her.

Lisabeth rushed over to the two of them, kissing Leila on the forehead and Jon on the cheek, and then pulled them close. Leila tried to squirm away, but failed. Jon's hand accidentally brushed against Leila's hair. Lisabeth let go, adjusted her braids, and observed the windowsill before looking back over at Jon and Leila.

"What's going on here? You're all wet, and what is all this?" she asked, taking a step back and pointing at the sink before resting her hands on her hips. Leila shrugged and went back to cutting the small branch, almost done.

"The branches are from the—" Leila started, staring down at the sink.

"Oh hell! Jon, the willow tree!" Lisabeth exclaimed, dashing over to the large window.

"Yeah, about that," Leila continued. "I took some twigs off the remaining branch just in case she doesn't make it—"

"Ugh. Damaged beyond repair," Lisabeth said, sounding crushed. "That other half could fall at any time. You know we're going to have to cut that thing down immediately."

Leila's heart wrenched itself in her chest, as the voices came crashing through.

NO.

Leila's knife slipped.

And sliced right into her hand.

"Fuck!" Leila screamed, pulling her hand back, whipping it through the air. She balled it into a fist, and when she unclenched it, saw the clean, straight line cutting into her palm, the meaty part right below her thumb.

"Leila, watch your lang—" Jon started, before gasping. "Oh God, Lizzie, get the car, before the storm comes back."

Leila slowly stretched out her hand and watched as the clean line opened and turned red. Blood poured down her hand and onto her forearm, and she shrieked, stepping back from the sink, covering her hand with the other.

Lisabeth rushed over to Leila, her eyes wide.

"It'll be okay, don't worry," she said quickly, and then muttered an array of swears as she darted towards the front of the house. Leila could hear the jingle of keys before the front door opened and shut.

"Water, here, let's get that under the tap," Jon said, bringing Leila closer to the sink. "Here, clean it under there and let me grab some paper towels. Put pressure on it."

Leila pressed down hard on her hand after the warm water coursed over it, and glanced out the window towards the willow tree in the yard. The sound of Lisabeth's car starting in front of the house and the angry beeping of the horn cut its way through the storm's momentary calm. It likely awoke the entire neighborhood.

"Here," Jon said, pulling her hand out from under the water. Droplets of blood spattered the perfect, white-tiled kitchen floor. "Here, let's wrap your hand up with these and . . . Leila? Leila!"

Everything around her zeroed out and felt as though it had grown farther away.

She breathed in, slowly, her heart hammering in her chest. Anxiety blossomed in her, hot and panicked.

Something broke.

She stared at that tree, the jagged cut that tore deep into the trunk, the bolt of lightning that had angrily torn half of it away for absolutely no reason. The other half, sprawled out on the earth, was probably food for the mulch machine stashed away in the garden shed, like Jon's neglected patch of vegetables along the side of the house. The mason jars were tiny in comparison, with their small branches protruding from the inch or two of water.

Maybe one would make it out of the ten.

Maybe none.

Lisabeth said they'd have to tear down the tree.

Damaged beyond repair.

Would Jon fight for the tree? Or would he just let her go, give in like so many others do when one person disagrees with the other?

Leila crumpled to the floor clutching her hand, and tears poured out of her eyes, a torrent the hurricane would have been envious of. She felt dizzy, her chest heavy.

"Leila?" Jon whispered. He squatted down and reached for her face, looking intently at her. "Sweetheart? Are you okay? Are you woozy? Is it . . . wait, the anxiety? Lizzie is better at that stuff than me, I'll get her, I . . . did you lose too much blood, what is happen—"

"You guys are j-just gonna cut her down," Leila said, sniffling. "You're just going to give up on her."

"What? No, no, only if we have to," Jon said, settling down on the floor next to her. He wrapped her up in his strong arms and hugged her tightly. "We'll do everything we can to make it work."

"I've heard that before," Leila said, choking back a sob, the emotions swelling in her chest. She resisted the urge to push Jon away.

"You've heard . . .?" Jon said before growing quiet. "Oh. Oh, Leila." The car horn honked outside, faster and angrier this time. "Bad timing, Lizzie," Jon muttered. Leila breathed in and out, still pressing one hand against the other, as Jon held her tightly.

"I'm going to take a wild guess here," Jon said, letting Leila go, his hands on her shoulders. He reached out and pushed her chin up, looking at her in the eyes. "And assume this is about more than just the tree?"

Leila sputtered out a laugh. "Yeah, no shit, Jon."

"Come on, we've got to get that hand stitched up before the storm hits again and we can't drive to the hospital." He stood up and held out his hand, motioning for Leila to get up.

"What? No. It's fine. I'm fine," Leila said as she scrambled to her feet and took a few steps back.

"Fine?" Jon asked, hands on his hips. The car horn blared. "Leila, I either saw your bone in your hand, or I saw *through* your hand to the white kitchen tile on the floor. We're going to the hospital."

"No, it's okay," Leila said resolutely. She'd spent years in the group home learning how to take care of herself, both physically when she got hurt, and emotionally when she felt discarded or in the way. "I don't need you to do that. I can take care of myself."

"You listen here," Jon said, his generally aloof tone gone serious. "Something breaks, we fix it. Together.

You—God, I can't believe this is about to come out of my mouth—you are not a tree, Leila. Not that tree, or any of these little guys you've got in the jars."

"Girls," Leila corrected, while trying to hide a quick sniffle.

"Yes, girls, lady trees!" Jon exclaimed. "Lizzie and I, we're not going to give up on you, you hear me? Come on. We need to go."

"No, no, don't," Leila said, clutching her hand and walking along with Jon towards the front door, eying the staircase to the second floor. "I'll head upstairs and wrap it up in an old t-shirt, it'll be fine."

Jon opened the front door to reveal an exasperated-looking Lisabeth sitting in the driver's seat of their Prius with the windows open. Leila saw the look of irritation on her face and winced, feeling the pain of previous drives like this one.

Away from a home.

Back to the group home.

Disappointed faces and tears.

"No, no," Leila muttered to herself, pushing back. "It won't happen again." She bolted towards the stairs. This was a good home. It felt right. The two of them, they were trying so hard. She could try harder. She could be what they wanted. "I'll be upstairs. I'll just grab a Band-Aid. I'll grab a Band-Aid and—"

"Damn it, Leila!" Jon shouted, walking in front of her, putting his hands on her shoulders again. She tried to stop herself from shaking but the tears still poured down her face. She was going to mess it all up. Again. She pushed against Jon, and then pulled, trying to go upstairs. Get to the bathroom. Find a towel.

Push these feelings away. Push it all away. She could do it. She just needed to be left alone. She didn't have to let it take over.

"I know I–I'm not perfect, I know I'm broken, I can do better and, and–"

"Stop it, please!" Jon pleaded. "Just stop it. Look at me." He pointed at Leila and then at himself. "Look at her." He did the same with Lisabeth, who now wore a quizzical expression. "We are taking you to get your hand fixed. Not because we have to, or because we're annoyed about it, or disappointed in some way. It's because we want to. We need to. If anything, I'm disappointed in myself for letting you use that knife in the sink."

"I'm not going. I can take care of myself–" Leila started.

"Leila. Leila, listen to me."

She stared. Jon's eyes glassed over. He looked on the brink of tears. But not the sort she'd seen so many times before in the eyes of other families who'd brought her in and changed their minds. Not the frustration or the anger that often brewed behind the eyes of those that had given up. Not the rage that surfaced when things weren't easy. It was a look of someone on the verge of heartbreak.

"We aren't leaving," he said, looking at her intently. "Well, we are, we're taking you to the hospital, and then we're coming back home. And maybe we'll stop by Sonic or Wawa on the way home. Whatever you want. Milkshakes. Hoagies. Hoagie milkshakes. Whatever. And we'll talk. And we'll laugh about this whole mess. And we'll think of a way to save your tree, even if it's just with the little cloned branches and—"

"It's not about the fucking tree!" Leila shouted through the tears.

"The *metaphorical* tree then!" Jon exclaimed, the tears now escaping from his eyes as he let out an awkward laugh. "We're in it to win it, darling. You're stuck with us. We're a family now. We are your parents. And we'll get through this."

"O-okay," Leila said, as Jon turned to walk her towards the car. He opened the passenger-side door, and gestured for her to get in. Leila got into the car clutching her hand, and Lisabeth reached over and fastened her seatbelt. Her braids tickled against Leila's face as Lisabeth got her secured.

"You alright?" Lisabeth asked, smiling gently.

"I think so," Leila said, wincing as the seatbelt pressed against her arm, pushing softly against her hand. She wriggled it free so she could keep applying pressure with her other hand. "It'll be okay, for the drive."

Jon popped back over to the passenger-side window.

"Hey Leila, fun fact," he said.

"Jon, come on," muttered Lisabeth. "Now is not the time."

"Now is precisely the time," Jon said. "Fun fact, Leila." He smiled.

"We're here for you, and we aren't going anywhere."

Relocating Year-Old Sapling
Posted by WithouttheY
JULY 24th, 2017 | 4:07PM
Hey forum! Anyone have solid advice on relocating a sapling? I've got a small one that's just starting to sprout roots, afraid I might shock it if I move it too fast.

> RE: Relocating Year-Old Sapling
> *Posted by WithouttheY*
> JULY 24th, 2017 | 4:09PM
> Oh! I should add that it's a weeping willow. And it means a lot to me, so don't give me any business about leaving it where it is or that it's an invasive species yada yada thanks.

RE: Relocating Year-Old Sapling
Posted by A Dash of Paprika
JULY 24th, 2017 | 4:27PM
Hey. Tomorrow. You. Me. The usual place. Text me.

> RE: Relocating Year-Old Sapling
> *Posted by WithouttheY*
> JULY 24th, 2017 | 4:30PM
> ;-)

RE: Relocating Year-Old Sapling
Posted by *Toothless*
JULY 27th, 2017 | 4:57PM
Actually, I did this once with a birch tree in my yard, my favorite kind of tree. But I believe you mean transplanting, not relocating.

> RE: Relocating Year-Old Sapling
> Posted by *A Dash of Paprika*
> JULY 27th, 2017 | 5:09PM
> Did you seriously just "well, actually" her? Seriously?!

> RE: Relocating Year-Old Sapling
> Posted by *WithouttheY*
> JULY 27th, 2017 | 5:10PM
> Hey thaaaaaaaaaanks for the condescending and unhelpful post there, Toothy.

>> RE: Relocating (EDIT: TRANSPLANTING) Year-Old Sapling
>> JULY 27th, 2017 | 5:27PM
>> Posted by *Toothless*
>> *shrug* that's what I'm here for.

RE: Relocating Year-Old Sapling
Posted by *The Professor of Pruning*
JULY 28th, 2017 | 6:27PM
Depends on how deep the roots go, really. As long as it small enough to dig up the entire root system, you should be fine. Luckily willow trees will

basically bloom from anything, including branches that just happen to fall on the ground.

Resilient, those trees are. (Note: This should be read in a Yoda voice.)

But, for the purposes of anyone else finding this post, make sure you take enough soil with the root system, go for at least a foot around. If there's too much resistance, you might have a large root in there. Take your time, you don't want to damage anything.

It's actually the best idea to transplant when the trees are dormant, in the winter or the fall, but I'm guessing that's not an option here. Once you've done the transplant, make sure you stake the sapling, as the roots won't have taken hold just yet.

> RE: Relocating Year-Old Sapling
> *Posted by WithouttheY*
> JULY 28th, 2017 | 7:39PM
> Oh wow! Thank you so much for taking the time to write all that. Thank you!

>> RE: Relocating Year-Old Sapling
>> *Posted by The Professor of Pruning*
>> JULY 28th, 2017 | 8:15PM
>> Good luck! Be sure to share some photos of the sapling in its new habitat!

RE: Relocating Year-Old Sapling
Posted by WithouttheY
JULY 28th, 2017 | 8:39PM
Totally!

RE: Relocating (EDIT: Transplanting Is What It's Called) Year-Old Sapling
Posted by Toothless
JULY 29th, 2017 | 9:07AM
Also make sure you fill the hole where you removed the tree, so no one falls in it. ‾_(:/)_/‾

RE: Relocating (Shut Up I Don't Care) Year-Old Sapling
Posted by WithouttheY
JULY 29th, 2017 | 10:02AM
OMG TOOTH GTFO YOU ARE THE ACTUAL WORST.

II

Leila held the medium-sized terracotta pot tightly and stared at the little tree. The baby willow was practically bursting out of it, small branches consumed by thick, green leaves. It looked nothing like the old willow, with its great branches and low, drooping foliage. It looked more like a brown stick with a giant, dirty, green cotton ball on top. Like green cotton candy, or maybe a Muppet.

Still, she loved it, odd as it looked.

Though it did give her pause.

It had only been, what, two weeks since the storm had torn through her family's yard? And here was the lone survivor of the yard, a small branch plucked from the downed willow, already growing a fairly strong, thin trunk and blooming with wispy leaves.

And whenever she was close to it, she swore—though she knew it was outrageous—she could hear the little tree growing. Little rustles and snaps, like it was stretching, reaching towards the sky right in front of her.

The rapid growth made no sense, but Jon and Liz both just shrugged about it. Leila left out the part where she thought she could hear it growing. "You've got a natural way with plants," Jon said, though his amazed eyes betrayed him.

Leila placed the potted tree on the floor, the ceramic hitting the wood with a light *plink*, and searched around in the pantry for her gardening tools. Eventually her eyes settled on a new-looking plastic bin labeled *Leila's Toys* with a little smiley face. She opened the plastic lid and caught a glimpse of small shovels and other gardening tools.

"Toys? Jon, come on," she said, rolling her eyes as she picked up the box.

"I'll be right back," she said to the willow tree, and made her way to the backyard. The house was narrow, and she had to weave in and out of the thin hallways to get to the back of the home. But it was cozy in that way. The old group home had been so big, all sprawled out, so many rooms everywhere. It was easy to avoid people. But here, it was kind of hard not to see her new parents at all times. She couldn't turn a corner without bumping into one of them, or sit in her room without hearing them talk.

It was strangely comforting. Nice, even.

She opened the door to the yard, a heavy weight in her chest at the sight of the place where the willow once stood. It'd been two weeks, sure, but the loss of the tree still scarred her, the same way it scarred the earth where it had stood. Heaps of dirt and piles of mulch covered the spot where Jon and Liz had the remaining tree uprooted, after one of the Urban Ecovist board members determined the tree wasn't going to make it.

But she had this little one now. A sapling of hope.

Jon stressed she'd need to keep it trimmed and main-tained. She could see it now, the entire yard becoming just her willow tree, the branches and thick, leafy strands taking over everything, which didn't seem like such a bad thing. But she understood the damage a large tree could do to these old Philadelphia homes. Especially a young one, with new roots digging into untouched places.

Earlier in the spring she'd attended a protest with Sarika near Fairmount Park, where trees hundreds of years old grew tall and strong, an almost-forest tucked away in the center of a giant metropolis. One of the oldest trees in the city was set to be cut down because the roots had taken hold of some water pipes. They'd made it a full two days at the protest, their parents coming by and dropping off snacks and blankets later in the evening with their gentle suggestions to come home. People who didn't have to go to school or work hung around for the remaining week and, thankfully, saved the ancient tree.

Leila chuckled, the memory sweet, but her laugh cut short when she picked up the sound of something on the wind. She listened, intently, and slowly placed the box down on the soft ground.

Whispering.

A laugh.

Th . . . wood . . . whe . . . hou . . .

She closed her eyes, gritting her teeth.

Sa . . . on . . . you . . .

"No, no, no," she muttered, placing her hands over her ears, the unintelligible whispering growing louder but still vague. "Not now, not right now." She took a deep breath and closed her eyes, visualizing the yard around her.

"Grass. Sky. Sun. Wind," she whispered, breathing slowly, and the voices faded.

She patted her pockets for her phone, and, finding nothing, went back inside, closing the back door behind her. She wanted to shut the voices out. Since the storm, the voices had taken on a new tone, with the hint of something strange that Leila couldn't quite figure out. Urgency, maybe? She hurried back into the living room, dipping in and out of the narrow hallways of the century-old rowhome, and dug around in her tattered messenger bag for her cell phone. Jon and Liz were out, collecting supplies for the yard and paint to touch up the house. She turned the phone's screen on, her hands shaking, and despite how her heart was racing in her chest, smiled to see a bunch of notifications waiting for her. Some alerts on the message board, the usual social media silliness, and most notably, a bunch of texts from Sarika.

> What are you doing?
> Why aren't you with me drinking coffee
> right now?!
> GIRL WHERE ARE YOU?

Leila smiled. Sarika was precisely the person she had planned to reach out to. Not that there was anyone else she'd talk to about it. With trembling hands, Leila responded:

> Having a moment. Can you come over?
> Like now?
> Please. Dropping everything.

Leila's finger hovered over the "depression" hashtag on Tumblr for a few second before she clicked it. A warning immediately appeared, filling her tablet's screen with a dark-blue background and bright-white text.

> *Everything Okay?*
> *If you or someone you know are experiencing some kind of crisis, there are people who care about you and are here to help. Consider chatting with a volunteer trained in crisis intervention or an anonymous listener at the following link.*
> *It might also help to fill your blog with inspirational and supportive posts from—*

She clicked "continue" to view the search results, pushing by the warning and the large "Go Back" button. She appreciated the friendly nudge, one that she'd given to other people in her group home countless times. She could be a person who listened, or refer them to someone else who could. As for Leila, she kept her secret with Sarika, the voices and the whispers and the soft laughter that edged its way into the corners of her mind. But here, on the Internet, she could look for others dealing with the same thing she was, see what they wrote, and sometimes, feel a little less alone.

A soft knock on the door shook Leila out of her mindless, hashtag-browsing trance. Nearly half an hour had gone by without her noticing. She leapt off the couch, and had barely turned the knob on the front door when it burst open and Sarika stormed in, a ball of concerned, worried energy.

"Leila!" Sarika exclaimed, running into her, giving her an enormous hug. "What's going on? How bad is it?" Sarika let go and stepped away from Leila, her big, brown eyes full and focused on her.

Leila smiled. There was a time when Sarika had been quiet and sheltered, arriving in the group home when she and Leila were a year short of being teenagers. Her hair had been matted, and those wide eyes of hers dark and sunken. She had looked as though she hadn't eaten in weeks, and shied away from everyone like a scared mouse until Leila had shared those books.

She grabbed Leila's hand.

"What's the deal?"

"Outside," Leila said, shaking her head as Sarika squeezed her hand. "I was going to go plant Major Willow." She nodded at the sapling, and Sarika followed her gaze, looking back at her with a smile. "That's a good name and you know it."

"Yeah, I do. Go on."

"It's just the usual voices, but . . ." Leila said, drifting off as though everything was just knocked out of her. Her shoulders sunk and she wanted to disappear into the folds in the couch. "This time, though," she squinted, thinking. "I heard a laugh, I think? And the whispers, they were . . . Sarika, I swear I almost understood them. I don't know. Something about woods? A house, maybe? It's like, in the back of my head somewhere, and I just can't pluck it out."

"Did you tell Jon or Liz yet?" Sarika asked, a warning in her voice.

"No," Leila said, sternly. "Hell no, of course not. Not when everything is going so well. I like it here. What if they send me back or something? Can they do that? Now that, you know, all *this* is a thing?" She motioned at herself and the house, and found herself struggling over saying the word *adopted*, just as difficult to push out of her mouth as words like *mom* and *dad*. "And this time, the thing is, I think . . . I think it wants me to follow it. The voices."

"Leila—" Sarika started, that warning tone returning.

"No, really, it's not like back at the group home or the other times in the coffee shop," Leila said, taking a deep breath. Back then, the voices were soft, distant, but still strangely welcoming. A curiosity, almost. Sometimes she welcomed the company, standing outside, listening to the muttering as she let the sun wash over her. Other times, she found herself holed up in the closet with Sarika, shaking, wanting them to go away, muttering words that she thought might keep her grounded, keep her safe. The voices came and went with the seasons, it seemed. They faded and disappeared with the winter, and rampaged back loudly in the spring.

"I mean, I'm not going to. Follow them." Leila stressed. "I'm not. But it feels, it felt . . . real this time."

"Listen," Sarika said, squeezing her hand even tighter. "You've pulled through it before. You'll get through it again. We'll just keep it between us, okay? Always."

"Yeah, always," Leila said, squeezing her hand back.

Although she wasn't so sure about that anymore.

These new labels, the whole *mom* and *dad* thing, it made things feel different. Complicated.

But Jon and Liz didn't seem like the types to drop her because something was wrong. It had nagged at Leila, ever since that day with the willow tree, the day of the hurricane. She'd cried the whole way to the hospital, and not because of the gash in her hand. If she could tell anyone about the voices, she would tell them. There was medicine for all this, wasn't there? They had money, at least it seemed like they did. They could make it all go away. They wouldn't send her back like others had, when they caught her sitting up in her bed, trying to speak to whoever was on the other line of those whispers, half-awake, half-asleep.

Leila looked down at the scar on her hand, tracing the jagged, white line that trailed along the natural patterns on her palm.

"Is it still happening?" Sarika asked, looking at her, eyes full of worry.

"No," Leila said, shaking her head, her curls jostling about. "It's gone. They stopped a little after I texted you."

"Oh my God, did you see what Toothless posted, about his internship essay?" Sarika said, and Leila found herself grateful for the immediate change of subject. Sarika was good at reading her like that.

"Internship essay?" Leila asked, grinning.

"He's trying to be a landscaping person in the park or something." Sarika laughed loudly. "The perfect job for that guy, I swear! He won't have to interact with a single human being."

"Did you read it?" Leila asked, curious.

"Of course not!" Sarika scoffed. "I should have flagged it as spam or something, but it's our solemn duty as board administrators to be better than the trolls."

"Mm. So true, so very true," Leila said, shaking her head in faux respect.

They sat there on the couch for a beat in silence.

"So do you want to read it right now?" Leila asked, smiling.

"OH MY GOD YES!" Sarika exclaimed.

They both pulled out their phones, laughing together madly, and Leila forgot about the whispering as they both flipped to the board.

THREAD: Internship Essay, Some Thoughts?

SUBFORUM: COLLEGE + GRADUATE SCHOOL

Internship Essay, Some Thoughts?
Posted by Toothless
JUNE 18th, 2015 | 2:04PM
Hey all. It should really come as no surprise to any of you who know me that I've applied to be an intern with the city's park service, helping maintain Fairmount Park. If you're not from Philadelphia, it's one of the biggest and the best urban parks in the United States. Anyhow, they're doing some new hip essay thing, where you only have to write like 250 words. So I promise it'll be short and painless. Thoughts appreciated.

"As someone who was born and raised in the Philadelphia region, I've come to admire the Fairmount Park system not just as an urban oasis, but as an emotional refuge. I come from a family of doctors and lawyers and other clichés, and since graduating high school, have been pushed to pursue the same path. But like the trees that grow in the deepest parts of the city's patch of wilderness, I refuse to be held back. My roots know where they want to go, and I'd like to take hold in Fairmount Park and help maintain the city's wild treasure."

> RE: Internship Essay, Some Thoughts?
> *Posted by NY in PA*
> JUNE 25th, 2015 | 3:04PM
> Best urban park system? Don't you mean Central Park in New York City?

>> RE: Internship Essay, Some Thoughts?
>> *Posted by Toothless*
>> JUNE 25th, 2015 | 3:06PM
>> No.

RE: Internship Essay, Some Thoughts?
Posted by Toothless
AUGUST 5th, 2017 | 2:04PM
BUMP. Hey everyone. So way back when I applied for this internship with the city, and never really updated it with much. But I got it. Two years later, but still. I got it. Thanks to everyone who sent me

private messages with notes and suggestions, and to NY in PA, you can go eff yourself.

"Ah," Sarika said, her mouth twisting up. "It's an old post from forever ago that he bumped up, look at the time stamp. Looks like he was just not-so-humble-bragging or whatever." She clicked off her phone and tossed it onto the sofa.

"Kinda sad that the only person who replied was that jerk with the comment," Leila said, flicking at the screen.

"Psh, is it, though?" Sarika replied. "He's usually the one that's the jerk. He deserves to get sassed. He's the worst."

"Good for him, I guess," Leila said, shrugging. It was hard to feel terribly excited for a guy on their message board who was so overly negative about absolutely everything all the time. Anytime someone had a happy announcement or planned a board get-together, he was there, trolling away, being a buzzkill. The board was supposed to be a happy reprieve from school and foster life. There they could rant and rage about the things that bothered them in the outside world, like the environment, local policies, and area parks, without being attacked by people *in* that outside world for wanting to share an opinion.

And the worst part was, he sometimes had interesting things to say, like this rough-draft essay of his. But of course that sort of stuff always got overlooked because no one liked him. Months ago, he mentioned saving that birch tree in his backyard. If Leila had to choose a second favorite tree, after her willow, it would be that one.

It was a tree that made soda. How do you not love that kind of tree?

Leila always shook it off. He was just some faceless Internet stranger, and it annoyed her that it was so easy to get worked up over someone she didn't even know a single thing about.

"Yeah, I guess," Sarika said grudgingly. "That guy is a tool."

"Tool!" Leila exclaimed at this, getting off the couch. She turned to Sarika, who stared at her quizzically. "Well, *tools*. Before I heard, well, you know"—Sarika winced—"I was planning to go plant Major Willow in the yard back here. Want to help me?"

"Oh yeah, totally!" Sarika said, grabbing her phone and stuffing it in her pocket. "You have any work gloves?" She held out her hand and wiggled her wingers, displaying bright-magenta nail polish decorated with bits of glitter.

"I've got you," Leila said. "Let me grab Major Willow, and we'll head out."

Leila wiped the sweat from her forehead and stretched, feeling pleased with herself, and resisted the urge to flash Sarika a scowl. There hadn't been any gloves in the box of gardening tools, and she wasn't about to waste another minute leaving Major Willow in that pot, even if it meant having to dig in the yard herself while Sarika gave her a mini photo shoot.

"I really like this one," Sarika said, pushing herself off the small porch swing in the yard, eyes set on her phone as she walked over, smirking. "See?"

She held out the phone, which showed Leila bent over fussing in the dirt, her butt up in the air.

"Give me that!" she shouted, laughing. Leila grabbed Sarika and wrestled the phone out of her hand, the two of them laughing, and then flipped through the remaining pictures. She stopped and smiled at one as Sarika looked over her shoulder.

"See, now this one isn't bad," Leila said, smiling and nodding. The photo showed her squatted down in the yard, digging in the small patch out back with one of the trowels. She was smiling, her hair looked great, and even her simple outfit, jeans and a loose-fitting, upcycled t-shirt from a nearby local thrift store, looked good.

"Maybe we can post that one on the board. I bet Toothless would be into it," Sarika said with a wink.

"Oh *hell* no." Leila rolled her eyes.

"What?" Sarika shrugged, her face a feigned expression of innocence. "I'm just saying, you are kinda nice to him sometimes. You guys direct message ever? Hm?" Her voice went up higher and faster with each little accusation. "Little private chat sessions? Just the two of you? Swap a few pics?"

"Sarika, please don't make me bury you under the tree."

"Okay, okay," Sarika said, hands up. "Maybe we post it for the others, though, just a little update on your sapling."

"Still no," Leila said, shaking her head. "Just a photo

of the tree, thanks. I prefer to keep things anonymous on the Internet." She didn't need a bunch of faceless strangers knowing what she looked like, especially when a lot of them lived here in the city—at least, according to the board and the sub-space they posted in.

She grabbed her trowel, walked back over to the sapling, and patted the soil down before staking the tree in place so it wouldn't move on a rainy or windy day. She gently tugged at the small willow tree, and, satisfied it wouldn't move, clapped her hands together to shake all the dirt off.

"She looks good," Sarika said, walking up behind her, placing her well-manicured hand on Leila's shoulder.

"Yeah she does," Leila said, smiling. She reached back out and ran her fingers through the young willow's leaves and thin branches, still bunched up in a green ball. For a moment, just a moment, she thought she felt the little tree rustle, like it was stretching up to greet her touch.

"Looks kinda like your hair, only green," Sarika said, before Leila could say anything.

"Oh wow, shut up," Leila said, playfully swinging at her best friend.

The wind around her whispered, the tone almost playful, whimsical, merry. She closed her eyes and shook her head, trying to block it out.

"You okay?" Sarika said, taking a step forward.

"I'm fine," Leila said. "I'm fine, it's alright. It'll pass."

Sarika hugged her close, and Leila whispered.

"Tree. Soil. Wind." She paused. "Friend."

Sarika gave her a little squeeze.

If she could survive uprooting, she could survive this new home.

She looked over Sarika's shoulder at the tree, and her best friend held her tight.

They would both survive.

Sarika Paprika

@TheSarikaPaprika

Heading to @AdamsPhillyCafe with my girl
@WithouttheY for the morning until lunch-ish.
Come and get it! #SarikaTheBarista

8/9/17, 7:47AM

37 Retweets 87 Likes

> Chris @ChristoferYurie   9m
> @TheSarikaPaprika @AdamsPhillyCafe OMG
> @LaurenGibs you see this? Let's go!

> Leila @WithouttheY   7m
> @TheSarikaPaprika @AdamsPhillyCafe Why you
> gotta put me on blast? I'm getting like a million
> notifications.

> Leila @WithouttheY   6m
> @TheSarikaPaprika @AdamsPhillyCafe WHY
> DID YOU RETWEET THAT NOW IT IS EVEN
> WORSE.

> Sarika @TheSarikaPaprika   5m
> @WithouttheY @AdamsPhillyCafe LOL

> Adam @AdamsPhillyCafe   2m
> @TheSarikaPaprika well the place is already
> starting to fill up. Great work.

III

Leila tossed her backpack onto a polished wooden table in Adam's, a nonprofit café on the edge of Philadelphia's Brewerytown neighborhood that employed foster kids. She slid onto the upcycled wooden bench, a reclaimed church pew, that sat along one of the windows. Adam's had a hip, earthy feel, and the entire café was painted in warm colors and decorated with art made by its patrons and workers, who were almost always one and the same.

Exceptions to the regular clientele came when people knew Sarika was behind the barista station, whipping up creations that otherwise weren't on the café's menu.

Like right now.

"Listen, I'm not judging or anything," Sarika shouted over the roar of the café's ancient, dying expresso machine. The old, metal, box-shaped monster made a cacophony of hisses and squeals as steam pushed out a valve on the opposite side. "Oh my God this fucking thing!"

"Sarika! Serenity, please," Mr. Hathaway snapped, peeking his head out from the small kitchen behind Sarika. The little, blonde mustache under his nose was already pushed up to the side as his mouth shifted up irritably. "Remember, we're here to learn how to communicate with—"

"With people," Sarika said. "Not with dying machines that refuse to let me finish this double mocha latte with a triple shot of expresso."

"Well if you would stick to the menu of—" Mr. Hathaway started.

"If I stuck to the menu of just plain coffee, iced coffee, and tea, we wouldn't do any business!" Sarika exclaimed while pressing an espresso bean holder into the whining machine, and cranking it in.

Leila stifled a laugh, watching the scene unravel from her seat, as Sarika shouted back at poor Mr. Hathaway. She made herself comfortable as the two of them battled, locked in their usual routine. Adam's was practically their second home, and not just because Sarika worked here, slinging coffee whenever she could, but because it was *meant* to feel like a second home for teens like them.

Leila nuzzled into the hard wall along the back of the once-church-pew-now-coffee-table-bench, and sighed as Sarika fussed with something behind the machine, causing steaming hot water to burst from the front. The steam hissed with an explosive smell of espresso beans and misty water, like someone had spilled a cup of coffee in the summer rain.

"Hey!" Sarika shouted at a random customer waiting in line, who looked up at her in surprise, pulled from his staring-at-his-phone trance.

"Would you come in here, if it was just plain coffee and tea?" Sarika asked. A number of anxious-looking people stood behind him, and Leila held in another laugh as their eyes darted about awkwardly in that trying-to-look-casual but please-don't-talk-to-me kind of way. Sarika leaned over her countertop, staring at everyone, and Leila smiled at the sight. Her best friend, intimidating a room full of people, leaning over the wooden countertop like a beautiful gargoyle.

"Uh," the man started.

"No," Sarika interrupted, pointing at him. "He wouldn't. You do the best business while I'm here." She smacked the machine and it let out a loud wheeze. "And you know it."

"Okay, okay," Mr. Hathaway said, waving a hand at her from inside the kitchen. "Do your thing."

When the crowd died down, Leila slid out of her favorite corner and headed up towards the barista station.

"So, like I was saying," Sarika continued. She glanced up at Leila quickly before smacking the machine while she cranked at levers and adjusted values, like a mad scientist behind a doomsday device. "I'm not here to judge. You're my best friend and I love you. But is this really the way you want to spend your last day before everything starts up? I know it's only summer programing, but really? Here? This café?"

"I can hear you over there," Mr. Hathaway grumbled. Leila and Sarika laughed.

"It's either here or at home on the boards," Leila said, shrugging. "Or wandering around the neighborhood alone. I promise, I'll get out more when enrichment or summer school or whatever it's called starts. I'll make some new friends from a different school or something."

"Eee!" Sarika let out a squeal that rivaled even the loudest noises the espresso machine could possibly make.

"I should stress that it's enrichment, and not summer school, though. And I seriously can't wait. Don't make too many friends. I'm selfish, and want you to myself." She continued fussing with the machine. "Why don't you grab an iced coffee or something, and we'll hang when rush hour officially ends? It's winding down but I'm sure more people are coming."

"Rush hour never ends when you're on the floor!" Mr. Hathaway shouted from the backroom, amidst the clatter of dishes.

"I know it!" Sarika yelled back.

Leila smiled and grabbed one of the ready-made cold brew coffees, another one of Sarika's many contributions to Adam's, and made her way back to the bench.

She sighed into her cold cup of coffee, nuzzling her back against the reclaimed wood wall, watching her friend hand out lattes and espresso shots and other cups full of caffeine as more people filtered in. She was totally in her zone, and it was beautiful.

The door to the café chimed, and Leila turned to watch the next businessman or businesswoman walk in, but what she saw almost made her spit out her cold brew.

A boy slightly older than Leila walked in, all cool and calm, a handful of fliers in his hand and a staple gun in the other. He approached the giant bulletin board located right next to the front door, where scores of fliers, post-cards, and business cards clung, offering up services for this or that, meetings, and events. He turned to look over at the register, squinting.

"Do—" Leila started, barely a whisper.

"Hey, Mr. Hathaway, is it okay if—" the boy started, a gruff edge to his voice, like he smoked a lot of cigarettes and was already paying for it.

"Yes, go right ahead, Shawn," Mr. Hathaway shouted back, still hidden in the kitchen.

"Thanks!" Shawn said. Before turning back to the bulletin board, he locked eyes with Leila. Her heart quickened for a moment, and sped up even more when he fixed his long, chestnut-colored hair, adjusting it with the hand that grasped the steel staple gun. He gave the impression he was invincible, with his dark-green eyes and freckled skin. His hair, cut down to his chin, tumbled back down around his face, moving right back into the position it was in earlier.

"Hey," Shawn said, nodding at her, the motion opening another button on his—she suspected purposely—wrinkled dress shirt that already had two undone, showing a glimpse of his smooth, slightly sunburned chest.

Leila died.

With that open button she died a thousand deaths.

"Wha . . . oh, hi!" Leila stammered.

"Thanks," Shawn said, smiling to reveal a lopsided grin that was undeniably cute.

"For what?" Leila asked.

"You were going to, you know, say something? Maybe ask if I needed help?" Shawn motioned, nodding back at the register and the barista bar. Leila followed his line of sight, and caught Sarika staring at the two of them, smirking. Sarika gave her a playful look and went back to fussing over the machine. This was going to be a conversation later.

"So yeah, thanks for that," he continued, still grinning.

"Oh yeah, n–no problem, really," Leila muttered.

"Cool," he said, nodding. "Well, see you around? Grab a flier, maybe come help change the world?" He stapled a few pieces of paper to the bulletin board in a practiced, quick motion, *chk-chk-chk*, and pointed at her, making a clicking noise with his mouth. "Later."

Leila scowled as he walked out the door. The moment was ruined.

That finger point and click. The hell was that?

What a douche.

What . . . hm.

What a cute douche.

"OH MY GOD DID YOU SEE THAT DELICIOUS BOY?"

Leila jumped in her seat, spilling the cold coffee all over the table, as Sarika stood over her gushing.

"He was totally checking you out!" Sarika exclaimed. "What did he say to you before he left? Did you get his number? Facebook?"

"No!" Leila said, standing up and walking around Sarika to the sugar and cream station to wrangle up a bundle of napkins from the dispenser. "I mean, yes, I saw the *delicious* boy," she said mockingly as she wiped up the coffee from the table. "But no, I didn't get his . . . Sarika, it looks like you have an angry mob of people waiting on you over there."

"Excuse me," a customer shouted from the line, his voice full of concern.

"They're fine," Sarika said dismissively with a wave of her hand, and Leila caught several seriously irritated stares. There were only four people in the line, but in a relatively small space like Adam's, particularly around the coffee bar, that made it look endless. "What did he say? What happened?"

"Oh, nothing," Leila said, balling up the coffee-soaked napkins and tossing them in a nearby bin. "Something about taking a flier and that he'd see me around."

"Okay, you go investigate the flier situation," Sarika said curtly. "I'll—"

"Oh my God, Sarika, what is happening over here?" Mr. Hathaway shouted, walking out of the kitchen to the ever-growing line of #SarikaTheBarista fans. Leila smiled. When you could actually see Adam Hathaway in plain sight, he was a good-looking guy. Slim and incredibly tall, with the sort of hipster, curly mustache you generally spotted all around the Northern Liberties neighborhood of Philadelphia, and brightly colored tattoos up and down his arms. A purple tentacle from the *Watchmen* comic curled around his upper bicep, easy to see when he wore a small t-shirt like today. His eyes were wide and panicked as he surveyed the customers that were shifting about anxiously.

"I'll get back to work," Sarika finished with a grin. "You go see what the deal is."

Sarika bounded back over to the espresso machine, leapt over the countertop, and started doing her thing.

Leila looked over the table for any leftover cold brew droplets before making her way to the bulletin board, where the cute tool had stapled a bunch of his fliers. It was odd, though. If someone wanted attention, they didn't use fliers that looked like they were made out of recycled bathroom paper towels, which is precisely what these seemed to be. Fliers were supposed to be bright colors, printed on resilient paper, drawn up with bold lettering. The ones that surrounded it were like that, advertising bands, odd jobs, a notice about saving a local endangered mouse, all printed in ways that demanded attention.

Leila plucked one of the incredibly bland fliers off the board, the paper stiff and dull as a brown paper bag.

JOIN THE BELMONT ENVIRONMENTAL ACTIVISM CLUB

Tired of watching Mother Earth suffer the wrath of man's careless nature?

- Sign up for the Belmont High School's Environmental Activism Club, or the B.E.A.C., and make a difference in the Philadelphia community. Open to ANY high school student, regardless of institution.
- First meeting kicks off this Wednesday at 3PM, at Belmont in Room 407. We'll be meeting every subsequent Wednesday through the summer and into the school year.

Be there!

Leila eyed the flier for a moment before tearing one of them off the wall and folding it into her pocket. Maybe he wasn't all that bad? That snap and click might have just been his carefree, earth-loving attitude. That was a thing, right? Maybe? In which case, he might be just her type.

Might be.

"WHAT DOES THE FLIER SAY?" Sarika shouted, appearing next to Leila.

Leila spilled what remained of her coffee, the cup hitting the ground with a *pang*, the cold brew staining the bottom of her jeans.

"YOU HAVE GOT TO STOP DOING THAT!"

Belmont's Environmental Activism Club?
Posted by WithouttheY
AUGUST 10th, 2017 | 9:07PM
Is anyone here a member? Me and Paprika are thinking of joining. First meeting this Wednesday. At least, first of the summer.

RE: Belmont's Environmental Activism Club?
Posted by A Dash of Paprika
AUGUST 10th, 2017 | 9:09PM
Yeah we are!

> RE: Belmont's Environmental Activism Club?
> *Posted by WithouttheY*
> AUGUST 10th, 2017 | 9:10PM
> You are literally sitting right next to me, and replying. Why are you even?

> > RE: Belmont's Environmental Activism Club?
> > *Posted by BroBoxOne*
> > AUGUST 10th, 2017 | 9:15PM
> > How do I get in on that? ;-P

> > > RE: Belmont's Environmental Activism Club?
> > > *Posted by WithouttheY*
> > > AUGUST 10th, 2017 | 9:17PM
> > > WOW. AND BANNED.

RE: Belmont's Environmental Activism Club?
Posted by A Dash of Paprika
AUGUST 10th, 2017 | 9:19PM
PERMABANNED. BANHAMMER
40,000. BANHAMMER OF THOR.
STRIKE UP THE BANNED.

> RE: Belmont's Environmental
> Activism Club?
> *Posted by WithouttheY*
> AUGUST 10th, 2017 | 9:21PM
> OMG STAHHHHP

RE: Belmont's Environmental Activism Club?
Posted by Sage Wisdom
AUGUST 10th, 2017 | 9:30PM
I think it's good you're joining a club, sweetheart.
It'd be really great for you to get there, meet some
new people, other kids your age. Do you like my avatar? What about my username? Do you get it?

> RE: Belmont's Environmental Activism Club?
> *Posted by WithouttheY*
> AUGUST 10th, 2017 | 9:09PM
> OH MY GOD! SAGE I KNOW WHO YOU ARE.
> GET OUT OF HERE!

RE: Belmont's Environmental Activism Club?
Posted by Sage Wisdom
AUGUST 10th, 2017 | 9:15PM
Hi! But do you get it? Sage, like the plant! And this is environment stuff!

RE: Belmont's Environmental Activism Club?
Posted by A Dash of Paprika
AUGUST 10th, 2017 | 9:17PM
I get it. "Sage" LOL.

RE: Belmont's Environmental Activism Club?
Posted by WithouttheY
AUGUST 10th, 2017 | 9:21PM
DO. NOT. ENCOURAGE. THIS.

FROM	SUBJECT	DATE
TOOTHLESS	HIGH SCHOOL ACTIVISM CLUBS So you're joining an environmental club at your high school? That's actually really awesome. I wish we had that sort of thing back when I was in high school.	8/10
WITHOUTTHEY	RE: HIGH SCHOOL ACTIVISM CLUBS Well you know, we'll see. It might be a total wash. Also, back when you were still in high school? How old are you?	8/10
TOOTHLESS	RE: HIGH SCHOOL ACTIVISM CLUBS Wow that probably came off way creepy. I'm sorry. I'm 19. Not an old creeper on a message board, I swear.	8/10
WITHOUTTHEY	RE: HIGH SCHOOL ACTIVISM CLUBS Suuuuuuuuuure. :-P	8/10

FROM	SUBJECT	DATE
TOOTHLESS	RE: HIGH SCHOOL ACTIVISM CLUBS I'm not! Here, I'll send you a pic as proof or something. Is that okay?	8/10
TOOTHLESS	RE: HIGH SCHOOL ACTIVISM CLUBS Hello?	8/10
TOOTHLESS	RE: HIGH SCHOOL ACTIVISM CLUBS Yeah okay I see where all of that went wrong.	8/10

IV

Leila lay awake in bed, staring at the ceiling in her bedroom. Despite the fact that she was living in a new home with a new family, the house was far from new. It was an old, built-around-the-founding-of-America, Philadelphia-style rowhome out in Manayunk, nearly three centuries old. The plaster ceiling was cracked, with thin breaks spreading out like spider webs. The lines moved from the ceiling to the wall, and bits of paint nicked out and threatened to fall with the slightest bump. She followed the lines with her eyes, like tracing a maze, trying to ignore what she couldn't stop hearing as the sun started to creep into her window.

The whispers.

Lay . . . whar . . . y . . . I . . . oh . . .

For whatever reason, the voices decided to be particularly loud this morning; and over the past two days, since hanging out with Sarika in Adam's Café and going through the motions at Summer Enrichment at Belmont, they'd suddenly become clearer. Every time she stepped outside, she could hear the unintelligible whispering on the wind, rattling in her mind, slowly morphing from multiple voices to what sounded like a single, resolute one. She closed her eyes, trying to push it back out, willing it to leave. It was bad enough that when the weather dipped, as autumn approached, so did her mood.

She gritted her teeth and squeezed her eyes shut.

Quiet. Soft. Dancing around her ears like a breath.

Lay . . . yuh . . . ter . . . us . . . oods . . .

"Bedroom. Ceiling. Walls. Plaster. Bed," she muttered, shaking her head.

Lay . . . yuh . . . ter . . . us . . . oods . . .

Multiple voices whispered like the deep exhale of several people after a long run.

"Go away!" Leila shouted, and tossed the sheets off her bed to sit up. The whispering vanished, the dissipation and resulting silence almost as loud as the voices themselves. She heard the sounds of footsteps briskly thundering up the stairs, and she grasped the bedsheets, tossing them back over herself as the door to her bedroom swung open.

"Leila?" Jon shouted, storming into the room with Lisabeth.

"Are you okay, sweetheart?" Lisabeth asked, sitting on the bed.

Leila feigned sleepiness, rubbing at her eyes and blinking.

"Hm?" she mumbled. "Yeah, I'm fine. Just a nightmare. Don't worry, Liz, just go back downstairs, I'll be down in a minute."

"It's okay, Mom," Jon said, patting Lisabeth on the back. Leila tried not to scowl. She wasn't ready for that word yet, and it wasn't fair that Jon kept using it whenever he wanted.

"O–okay," Lisabeth stammered, and Leila could

practically hear her eyes starting to glisten. Damn it. The M word always brought her to tears, albeit adorable tears. Leila's mouth felt like it was torn between frowning and smiling at all of it. On the one hand, she still wasn't ready for any of that. On the other hand, she had to admit, it was sweet.

But she couldn't do it yet.

Not yet.

Jon stood aside, letting Liz walk through the door first, and then followed suit.

He peeked down the hallway and then turned back to her, whispering, "She made pancakes and bacon, if you're up and hungry." Leila knew it was more him asking her to please join them, and less him just letting her know the deal.

"I'll be down in a second," Leila said, and Jon walked out of the room, his footsteps matching Lisabeth's as they descended the staircase.

The rowhome's kitchen was just big enough to fit a little dining table and three seats, the fourth edge of the table pressed up against a wall. From the kitchen window Leila could look outside and see Major Willow, and she hoped the little tree was taking root okay. She visited her twice a day to make sure she was safe and secure in the new plot of dirt. Leila was still torn as to whether or not it had been a good idea, planting the little tree there. The potential for the roots to wrap around something was so very real. But it would have to do for now.

Leila shrugged and adjusted her light box, shifting it over a little to make room for her plate of breakfast. The light shone right at her, beaming from the vertical, steel box. They'd fallen into a comfortable routine, sitting down at the kitchen table together in the morning, Jon reading his papers, Liz and Leila fussing with their phones, while the box beamed on Leila for a solid fifteen minutes. When they hit the halfway mark, right around seven minutes or so, conversation usually broke out, and for the most part phones went away and it was time for breakfast.

Leila didn't show it, but she was relieved that Liz cooked today. Jon's last experiment with waffles resulted in waffle batter burnt so solid, it could have been used as ice cube trays.

"So, how's enrichment been?" Lisabeth asked, pushing a plate of eggs and bacon across their small kitchen table. "Still into it?"

"Not bad," Leila said, taking a bite of bacon, and trying not to audibly sigh at the burst of salty and sweet flavor exploding in her mouth. "It's mostly been me and Sarika hitting the school gym, which is ridiculously huge, or holing up in the library. And then there's Adam's at the end of the day."

"So you're basically spending summer the way you would have anyway. Books, coffee, Sarika," Jon said, his newspaper rustling as he talked. "Why don't you meet some people? Make some friends at the enrichment program. Aren't there kids from all the regional schools in there?"

"Meh," Leila said, taking another bite of bacon. "People

are kind of the worst. I'll stick to my routine, thanks. Routine is comfortable." She tapped the metal side of her light box.

"That's one of the building blocks of a good marriage," Jon said, a smile in his voice.

Lisabeth laughed and threw a bag of tea at Jon's head.

"What about that club, though?" Lisabeth asked, reaching for some more pancakes. "You know, the one with the Captain Planet kids that you're all geared up about."

"Oh, no, that's nothing," Leila said as Jon put down his newspaper, looking at her with increased interest. He folded his arms and lifted his eyebrows. She was sure a bad nature pun was coming. "Also, come on, Captain Planet? No one knows what that is anymore."

"Sure they do," Lisabeth said, leaning back in her chair. She took a bite of a pancake, and one of her braids slipped out of the headscarf they were wrapped up in. "Ah, shoot." She fussed with it as she continued talking. "I bet it's only a matter of time before Netflix reboots it or something."

"We haven't even met yet. So, we'll see how Captain Planet-ish the group is," Leila said. "But I'm going to ride my bike over to enrichment this morning, along the Schuylkill Trail, if you want to, I don't know, take the ride with me?"

Leila shook her head, annoyed with herself at making it more of a question than a request, her voice turning up with her insecurity. She'd had a hard time trying to bond with any of the foster families, and now that she was actually adopted . . . she tried to push the dark, swirling feelings inside down deep someplace, and open herself up to all this. They *wanted* her. But the feeling of needing them pushed itself up. It pressed.

Accept me.

Don't push me away.

I want to be here. I don't want to be alone again.

"Sure, that sounds lovely," Lisabeth said with a smile.

"Awesome." Leila looked at her watch and flicked off the light box. "Thanks for the breakfast, Liz." She stood up, pushed her chair in to the tiny table, and pulled at the power cord, popping the plug out of the wall beneath the table.

Lisabeth paused, standing there with an expectant look on her face.

"What is it?" Leila asked, as she started to pull the cord up from under the table, coiling it around her arm.

"Nothing," she said, her voice gone quiet. "I'll go get dressed and grab my helmet." With that, she got up and made her way out of the kitchen, the sound of her feet soft against the steps leading upstairs.

Leila put her light box under the table and looked at Jon, who glanced up from his paper with that look. The one he'd been giving her the past few months. Leila grabbed her dishes and stormed over to the sink, tossing them in with a loud clatter.

"I can't say it," Leila said, standing at the sink. She looked up through the window at Major Willow outside. She looked at her palm, the scar shiny and pale against her skin. "I want to, but I can't. Not yet."

"I don't know what you're talking about," Jon said.

Leila turned around and caught him as he reached for his coffee before taking a long sip.

"You do though. I know that look. I know what you're thinking," Leila said, leaning against the sink. "Sarika, her family had the same problem, you know? Last year, her parents kept trying to get her to say it. And it's just hard, Jon, you know?"

"I don't know, though," Jon said between sips of his coffee. He placed his paper down on the table and looked at her, his mouth turned into a soft smile. "Leila, I've had a privileged life. I'm aware of it. Your moth—" He stopped himself, closing his eyes. "Lisabeth has taught me to look at what I have differently. My family? I was lucky. Her family, not so much."

"Oh?" Leila asked, her heart hammering. She walked back to the kitchen table and sat down, nudging her chair closer, the wood of the chair scraping against the hardwood floor with an audible squeak.

"I'm not the one to talk to you about it," Jon said, shaking his head. "That's between you two, really. I don't want to take that away from her, it's not my place. Let's just say I used words like "mom" and "dad" quite often growing up, throughout my whole life. She," he looked up and out of the kitchen, towards the stairs. "She didn't get to."

"That's," Leila started, her chest feeling heavy. Lisabeth didn't look like she'd lived with the weight that Leila had, and the revelation left her surprised. "I don't even know what to say."

"Sometimes it's better just to listen," Jon said, picking

his coffee up again, lifting it in a faux toast. "Liz taught me that."

"How does all this," Leila said, gesturing between the two of them and then at the stairs, "not wear on you? I swear, I never see you cry or anything. You just make jokes all the time."

"Defense mechanism," Jon said, shrugging while sipping his coffee again. "I save all the heavy emotions for later. Bottle it all up and cry in the shower."

"Oh my God, Jon." Leila laughed, happy for the levity in the air.

"So this club of yours," Jon started, changing the subject. "What's the story? First you ban me from your message board, which was mean by the way, and now, why are you trying to hide it from me? It sounds fun."

"Listen up, Sage Wisdom," Leila said, pointing a finger at Jon. "I just don't want you making a big deal out of it or anything. Or trying to, like, come join it or try to supervise it or whatever."

"What?" Jon gasped. "I'd never do that."

Leila gave him a stare.

"Okay, maybe I would, but okay. Okay. I'll respect your privacy," Jon said, smiling from behind his newspaper. "Besides, there's far too much going on with all this stuff: the teaching, trying to cover what's going on in the park. You know they're trying to build *in* the park? And then there's this whole visitor's center and field mouse debacle up near East Falls." He slapped at the newspaper and put it down. "And that abandoned bird conservatory for wounded raptors. Well, practically abandoned. I might do a story on it, but there's all this conflict of interest and . . ."

He sipped his coffee and cleared his throat.

"Ah, darling," he said, grinning over his paper and shaking his head. "It's tough work, trying to save the world with words."

"Someone has to do it though, right?" Leila didn't so much ask as say.

"Damn right." He lifted his coffee cup and Leila toasted hers with his and took a sip. "So wait, this club. I digressed far too much. What's the story?"

"I don't quite know yet." Leila shrugged, trying not to think of the mysterious, cute boy from Adam's Café, with his messy, brown hair and sun-kissed skin that made him look like he'd just spent a long day the beach. "No one on the board"—she scowled—"which, by the way, stay off of. It's anonymous."

"Oh, I couldn't help myself." Jon chuckled. "And did I say your name on there? Clear the browser history when you use the downstairs computer next time. Life lesson."

"Anyway, no one on the message board knew anything about it," Leila continued. "Sarika thinks it'll be good for me, though. I do too, I guess. I mean, those are my kind of people, just this time, IRL."

"Earl?" Jon asked.

"No, I-R-L," Leila said, rolling her eyes. "In real life. Come on, you aren't *that* old, you know what that means."

"Ah, yes," Jon said, taking a sip from his coffee. "Well, I hope Earl is nice to you."

Leila balled up a napkin, tossed it at Jon, and got up from the table.

"Time to get ready," she said, pushing her chair in. "See you after school or whatever."

"Tell Earl I said hi," he said, lifting his newspaper up.

"Just stop," Leila said, making her way down the hall towards the stairs.

V

"Remind me why we need lockers again?" Leila asked, fiddling with the combination code with one hand while fussing with her hair with the other. Her bike helmet was wedged under her arm, her small backpack on the hallway floor. "I mean really, its *summer* enrichment. Does anyone even have *books*?"

"If anyone needs a locker during all this, it's you," Sarika said with a smirk, before falling back and leaning against the locker next to her with loud *pang*. She pulled Leila's helmet out from under her arm and held onto it.

"Thanks," Leila said, her locker finally swinging open. There were a handful of leftover stickers all over the inside from whoever had it last. Leila scowled at the multicolored dolphins and kittens coated with rainbows and glitter. "Look at all this. It's like a time machine. Lisa Frank is not my thing."

"It looks like a unicorn threw up in here. Or maybe exploded and died," Sarika said, eying up the inside of the locker. "We'll have to redecorate, especially if you're gonna show up looking like this every other day."

"What's wrong with this?" Leila asked, offended.

"You have helmet hair," Sarika said flatly. "You're a girl with a 'fro with helmet hair. All out to the side, like this, like you slept with a book on top of your head. Not acceptable."

"Yeah I suppose you're—hey!" Leila exclaimed, as someone slammed a shoulder into hers, sending her crashing against the door to her locker. Two girls about her age walked by laughing to one another, as a third trailed pensively behind. Leila spun around and glared at them just as they stopped.

"Oops, sorry," a blonde girl with a white-and-black striped skirt and a makeup clutch under her arm said. "Didn't see you there. Usually this one is all by herself. Finally make a friend? How cute."

Leila turned to Sarika, who had backed against the locker, glowering at the three girls as they approached. Two were tall and blonde, and the one talking to them was clearly the alpha of the pack. The other, mousey with brown hair, smirked but stood back, as if she was a spectator to the whole thing. Leila locked eyes with her for a moment, and the girl turned away.

"Screw off, Jessica," Sarika spat.

"Or what?" Jessica snapped back. "You'll report me? This isn't Central. No one here knows me. And I own this school."

"Please. You were nobody there, and you're a nobody here." Sarika crossed her arms and stuck her chin up. Jessica took a threatening step forward, and Leila moved closer to Sarika, feeling her body tense as the blonde girl loomed over her.

It was Sarika's first year at the group home all over again. Sarika, small, slim, her eyes wide and terrified; Leila, tall, strong, ready to tear down anyone who dared pick on her friend. Or, in the event she wasn't around, avenging her when they picked on her without her watchful presence.

Only it wasn't.

Sarika stared hard at Jessica as the tall girl, her eyes blue and cold, bore down on her. The girl Leila had grown up with, scared and reserved, who used to panic and hide behind her, was gone. Here she stood resolute, unafraid, unmoving.

Un-Sarika.

"What?" Sarika asked, a smirk on her face. "Come on. Do it."

"Jessica," said the mousy girl, who stood a few feet away clutching her books. "Jessica, come on, maybe we should–"

"Shut up, Gwen!" Jessica snapped, pointing a finger at the brown-haired girl, who promptly shrunk back and pressed herself against the lockers on the opposite side of the hall. Jessica glared at Sarika. "I should be at home basking in the sun by my pool. Instead, I'm stuck here with these two, and spending my summer in this hole because of you, you fucking Paki–"

Sarika swung the backpack on her shoulder, the fabric and books making an audible *whoosh* from the speed, and connected squarely with Jessica's head.

"Sarika!" Leila shouted.

"Jessica!" Gwen and her still-unknown friend exclaimed.

Jessica hit the hallway floor with a bang, her makeup

bag clattering across the tile, eyeshadow palettes and lipsticks skittering and clinking against the lockers. She rolled onto her back, stared up at Sarika and Leila with wide and horrified eyes, and wiped a streak of blood away from her nose. She looked down at her hand and back up at Sarika, and moved to stand up, her eyes now angry and fierce.

Sarika jumped on top of her and gripped Jessica's wrists, pinning her to the ground.

"Say it again," Sarika said, almost a whisper, but loud enough that Leila heard it over Jessica's friends' panicked muttering. Leila turned to look at them, and they promptly took a step back.

"SAY IT," Sarika roared, her voice echoing in the still-empty hallway.

Jessica stared at Sarika, a line of blood trickling out her nose. The two of them breathed hard.

"You're, you're fucking crazy!" Jessica blubbered.

"Sarika?" Leila ventured, taking a step towards her friend, placing a hand on her shoulder. "Come on, let's go."

"I didn't think so," Sarika spat, glaring at Jessica. She looked up at Leila, who hardly recognized her closest friend. Sarika's thick eyebrows were furrowed angrily, she was breathing heavily, everything about her screamed rage. She got off Jessica, who promptly scurried off to her friends.

"I'll get you for this," Jessica said, pointing at Sarika angrily. "You're lucky your new friend is here." She stared at Leila.

"Damn, that's enough, Jessica," the unknown girl muttered. "Let's go—"

"I say when it's time to go, Rebekah," Jessica said, glaring at her supposed friend. Who talked to their friends like this? "And new girl? Do yourself a favor. Pick up some of my makeup, and fix that fucking face of yours."

Instinctively, Leila lifted a hand and pressed it against her own cheek. She felt heated all over, felt a warm defiance course through her body.

"It's a birthmark," Leila said, trying to control the rage she felt brewing up inside of her. It'd been bad enough getting this nonsense from other kids and teens in the group home and at school, but not from some girl who just got her ass kicked by her five-foot-two best friend.

"Well it looks like someone burned you," she snapped, crossing her arms and looking her up and down.

"Didn't you already learn your damn lesson?" Sarika shouted, moving to rush at the girls, who flinched back. Leila reached out and grabbed Sarika, throwing her arms around her into an awkward hug from the back.

"Come on, girl," Leila whispered. "It isn't worth it."

"Hey!" someone shouted.

"Shit, Dr. Rich is here for the summer?" Jessica muttered.

Leila turned and caught sight of a man hurrying down the hall, another trailing behind him. One had a small belly and was dressed in red-and-black plaid and blue jeans like some kind of lazy lumberjack, the other was dressed in a tweed jacket complete with patches, a vest, and a bright-yellow tie.

The lumberjack hustled ahead.

"Just what the hell is going on here?" he asked, glaring at Jessica and then at Sarika. "Haven't the two of you gotten into it enough?"

"She started it, Dr. Rich!" shouted Jessica, holding a hand up to her bloody nose.

"She's lying!" shouted Sarika, struggling to free herself from Leila's grasp.

"My dad and his lawyers will be down here so fast you won't—" Jessica started.

"Cut it out!" Dr. Rich shouted, standing in between Leila, Sarika, and the three girls. "You three, get to your sensitivity class, or I swear to God, you're finished in this school district, and no, I don't give a damn who your father is, Jessica. And you two," he started before his eyes settled on Leila. "Wait, who is this? Who are you?"

"Leila," Leila said, letting go of Sarika, who brushed herself off. "I'm, uh, I'm new."

"Clearly," Dr. Rich said. "I'll be keeping an eye on you. You too." He nodded at Sarika.

"Are you two here for summer school or something?" the smartly dressed teacher asked, stepping up next to Dr. Rich and staring at Sarika and Leila.

"Chet, why?" Dr. Rich muttered, his hand slapping against his forehead.

"For your information," Sarika spat. "We're in the enrichment program. For fun. They're the ones here for punishment. Don't assume we're in summer school just because we're the first brown people you've spotted today."

"Oh, damn," Leila muttered.

"That's not what . . ." the other teacher stammered, looking from Leila and Sarika to Dr. Rich, who shrugged his shoulders in response.

"Maybe you should consider sending your teachers to sensitivity training, too, Dr. Rich," Sarika said, her voice oozing sarcasm.

"Okay, okay," Dr. Rich said, his hands up. "That's enough. You." He pointed at Jessica. "My office. That goes for you, too." He nodded at Sarika. "We'll talk this out." He turned to the teacher, and shook his head. "Chet, you're a piece of work, you know that? We'll have a conversation about this later. Sarika, Jessica, put your stuff away. See you in fifteen minutes."

"You're not going to call our parents, are you, Dr. Rich?" Jessica asked, her voice full of worry and concern, her eyes sad and pleading. In a flash her face turned dark and sarcastic. "Well, my parents, I suppose. Might be hard to find hers."

Sarika lunged again and Leila pulled her back as she lashed about, though Leila had a serious urge just to let Sarika tear her apart.

"Sweet Jesus, make that FIVE minutes, you two." Dr. Rich said, shooing Jessica and her girls towards the end of the hall. "I'll be waiting."

Jessica and the girls walked away, but not before turning around and smiling at Sarika and Leila. Jessica and Rebekah both gave them the finger as they twirled about, making their exit.

"Damn it," Sarika muttered, pounding a fist against a

hard metal locker and turning to Leila. She peered into Leila's locker and scowled. "We should really decorate in here. I mean, I know you only have this locker for the next few weeks or so, but still, might as well make it feel like home."

"Oh, no, you think you can get in a fight and curse off in front of a teacher, right next to me, and just change the subject to this?" Leila asked, leaning back against the lockers. Sarika shrugged.

"Listen, we've had years of life experience with prissy kids who think they can shove us around for being different from them. So to hell with them, not worth our time," Sarika said, scowling again.

Leila gave her a look.

"Ugh, fine," Sarika huffed. "Those three? I'll give you the quick-and-dirty rundown, and then feel free to forget their names. They've only stuck with me because I've been around them for two years. Jessica De La Costa, the tall one of the bunch. She's the leader, and the worst of them all. We got in a fight at the end of the school year, like right in June, and she and her friends are here for racial sensitivity training or some such bullshit that will inevitably fail."

"Wait. You got in a fight?" Leila asked. "Why didn't you tell me?"

"I don't know." Sarika shrugged. "I mean, you and the Klines? You had more important things on your mind."

"You'll always be first, you know that." Leila smiled. "Just because things are complicated, doesn't mean I don't have room for more complications."

"Well, get ready," Sarika said with a scowl, "because it's going to get more complex with those three rampaging around. So we got Jessica, and then there's Rebekah Mamakas, she's the shorter one with the freckles. And," Sarika paused, as if collecting herself, her eyes closed.

"What is it?" Leila asked. Sarika lifted a hand.

"A moment, please," Sarika said, clearing her throat. "For the third one. Dramatic pause: Gwenyffer Stillwater."

A beat passed before Leila and Sarika erupted into laughter.

"Gwenyffer?" Leila sighed. "That's actually an awesome name. Like she could be a singer or a model."

"Too bad it's wasted on her. She doesn't talk much, just follows those two around. I don't even think she likes them, but it doesn't matter. Makes her just as bad as the rest of them for not saying anything," Sarika said, the laughter fading. "Look, I didn't go through all those shitty fosters and get my ass kicked back in the group home all those years to be kicked around now. Especially by girls like that who think they rule this place because *oh look at me my father owns three homes with a million bathrooms* or whatever. And neither did you."

Leila nodded, surprised at this fury coming out of her best friend. She felt a familiar pang in her chest, remembering Sarika with the bruises all those times she hadn't been around to protect her.

"For them, yeah, this is a fun excuse to goof off, maybe meet some boys, maybe give out a few hand jobs in a stairwell, and ignore this 'training' they're supposed to get. Which, let's be real, will never help anyway," Sarika said, smirking and doing air quotes. "Don't let them think they're better than you. Or us. 'Cause they aren't."

Sarika reached into her backpack and slapped something against the inside of Leila's locker, which clicked against the metal inside with a bang. She moved her hand to reveal a mirror, stuck to the metal with a magnet, covering up all the rainbow glitter stickers. It was bland, the frame made out of a sand-colored wood. Leila peered in and looked at herself, at the splash of pale beige that made its way up the side of her face like a handprint and the dark freckles that flecked the sides of her nose and flowed over the top of her cheeks.

"Maybe I *should* try some makeup," Leila said, raising a hand over her face to block out the mark on the lower part of her left cheek. "What do you think?"

She looked at Sarika, who stared at her, aghast.

"I'm just saying," Leila said, shrugging. "New school for the summer, new me. Who would know?"

"*You* would know," Sarika said, sternly. "You would. That is not why I dramatically slapped a mirror inside of your locker. You were supposed to look at it and be all, 'Wow, I'm hella beautiful the way I am. Fuck those girls.' And then walk away with me to some kind of bad-ass friendship soundtrack."

"Come on, I'm just—"

"Friendship. Soundtrack," Sarika said, stressing each word. "Never change. What did we learn from *Rappaccini's Daughter* in English last year?" Sarika grinned, and Leila scowled. She knew she hated that story.

"Oh no," Leila said, crossing her arms and closing her

locker. "No, no. Not that short story. Every single foster parent and well-meaning teacher ever has tried to shove that fable down my throat, I won't hear it from you."

"I'm just saying, if we got anything from that story, it's that if you put makeup on over your skin, you'll die."

"That . . . that is not what that story is about," Leila said, smiling.

"Come on," Sarika said, offering up an arm. Leila looped her arm through. "Come walk me to the firing squad, and then let's go check out this environmental activism club thing, and see if that delicious boy is here today."

Luckily, Sarika's meeting with Dr. Rich only lasted a few minutes, and she got off with a warning. Room 407 was located on the clear opposite side of Belmont, in the upper corner of the school on the top floor, next to a number of classrooms that looked as though they were set up for labs. Leila guessed the various chemistry, physics, and biology courses were secluded in this section of the school in the event anyone blew something up—or a high school teacher decided to start making drugs to save his sick family.

Leila eyed all the bulletin boards that lined the rather quiet hallway around the science classrooms, tacked up with fliers for the Environmental Activism club, notes about field trips, a bicycle for sale, and details regarding September classes. Botany, astronomy, lots of classes that she'd totally take that ended in "y," if this was the school she was actually attending instead of Central across town.

Sarika opened the door to the classroom first, and Leila followed.

Instead of conventional desks, the room was full of large laboratory tables, with pipes and valves on the surface for Bunsen burners and experiments. A handful of students already sat at a few of the tables, and they all turned to look at Sarika and Leila as they walked in. Leila offered up an awkward wave and looked at Sarika, who rolled her eyes as they made their way to a free table and two empty lab stools.

Leila scooted the stool up against the table and resisted the urge to squirm about. The wooden stools weren't exactly comfortable. She leaned on the table, the black surface cold and comforting against her bare arms, and felt some odd scratches and scuffs against her skin. She looked down at the slab.

An array of names and dates were etched into the table, some with elegant care and precision, others carelessly scrawled.

A.K. ♥'s S.R. 4 EVR: *Class of 2001*

DOWN WITH SCIENCE

Mr. Chet is a total babe, 10/10, would ba—

The door to the classroom swung open while Leila traced the etched carvings, and in walked Shawn, the "delicious" boy from the café. He had a beat-up backpack slung carelessly over his shoulder, beige and worn, like something from an army surplus store. His chestnut hair hung over his face as he sauntered in. He tossed his backpack on the teacher's desk in the front of the classroom and sat down on it. He looked up and ran his hand through his hair, pulling it away from his face, and smiled at everyone in the room. His teeth were a shocking white, and he had a single dimple like a crater on the left side of his face.

He looked right at Leila, and she felt herself blush just as an elbow nudged her in the side. She turned and glared at Sarika, who in turn stared at her with wide eyes and an open mouth.

"Welcome everyone, I'm Shawn Kennedy. Welcome to the first meeting of the Belmont Environmental Activism Club, or B.E.A.C., as we generally call it. Like a bird's beak, but with a C." He looked back at Leila again, smiling, and Leila felt the warmth returning to her cheeks.

"I see a couple of new faces in the room," Shawn continued, "as well as a bunch of returning ones, which is good to see. You should know that even after the enrichment is over, no matter what school you're at, you are welcome to attend our meetings and events. We've got a lot of work to do this year and need all the help we can get, from changes being made in Fairmount Park to protests along the Schuylkill River regarding some of these outrageous new fishing laws."

"Yeah!" a girl with bright-red hair shouted from up in the front the room, slamming her fist down against her desk.

"Down with those corporate scumbags and their machine!" snapped someone just one row ahead of Leila and Sarika. He turned and nodded to someone else sitting in the classroom, his long hair dancing about on his head.

Mixed in with the cheers and shouts were a couple of

halfhearted grumbles muttered around the lab, some of the students staring down at their hands or awkwardly at one another.

"Hey losers!" a familiar voice piped up. Leila looked towards the door to spot Jessica and Gwen standing in the door frame. Jessica had her arms crossed and a smirk on her face; Gwen lingered behind, her eyes darting around uncomfortably.

Sarika moved to get up off of her stool, and Leila held a hand out to grab her shoulder. She shook her head. She seriously didn't need to get in any more trouble today, and the last thing Leila wanted to do was keep drawing attention to herself.

"Corporate scumbags? Really? The developers working in Fairmount Park? And what's the big deal? It's just a few fish in the river. If people want to eat all that mercury, let them. The people working on this stuff can't be all bad," Jessica continued as she walked in. Gwen trailed hesitantly behind her. "You should know more than anyone."

Shawn sighed and nodded at the rest of the club.

"For those of you who are new, this is Jessica and Gwen. Jessica's father is also, well, something of an activist, I suppose."

"You suppose?" Jessica scoffed. "Please. Who do you think helps fund you and your father's precious vacations?"

"They aren't vacations, we're raising awareness for—"

"Right, while enjoying the scenic oceans and warm waters, while—"

"Your dad only does it for the tax write off, Jessica," Shawn suddenly snapped, his demeanor gone sour, the playful expression on his face vanished. "He doesn't give a damn. You know that, I know that, and furthermore—"

"Does he know you know that?" Jessica asked.

Shawn stared at her.

"Does he, does my dad, know that your father thinks he does this for the tax benefits?" Jessica continued, taking a step.

"Jessica, I don't speak for my—"

"Whatever," Jessica snapped. She turned and looked around the room, her eyes settling on Leila and Sarika. She glowered and waved her hand around dismissively before turning to Gwen. "Let's grab a seat."

"What?" Sarika said, deadpan. Leila nudged her.

"Jessica, can we not do this?" Shawn said. "I mean, really, you don't want to be here."

"Maybe I do," Jessica said, walking towards the group. She grabbed one of the tall stools. "Come on. I know you want me. Here, that is."

She grinned, and Leila felt a rush of jealousy course through her. Clearly the two of them had some history.

"You should leave," Shawn said, turning away to look back at the group. "I mean, I can't stop you from joining B.E.A.C., but this isn't what you want. And I'm certainly not what you want. You made that pretty damn clear."

An awkward quiet fell over the room. Sarika nudged Leila.

"Daaaaaamn," Sarika mouthed silently.

Jessica stood up quickly and glared at Shawn, who continued to look away.

She kicked her stool over, causing everyone in the room to jump.

"Fuck you. Fuck you and your dad's bullshit causes." She looked over at Sarika and Leila, her eyes narrowing. "The hell you looking at, huh? All of you? Fuck this. I'm going to go throw aluminum cans out of my SUV into a pond full of manatees, you tree-hugging freaks. Let's go, Gwen."

Jessica bolted out of the room, knocking over a few more stools as she left. Gwen hurried behind her and awkwardly tried to pick up a few of the seats.

"Gwen!" Jessica snapped, peeking back into the room. "Leave them!" Gwen looked over at Jessica and then back at the classroom, her eyes flashing what looked like a silent apology.

Shawn buried his head in his hands and breathed in deep, and looked up back at everyone, his mouth a narrow line. He cleared his throat.

"So . . . me and Jessica broke up," he said, his mouth curving up in a half smile. A couple of chuckles broke out around the room as he stood back up, shrugging. "Look, I, um, I know her dad sometimes helped out with some of our trips and what-not through the school year, but nothing is going to change. I've still got some fun things planned this year."

Shawn's voice faded as he went on about the club, and Leila stared ahead, feeling a bit disappointed. What kind of guy was he if he dated a girl like that? Too bad.

Shawn walked towards the back of the classroom,

closed the door tightly, and then strolled back over, shrugging.

"So, unfortunately, this will sadly be my last year at the helm, and I hope one of you will take the green throne after I move on and graduate." He hung his head down, shaking it solemnly. Leila glanced over at Sarika, who exchanged looks with her.

Green throne? Was he for real?

"Boo!" shouted a few of the students sitting closer to the front of the room. Shawn smiled and waved them off.

"There will be time for mourning later," he exclaimed, looking back up. He held his hands in the air, as though to calm the masses before him, even though there were only a dozen or so people in the class. Then he sat back down and rubbed his hands together. "The drama is over, and today, we get to know the new recruits. The acorns, if you will."

"Hah! I won't," Sarika said with a smirk.

Leila laughed and nudged her, and the rest of the students who had assembled turned and looked at them with a mixture of bemused expressions and utter horror.

"What?" Sarika snapped at one of the students glaring at her. The student turned away quickly, looking back at Shawn. "I'm not a boring average nut from off a tree. Neither of us are. Me and this girl are more like hazelnuts, thank you."

"Well then, I suppose we can start with the two of you," Shawn said, hopping back off his desk and standing in front of the class. He extended a hand. "Or, how about I start and break the ice. Me, I'm Shawn Kennedy, president and founder of the B.E.A.C. here at Belmont High School." He started to pace in the front of the room, hands behind his back. "In addition to all that, I'm captain of our lacrosse team, and vice president of the student government."

He walked back over to the desk and sat back on it.

"That about sums me up, I suppose. Anyone care to go first?" He looked around the room. No hands raised.

"Sure, why not," Sarika chimed in, standing up. She gave a little wave to everyone in the room and then sat on the edge of the lab table, crossing her legs and leaning back on the black surface. "So I'm Sarika Krishna. Not super into the environment, but I am really into coffee—"

"Ah, the plague that hurts the planet." Shawn interrupted, a disapproving look on his face.

"Excuse me?" Sarika asked, hopping off the desk.

"Just saying, those coffee farms decimate the planet." He shrugged and smiled at her. "And those instant coffee pods people love using these days, so much waste, so much—"

"Whatever," she snipped. "I'm into coffee; specifically, if you'd had let me finish before 'actually-ing' me, the sustainable kind. Coffee that comes from small communities, harvested from individual farms, roasted locally and sourced with minimum damage to the land. So sure, I guess I'm into preserving the environment, but I'm a little more interested in how saving land helps save and preserve ways of life."

"Ah," Shawn said, looking down at his hands. "Well, that is interesting. I'm sorry."

"Accepted," Sarika said curtly.

"Geez, Sarika," Leila muttered.

"Hey, no one gets to "well actually" me and get away with it," she said, crossing her arms and looking back up at Shawn. "So yes. I'm here for that. There's an excellent coffee community in Philadelphia, and I'd love to learn more about preservation and environmental science, and how that can help me be a bigger part of it. And, of course, I'm here for this one." She nodded at Leila and grinned.

"Damn it, girl," Leila groaned, burying her head in her hands.

"Ah, yes," Shawn said, and Leila could hear him grinning. "I believe you're up, and that we've met before, no?"

"Yes," Leila said into her hands, wanting the earth to open up and swallow her.

"Well?" Shawn asked. Leila looked up, and there he was, at his desk, his hand out, welcoming. He was smiling that lopsided smile, and she forced herself not to sigh.

"Hey all," Leila said, sitting up. She waved to the faces that had turned to look at her. "So yeah, hi. I'm Leila, with an I and not a Y. Um."

She looked around at all the eyes staring at her, and felt that warmth returning to her chest, bubbling up. The pressure and the anxiety that brewed in her when around too many people she didn't know. She could feel her heart speeding up, her breathing quickening.

Leila glanced at the door leading out of the science lab, and moved to walk away from the desk. Sarika grabbed her arm.

"Hey, come on now," Sarika said, her voice soft.

"I just don't think I can do," Leila looked up at the class, their eyes all on her, as she whispered to Sarika, "all this, you know?" Shawn stared at her, his eyes soft without any trace of judgement, none of that awkward pity or concern. His eyes sparkled. It calmed her down in an odd way, and she took a deep breath.

"Come on," Sarika repeated. "It's just like, you know."

Leila looked down at Sarika, who nodded her head.

"It's like group." Sarika muttered.

Ah.

She did know.

The long talk sessions at Adam's Café, foster kids and recent adoptees, bonding together, talking long and hard into the evening. Parents that walked away, foster families that didn't work out. Stories of estranged siblings and runaway friends were frequent and heartbreaking, but the words poured out as long as there were people around to listen.

"Sorry, I, um, I don't speak in front of people all that often," she said, laughing awkwardly. She took a deep breath, and felt Sarika squeeze her hand. "I just, you know, care a lot about what happens to our world. When you spend most of your life moving here and there, with new families and new schools, you learn to find something to stay connected with that's a constant."

She blinked away tears that threatened to show themselves and cleared her throat, the mixture of digging up a personal story hitting hard with the anxiety of being around so many new people.

"You can do it," Sarika whispered.

"Anyhow, that constant for me is, well, all of that." She nodded at the windows in the back of the lab, which overlooked a patch of trees in a park near the school. "The trees, the outdoors. The world under my feet. Things that are solid and hard to move, difficult to change. And the things that want to change them, change them in a negative way? Well, I'd like to be there to stop it. To preserve something."

She looked up at Shawn and saw his gaze full of something a little deeper. Admiration, maybe? She felt a gentle touch on her forearm, and saw Sarika still holding her, smiling softly. She nodded at her friend and looked back the room.

"So yeah, that's why I'm here. I um, saved a willow tree recently." She shrugged. "Sometimes you have to start small. Although, it didn't feel small for me. I loved that tree."

"Thank you for sharing," Shawn said, his tone gentle and soft.

"Man, I'm just here so I have something that looks good on my college application," muttered one of the students up front. Leila let out a laugh, and the redhead in front of the room threw a pen at the kid, the plastic clattering across the science lab's hard floor.

"Thank you, Mikey," Shawn said, shaking his head and smiling. "Let's continue around the room."

Shawn made his way around the room, pointing at this student and that, each with their own story of why they cared about the planet and what they were doing here. Leila listened, occasionally interrupted by a playful nudge or snarky comment from Sarika, but mostly, she watched. She stared.

At Shawn, and how he kept talking to everyone else but never seemed to take his eyes off her.

Alternatives to the Raptor Trust in Fairmount
Posted by Toothless
AUGUST 14th, 2017 | 7:02PM
Hey all, odd question. I've come across this wounded bird that I'd like to help out, but the Raptor Trust in Fairmount is shutting down, as I'm sure many of you have heard. Does anyone know any solid alternatives, particularly places that won't euthanize an animal that can't be recuperated?

RE: Alternatives to the Raptor Trust in Fairmount
Posted by Jill the Birder
AUGUST 14th, 2017 | 7:09PM
You could try the Roxborough Animal Habilitation Center. Depends on the bird, I think, but I know they take just about everything. I saw a turkey vulture there once that would never be able to fly. Just lives there. Seems happy. As does the peacock who chased my car.

> RE: Alternatives to the Raptor Trust in Fairmount
> *Posted by Toothless*
> AUGUST 14th, 2017 | 7:09PM
> LOL, that peacock story. Thanks Jill. This really helps out a lot.

RE: Alternatives to the Raptor Trust in Fairmount
Posted by A Dash of Paprika
AUGUST 14th, 2017 | 8:09PM
What did you do to that poor bird, Toothy?

> RE: Alternatives to the Raptor Trust in
> Fairmount
> Posted by Toothless
> AUGUST 14th, 2017 | 7:02PM
> Har har. Nothing. I'm trying to save him.
>
> RE: Alternatives to the Raptor Trust in
> Fairmount
> Posted by A Dash of Paprika
> AUGUST 14th, 2017 | 7:09PM
> Since when did you grow a heart?
>
> RE: Alternatives to the Raptor Trust in
> Fairmount
> Posted by WithouttheY
> AUGUST 14th, 2017 | 7:15PM
> Come on Paprika, chill.

FROM	SUBJECT	DATE
TOOTHLESS	Thanks You know, for all that.	8/14
WITHOUTTHEY	RE: Thanks *shrugs* not a big deal. We all get carried away sometimes.	8/14

VI

"Wait, so nothing? Nothing at all?" Sarika asked as she poked at the chicken nuggets on her lunch tray, scowling.

"Not yet," Leila said, shrugging and taking a bite out of a nugget. "Try one, they aren't terrible."

"I don't trust meat that isn't shaped like actual meat," Sarika said, grabbing a french fry off her plate and dipping it in ketchup. "It isn't natural."

"You're serious?" Leila asked. "You just dipped a rectangle made of potato starch into a puddle of paste that contains some tomato, but mostly tons of artificial chemicals. Let's not talk about natural vs. unnatural here. This isn't hair."

"Yeah, but french fries are fucking delicious," Sarika said, eating the whole fry in a single bite. "They are excellent ketchup delivery systems. Right?" Leila gave her a look, and Sarika grabbed the ketchup packet and looked at the back, her expression immediately souring. "Oh. Well, whatever. I'm a hypocrite, lock me up. Anyway, I still can't believe the two of you haven't talked since that first meeting. That tension in that room was thick."

"You think so?" Leila asked, even though she knew. She could tell that Shawn was into her, the way he stared at her from across the room and the awkward way he said goodbye at the end of the meeting, complete with way-too-long *see you laters* and an extended handshake that implied maybe a hug could have happened.

"Oh, yeah, definitely," Sarika said, swirling another fry around. "Maybe he's waiting for you to make the first move or something. Trying to be all mysterious or hard to get or something."

"Well, he's going to be waiting a long-ass time," Leila raised one eyebrow, "what with that whole mess involving that friend of yours."

"Ha ha," Sarika said, rolling her eyes. "I wouldn't hold that against him. I've been dealing with Jessica and her clique for a while now, and I've never even seen him around. Not at after-school events, or picking her up. Nothing. I think they were secret or something." She shrugged.

"I still can't believe you didn't tell me you had some bullies picking on you." Leila shook her head.

"You can't protect everyone," Sarika said, reaching across the table and giving Leila's hand a squeeze. "I didn't need saving."

"Okay, okay," Leila said before grabbing another nugget.

"You should at least come on the field trip," Sarika continued, burying another french fry in ketchup, the lightly burnt potato slice coming up entirely red. "I mean, if anything, that'll be a good opportunity for you two to talk, maybe sneak off into the woods."

"Field trip?" Leila asked, ignoring her suggestion. "I didn't hear anything about that."

"Wow, you really were out of it." Sarika laughed. "He handed out those slips?" Leila shrugged and Sarika abandoned her fries to dig through her backpack.

"Behold, the permission slip," Sarika said, pulling a piece of paper out of her backpack and waving it about triumphantly. "Fairmount Park field trip." Leila plucked the piece of paper out of Sarika's hands and read it, trying not to frown.

"You know we can basically walk to Fairmount Park whenever we want, right?" Leila asked, handing the slip back to Sarika. "It's like, right there. You can probably see it right outside the windows here in the cafeteria."

"But on this trip, you'll get to see so much more," a voice chimed from behind Leila. She turned around to spot Shawn smiling his lopsided smile, his long hair dancing over his eyes as he gazed intently at Leila. She felt herself going flush and turned back to Sarika, who was grinning.

"Mind if I sit?" he asked, a bagged lunch in his hands.

"Yeah, no sure, go ahead," Leila muttered as he settled down next to her.

"Sarika, right?" he asked, pointing at Sarika with a snap and a click sound from inside his cheek. Sarika frowned and Leila flashed her a quick please-be-nice look. Sarika's expression immediately softened, though her smile looked forced.

"Yes!" Sarika exclaimed. "Nice to see you again."

"You too," Shawn said, nodding. He turned to Leila. "So the field trip. Like I said at the meeting, we're not, um, as funded as we were before for . . . personal reasons."

Shawn stumbled over his words, looking progressively more awkward as he tried not to mention Jessica. "We're going to do a little community service as part of their summer clean-up day, cleaning the grounds around the Shofuso house. We'll even get to work with the koi pond. And then tea and a Japanese lunch in the house.

"Manual labor, Shawn?" Sarika snarked, gobbling another fry. "Really?"

"Hey, I'm trying here," Shawn said, stealing a fry off her plate with a defiant smile before turning back to Leila. "Have you ever been there? How long have you even been in Philadelphia?" He put his elbows on the table and held his head in his hands, smiling, his eyes piercing into her. Again, Leila felt flustered at all the attention.

"No, I haven't. I've lived in the city a while, in . . . a few places. Can we"–Leila glanced at Sarika, who exchanged a knowing look with her–"maybe talk about something else? What's the deal with that house?"

"Oh, Shofuso is a Japanese teahouse in the middle of the park," Shawn said, his eyes alight. "They have all these beautiful plants, a nice-sized koi pond. Oh, it's just gorgeous. And we get to help keep it that way. Bit of community service in lieu of, well," he glanced at Sarika and shrugged. "I don't know. Other trips we might have taken if we had the funds. Maybe the aquarium over in Camden or something like that."

"Cool, that's still really, you know, cool. And neat. Neat and cool." Leila looked over at Sarika, who looked as though she might burst from the laughter she was holding back.

"Well, I'll leave you two to finish your lunch." Shawn looked at the trays and stood up, grabbing his brown bag from off the table. "School isn't so great with the vegan options, so I've got my own here. Gonna bike over to the park and then head home. Leila, you ride, right? I thought I saw you the other day."

"Oh!" Leila exclaimed. "Yeah! Almost every day."

"You know they close the roads around Kelly Drive on Sundays, up around Fairmount Park and the river," he said, smiling again. Leila felt her heart quicken. "If you're free, maybe we could go on a ride? Grab something to eat? It's really lovely."

Leila looked over at Sarika, who nodded her head yes just barely, and turned back to Shawn.

"Sure, I'd love that," she said, grinning.

"It's a date then," he said with a wink. He snapped his fingers and pointed at her, making that click sound with his cheek. "I'll text you later, I've got your contact info thanks to the club signup sheet. Catch the two of you later."

Leila watched him as he walked away and out of the cafeteria and the large doors swung closed behind him. She turned back to Sarika, who was now glaring.

"What?" Leila asked.

"Nothing, nothing." Sarika shrugged. "He's totally hot. But, I dunno, something is off about him. And that finger snap and clicking noise?"

"I know, I know," Leila said, shaking her head. "But maybe—"

"Don't you say it," Sarika said.

"I can—"

"Don't!"

"Fix him."

Sarika leapt to her feet, and then feigned flipping the lunch table over.

Sarika Paprika

@TheSarikaPaprika

Let's take a poll. If you date someone, is it possible to "fix" them?

Yes	13%
LOL NOPE	87%

19,293 Votes – Final Results
8/12/17, 9:47AM
1,283 Retweets 3,031 Likes

> Leila @WithouttheY   7m
> @TheSarikaPaprika this is the subtweet to end all subtweets.

> Sarika @TheSarikaPaprika   5m
> @WithouttheY ‾_(:/)_/‾

VII

Leila awoke with a gasp.

Today was the day.

She darted over to her dresser and dug through to find the perfect outfit for a long bike ride and a picnic—just a simple pair of worn-in jeans (ones she'd worn almost every day last week) and a black t-shirt with a white graffiti heart on it. After a quick shower, she grabbed her phone and darted down the stairs to tune up her bike.

With an audible click, she woke up her phone and went to the messages, where she was surprised to find she had several waiting. They were all from Sarika.

> **On my way to Adam's. Can't do make-overs. Lots of call outs. Don't be mad.**

> **Don't get crazy. You're bike riding, you don't need the makeup.**

> **You bike ride, you sweat, makeup night-marishly leaks off your face.**

> **Remember the short story? No makeup. You'll die. Don't die.**

Leila laughed and texted Sarika a quick heart ♥ and

made her way into the kitchen. Jon and Lisabeth were already in there, drinking coffee. Jon had today's newspaper in his hands, his spectacles on, and appeared as though he was ready to spend his entire day there. Lisabeth was flicking her finger at a tablet, making quick work of whatever was on there, her expression clear. She'd be done soon, there were things to do. People to see. It was a determined expression that Leila frequently saw, the look of someone who always had a goal, who was always chasing something. She loved it.

Leila reached under the kitchen table, hauled her light box up and onto it, and plugged it in. The bright light beamed over her face as she looked away from the soft glow and settled into her chair. She pulled out her phone, flipping through a few news blips and her social media.

"So," Jon said, and without looking up slid a piece of paper across the table. "Here's your permission slip that you left on the fridge, signed and good to go. But I can't imagine why you need one of those. It's just the park. Have fun today."

"Jon, it's Sunday," Leila said, taking the slip and shoving it in her pocket. She reached out and grabbed some orange juice on the table, and started pouring herself a glass.

Jon flipped his paper over and looked at the front.

"So it is!" he exclaimed, before going back to the stories inside. "Ah, the joys of summers and academia."

"Yeah, you go on about that," Lisabeth said, putting her tablet down and swatting at Jon's newspaper. "Some of us have to go into work and have to keep track of things. Like, you know, days of the week, the household budget, the electric bill." She kissed Jon on the forehead and made her way towards Leila with an empty mug in her hand. "And where are you off to? Shouldn't you be sleeping in, reading your message boards? Or are you off to the farmer's market for some more plants for this one to murder?"

"Hey, I don't murder them," Jon said. "They die from neglect."

"No, I . . ." Leila muttered. "Well, there's this . . . I'm going on a bike ride with . . ."

Lisabeth put down her mug and turned to Jon.

"My God," Lisabeth said, grinning from ear to ear.

"No," Leila said.

"You have—"

"Just stop."

"A DATE?" Lisabeth exclaimed.

"Shall I fetch my shotgun?" Jon asked, still looking into his paper. "That's what father-type figures are supposed to do in this situation, yes? I've seen movies. I did research."

"Tell me everything," Lisabeth said, turning to refill her coffee mug and utterly ignoring Jon. "Do you want any coffee?"

"No, I'm fine," Leila said, feeling flustered. "And he's just this boy from school. He runs the environmental activist club I joined with Sarika. And he asked me to go on a bike ride."

"And? What's his name? Where's he from? What grade is he in?"

"God, Liz. He's actually a teacher. From New Jersey. He's thirty-seven."

"Ah, excellent," Jon said from behind his paper. "Gainfully employed. I approve."

"Jon, you are not helping," Lisabeth frowned. "Come on, Leila, humor me."

"It's just . . ." Leila closed her eyes, the bright, soft light from her light box lighting up the back of her eyelids. She knew Liz was trying hard, and that her intentions were good. She could feel the anxiety rising up in her, and she wrestled against it.

Don't push her, don't push her away.

"Okay, his name is Shawn. I think he lives downtown, in the actual city, down in Queen Village. He said his parents have one of those green-energy, solar-paneled homes. Jon, you'd probably like him."

Jon shrugged.

"That's his jealous shrug," Lisabeth said, grinning.

Jon shrugged again.

"I was thinking that, maybe . . ." Leila looked down at her hands. "Liz, you're good with, you know, makeup and stuff. Do you think I should—"

"Not a chance," Lisabeth said, putting down her coffee mug. She looked at Leila with focused, affirming eyes. "I see where you're going with this, and no. Don't do it."

"But what if he doesn't like all, you know, all this." Leila pleaded, waving her hand in front of her face. Tears threatened to stream out of her eyes and she shook them back. It was frustrating, wanting to be true to herself and not cover up anything, but still wanting to be liked. And all of the "if he doesn't like you for who you are" speeches didn't quite cut it, even if she knew in her heart they were the truth. It didn't change the way she felt.

"Should I leave? Do you need girl time?" Jon asked, putting down his paper. His tone lacked the usual humor, he was actually acting serious.

"No, it's fine," Leila said, suppressing a sniffle.

"Listen. I'm not going to pepper you with clichés," Lisabeth said, practically reading her mind. "But say you do put on a little concealer on the birthmark. And he likes it like that. And wants you to keep it like that. That's you. And you can't cover up a part of who you are forever, particularly for some boy."

"You never, I don't know, changed anything for . . ." Leila looked over at Jon.

"Alright, that's my cue," Jon said. He folded up his paper and tucked it under his arm, his chair squeaking as he got up.

"Jon," Leila ventured. For a moment, just a moment, the word *dad* had come dangerously close to slipping out, and her heart quickened.

"You two talk, I'll finish my paper on the porch." He smiled and hurried out of the little kitchen. Lisabeth stood up and wrapped an arm around Leila, hugging her from the side. Leila stiffened as though ice had shot through her veins, but she pushed through it, trying to soften herself up, lean into the hug.

"I think everyone changes a little bit when they end up together, you know?" Lisabeth said, giving Leila an extra squeeze before letting her go. She crossed her arms and looked where Jon had walked. "That one. He used to crack his knuckles a lot, channel surf, little things like that which sort of annoyed me. You adjust. You don't change. There's a difference."

Leila grinned, and this struck an odd chord with her, as she'd basically done precisely the opposite her entire life. It was the sort of thing you learned in the group home when prospective parents came by. To act a certain way, talk a certain way, dress a certain way. When they took you home, you changed, behaved more like them. Like their kids. Talked and acted "normal," whatever that was. It was easy to be herself around Sarika, and for the first time, thanks to their gentle nudging, she'd been mostly herself around Lisabeth and Jon.

Everyone else though . . .

"So, no makeup?" Leila said, looking at Lisabeth.

"No makeup."

"Then why bother with it at all, ever? Any kind of makeup?" Leila gestured at her face.

"None of that covers up anything, really. The little things." Lisabeth said. She walked over to the coffee maker and cleared out the grounds, and her thick braids swung around her head every time she moved. Her eyes sparkled with adoration when she looked back at Leila, who blinked and tried to ignore the heavy feeling in her chest as Lisabeth stared at her. Without makeup, and maybe if Liz wore her hair a little differently, well, they looked a lot alike.

She could easily be confused for her biological mom.

A blast of warmth shot through Leila and she had to turn away.

"It's for you, and it accentuates what's already there," Lisabeth said, sitting back down and putting a hand on Leila's shoulder. "And what's there is beautiful."

"Okay," Leila said, nodding. "I'm, um, I'm going to head out, meet up with Shawn."

She pushed her chair out and grabbed her bike helmet off the rack near the back door, pushing it down over her hair and onto her head, clicking the strap in place. She smiled as bits of hair pushed their way up through the spaces in the helmet, and glanced at Lisabeth, who stared, aghast.

"What?" Leila said. "I'll fix it later."

Lisabeth shrugged.

"You said it yourself," Leila said. "Never change, remember?"

After several minutes of awkward wrangling and twisting, Leila finally managed to squeeze her bike out the front door. It was a tedious routine. The hallways of the home were narrow, and the only place for her bike was hanging from the wall in the living room, far away from the door. Jon suggested locking the bike up out in front of the house, promising there was no way it would get stolen, but she'd heard that before.

Her bike, named Marigold after the seeds Frieda and Claudia sell in *The Bluest Eye* to purchase a bicycle, had been with her through too much to risk losing it. The group home, foster homes, and now this one. She wasn't about to lose her to people who wouldn't appreciate her fading paint, her slightly dented tire that wobbled a little bit, and the brakes that were somewhat spotty.

"Alright, let's do this," Leila muttered, swinging her leg over the thin bike frame. Straddling the bike, she pulled her phone out of her jeans pocket and clicked it on to double check where she was going, flipping to the texts Shawn had sent her earlier in the day.

> **Let's meet over at the Art Museum, and we'll roll out from there.**
> **Meet you there around 3PM? Ride our bikes through golden hour?**
>
> **Sounds good, see you soon!**

She stared at the phrase "golden hour" quizzically for a moment, as confused about it now as she was when she got the text, before shrugging her shoulders and putting the phone back in her pocket.

With a few quick huffs, she was off.

LEILA: Hey what does "golden hour" mean?

SARIKA: What?

LEILA: I don't know. Shawn said something about it in his text. Riding our bikes through it.

SARIKA: Oh.

SARIKA: Damn girl, it's going down.

LEILA: What?!

SARIKA: ;-)

LEILA: What does it mean?

SARIKA: Not telling, but you're gonna like it when he does it. Mm. Rawr.

LEILA: Oh my God stop it what is it.

LEILA: No seriously I'm like a block away from my house still and about to go home.

SARIKA: Hahahah it has to do with taking pictures.

SARIKA: Golden hour is like, that time when the sun is at its best.

SARIKA: Probably wants to take cute snaps together on Instagram or something.

LEILA: Ohhhhh.

SARIKA: You thought it was some weird sex thing.

LEILA: I hate you. ♥

SARIKA: ♥

VIII

Leila pushed forward on her bicycle as the wind tickled her skin. She had always felt that Philadelphia's end-of-summer-here-comes-fall weather had a special magic to it. It was unpredictable. Sometimes Mother Nature was kind, with cool breezes and temperatures that usually came in October, ushering in the crunch of multicolored leaves and the smell of tiny fireplaces. Other days, it felt like it hammered home the remains of summer, with blistering, unforgiving heat that rose up in waves off the cobblestone streets and burnt-brick sidewalks. Back at the Kline's, air conditioners and space heaters waged a noisy war with one another in the old, historic home, despite the fact that one side was always going to lose.

Today felt like it was a lucky day, with surprise fall weather, just minus the changing, vivid landscape. Leila rode her bike out from home and through the brown-stone-lined streets, and flashes of murals greeted her as she pedaled along the bike lane. Fearless alongside speeding cars and motorcycles, Marigold's threadbare tires pushed hard against the city asphalt. Philadelphia. The City of Murals. From the large-scale paintings that took over the sides of entire buildings to the smaller ones decorating the ends of rowhomes, they were everywhere, impossible to miss, and were always a welcome distraction on long walks or quiet bike rides.

She took a hard left onto the Benjamin Franklin Parkway as she rode away from the Center City region of the city and towards the Art Museum neighborhood, and went up the long strip of road that led up to the Philadelphia Museum of Art. A mile of museums, with beautiful buildings that thrilled her. Like the Academy of Natural Sciences, a place dedicated to the history of the planet, with dinosaurs, plants, weird insects, and live animals. And then there was the Franklin Institute, a science museum that she and Sarika used to get lost in on school trips, ducking in and out of a giant, to-scale human heart you could walk through and hole up in. Museums dotted the mile, most of which were easier to visit in the evenings, when tickets were discounted and the lighting was low. It set the mood for some and dished out the opportunity to hide, or sneak in, for others. At the end of the mile was the museum that housed most of the artwork in the city.

Leila squinted as she approached the Philadelphia Museum of Art, looking for a sign of Shawn. She cursed herself as she stopped her bike and leaned it against one of the columns by the long steps leading up to the museum. Why hadn't she asked him what he'd be wearing, or maybe something about his bicycle? Even at this hour on a Sunday, late afternoon when you'd think people would be snuggled in on a blustery day or grabbing brunch someplace, the front of the Philadelphia Museum of Art was swarming with people. Runners used the stairs as a workout routine and tourists meandered about, absorbing everything with their cameras and smartphones, and some, embarrassingly, with their giant tablets. Leila grinned at an older man holding up an enormous iPad to take a picture. She opened her backpack and had just flushed her phone to text Shawn when the wind picked up, tickling her neck.

Carrying the voices.

Ley . . . ga . . . co . . . hel . . .

They came in and out, half-formed words that sounded like they were on the other end of a bad cell phone connection. Leila winced and closed her eyes, gritting her teeth against them. She thought of what was around her. Get grounded. Be present. She whispered to herself.

"Museum. Stairs. Concrete. Leaves. Bike."

Suddenly a hand grabbed at her shoulder, the fingers grasping tight.

"Get off!" she shouted, and swung at the hand's owner, her fist connecting squarely with a shoulder. She bounced back, and despite the stinging pain that buzzed along her knuckles and down into her wrist, balled her fist up again to strike again. The figure stumbled back and fell onto the hard stone steps, their backpack slapping against the beige stairs.

Their beat up, slightly military-surplus-looking backpack.

Leila groaned.

Oh no.

It was Shawn.

"Damn!" he shouted, looking up at her with pained eyes as he got back to his feet, brushing himself off. A few people scaling the steps slowed to look, and then kept going. "You sure know how to throw a punch."

"Oh, hell," Leila muttered, walking over to him and flexing her fingers in and out. "Sorry, I really don't like people sneaking up on me."

Her thoughts ran.

Or touching me. Or looking at me. Or speaking to me.

"It's, uh, nothing personal." She shrugged.

"Noted, noted," Shawn said, gripping his shoulder. He smiled that crooked smile of his and ran his hand through his hair. Leila relaxed a bit, and then tensed back up immediately as a runner brushed by her, bounding up the stairs.

"Excuse me!" he shouted as he darted by, leaving the smell of sweat and coffee in his wake. He moved strangely fast for someone with a medium-sized cup of coffee in his hand. He made quick work of the stone steps with his bright-red sneakers and neon-yellow, stretchy pants.

"Watch it!" shouted Shawn, and the runner turned back for a second, locked eyes with the two of them, and turned back, continuing up the stairs while sipping from his coffee cup.

"Ass," Shawn muttered. He turned back to Leila and smiled. "Question: And I'm sure you have, but have you ever, you know?" He nodded at the stairs and grinned.

"What?" Leila asked.

"I mean, I guess it's kinda silly," Shawn continued,

gesturing over at the stairs, that confidence he seemed to ooze fading just a little.

Leila looked over at the stairs and up to the top, where the coffee-drinking-while-running guy had reached the final step. He placed his coffee down and jumped up and down, his fists in the air, and promptly knocked over his own coffee with a careless foot. She laughed as the man muttered some kind of inaudible swear, bending down to fumble with the coffee which was now making its way down the steps, streaming and hot. Served him right.

And then someone next to him did the same thing. Jumping up and down, fists in the air.

And then a couple, who promptly kissed at the top of the stairs.

And another person, cheering alone.

Something clicked.

"Oh," Leila said, turning back to Shawn. "You mean the whole *Rocky* stairs run thing? You know a couple of years ago, someone knitted a sweater that said 'See the Art' on that statue, right?"

"Yeah, I saw that on Tumblr," Shawn laughed, looking over at the nearby statue. A massive statue of Sylvester Stallone as the iconic underdog boxing champ, Rocky, stood on a small platform in bronze. Tourists were lined up to take photos of it, and a family posed in front of it, two parents and their two children, all their hands raised. A man took the photo and handed it to one of the kids, who looked at the picture and smiled brightly.

"Come on, it'll be fun," Shawn said, his voice practically

a nudge. "You're new to the city, right? Or is it just the school? It's like, a total rite of passage."

"Shawn, you, um," Leila started before fading off. "You really don't know that much about me just yet. I've lived in Philadelphia almost my entire life. My . . . um, adoptive parents and I don't live that far, we're right in Manayunk."

"Adoptive parents?" Shawn asked, his eyebrows arching up. "I didn't know you were adopted. Were you born here? Where in Philly were you before you were adopted?"

"Little bit of everywhere?" Leila said, shrugging, trying to steel herself against the questions. "My old group home is down in South Philly, not too far from the stadiums. I lived with one foster family in Frankford, another in West Philly." She looked up at Shawn to find his mouth open, agape. She fought the discomfort rising in her chest as the thoughts of each of those places rushed in. The couple in Frankford filed for divorce shortly after bringing her home; evidentially having a kid wasn't a good way to save a marriage. The family in West Philly had a number of foster kids, and were clearly in it for all the wrong reasons. She'd heard about that before, seen kids come back to the group home with stories of homes far too full of children and never full enough of love.

"Yeah, like I said, there's a lot you don't know." She sighed, feeling the return of the pressure from that meeting last week, in that classroom with all those eyes on her. People ran by, charging up the stairs, or casually strolled too close, holding hands, bodies and backpacks brushing against her. "Maybe, um, maybe this wasn't the best idea."

Leila felt a rush of warmth course over her, the anxiety

heavy and hot. All these people everywhere, all these things to talk about, secrets she didn't really want to share with anyone. Was this what it was going to be like? Dating? Meeting boys? That wasn't something she did back at the group home, back at any of the old schools she'd gone to, where things were temporary. Where questions were even harder to answer. And making friends other than Sarika or the people at Adam's Café? She'd have to explain things to them. Her life.

"Wait, no," Shawn said, holding out his hand. Leila flinched, and Shawn retracted. "I just . . . that's what dates are for, right? Getting to know each other and all that?"

"I suppose," Leila said, fighting the urge to shrink back into herself.

"I mean, you already know a, um, rather embarrassing thing about me. You saw it in the class, with, you know." He shrugged, stammering a little. "She who will not be named."

"Your ex-girlfriend isn't Voldemort, Shawn." Leila laughed, shaking her head. "There are far worse villains in the world." She thought back to the incident in the hallway with Sarika. "Though I suppose not too many." She grinned.

"I knew I liked you," Shawn laughed. "Look. You shared some truths with me, and I'll share one with you," Shawn said, extending his hand again. Leila looked at it hesitantly, and then up at his face. His smile was warm, that dimple a crater on the side of his mouth, his eyes kind and welcoming. Leila closed her hand into a fist, backed up, and then opened it, grabbing his hand.

Shawn pulled her forward, and Leila felt her whole body tense up.

"What are you–" she started.

"I love those *Rocky* movies, but I've never run the steps. I tell people I have, but I haven't," Shawn whispered into her ear. The tension in Leila's body faded a little as Shawn spoke and softly laughed during his confession. "The first one is amazing, and the next few get worse and worse, until you get to the masterpiece that is *Creed*, that is. But I love them. Even the part with the robot in *Rocky IV*."

"There's a robot?" Leila whispered back. She thought about pushing him away but stayed close, listening to his whisper, feeling a rush of warmth to her cheeks at the smell of his shaving gel, like cinnamon and vanilla.

"There is, and it's terrible." He backed away, smiling, and Leila exhaled with a sigh, a rush of warmth all over.

Shawn took her hand.

"Now come on," he said. "Take a little run. I've always wanted someone to do this with me."

He squeezed Leila's hand encouragingly and put one foot on the first step leading up to the Philadelphia Museum of Art.

"Can we go see the art another day?" Leila asked, pulling back a little.

"We can do whatever you want," Shawn beamed.

Leila looked back to the Benjamin Franklin Parkway, the long strip of road leading towards Philadelphia's City Hall. Museums were off to the right and the left, and the street was lined with flags of every country, high and waving in the chill breeze. She stared at them, and for a moment, wondered if her flag was in there someplace, representing wherever it was she had come from. It was a mystery to her, though she'd made assumptions and lied about it before, to the endless wave of too-curious people who tended to ask the annoying "but where you are *from*?" questions. One of the joys of being adopted. So many questions, so few real answers.

She turned back to Shawn, who still smiled warmly.

"Race you to the top!" she shouted, letting go of his hand and darting madly up the stairs.

Leila stumbled almost immediately as she took off up the stone steps. Shawn hurried behind her, yelling shouts of concern as she regained her footing and kept going. She didn't turn around, instead, focused on the surprisingly small and narrow steps leading to the museum. They looked a lot wider when you weren't running madly up them, but now that her feet were hitting the hard surface, she realized how thin they were, barely able to hold an entire foot, mostly just the tips of your toes as you moved up quickly. No wonder people exercised on this.

When she reached the top, she caught the view of the city and gasped. She could practically see the tops of the flagpoles now, and the surface of the multicolored pavement that led away from the museum looked far more stunning when you stood above it instead of on it. Shawn reached her side, huffing, puffing, and coughing. He dry heaved and sat down on the top step. Leila struggled not to laugh.

"Are you okay?" she asked, sitting down with him.

"Yeah, it's just . . . I don't really . . . run that often," he stammered in-between deep breaths and coughs. "Or . . . um . . . at all. You really . . . really know what you're doing there." He looked up at her, his face bright red and eyes watering. "I'm, uh, I'm a little . . . embarrassed . . . right now."

"You're fine, it's fine," Leila said, nudging him with her shoulder as they sat on the top of the steps. A young couple ran up by them, and instead of sitting down, stood up and pumped their arms in the air. They kissed, and Leila felt that rush of warmth go through her again. Was this what was supposed to happen after the run? Was this some kind of cute setup? Leila steeled herself, adrenaline still pumping, the anxiety washed away with a fierce, almost rebellious feeling after running up the stairs. She breathed in, leaning towards Shawn, her lips parted.

"Shawn," Leila started, thinking of what felt like an almost-kiss at the bottom of the stairs, a rush of heat in her chest.

Shawn dry heaved, louder this time, and coughed heavily. He spit a large glob of saliva onto the sand-colored steps and looked back up at her, wiping at his face.

Okay, yeah, no kissing.

"I'm sorry, I'm sorry," he muttered. "This was a bad idea. I ruined the moment."

"No, no," Leila said, feeling bad for the guy. He had seemed so confident. "This was great. I feel great. I think I needed this." She leaned against his shoulder, staring out at the cityscape, and he took her hand. "Are you, um, going to be okay for the bike ride after this?"

"Oh, God," Shawn muttered, coughing again.

"I'll give you a few minutes," Leila said, patting his hand and leaning against him. She could feel him holding back his coughs, his body shaking as he held his mouth shut. She saw his eyes water as he stared forward with determination.

"You can, like, cough and stuff, you know," Leila said as he held in another cough. His body quivered, and his throat made a weird sound as he held it back.

"What? No. I'm fine."

Leila patted him on the back.

"I'm—"

And then Shawn threw up all over the Philadelphia Museum of Art's steps.

"You know, I have to hand it to you, this is a nice spread," Leila said, smiling at the array of nibbles Shawn had placed on the picnic table. Just a few feet away from the end of the Reading Terminal Bridge, all the way up Kelly Drive, were a number of small picnic tables and benches, a perfect place for taking a breather and having a bite. The wood on the table was old and splintering, with cracks and holes from decades of rain on the untreated wood.

"I do make a mean picnic," Shawn said, grinning. "And you know what I really love about this spot?"

"Oh? What's that?" Leila asked. She could guess. It seemed like a cliché spot for making out, though that was absolutely out of the question after the incident on the museum steps. This, though, this was beautiful. The historic stone bridge in the background, the overlook above the water, the handful of people nearby and cyclists on the bridge pedaling off to places unknown. There was so much life here.

"These picnic tables," Shawn said, proudly. "All natural, these guys. Old. They might be falling apart, but they're real. Did you know that some picnic tables, the ones that are made of processed, treated wood, have deadly chemicals mixed in with the lumber? That stuff leaks out in bad weather, hits the aquifer, and gets into the water. It poisons children and animals. Oh, I could go on."

"I'm sure you can," Leila said, smirking.

"But enough of all that," Shawn said, waving his hand dismissively at the table and grabbing a slice of apple from his snack spread. "Back at the stairs, before I got all, well, you know," he grimaced. "You brought up something about being adopted? Living around the city?"

"Uh, yeah," Leila said as she finished chewing a bit of cheese. "I basically grew up in a group home. I had a few near misses with foster families, but, you know. Sometimes things just don't work out."

"How so?" Shawn asked, leaning on the table, looking at her intently. Leila flushed a little. He looked at her with such interest, like she was the only person in the world, his hazel eyes so focused.

"It's just—" Leila stammered.

"I'm sorry if I'm prying. It's just, you know, not my world," Shawn said in an almost-question. "I want to know you, you know?"

"Sure, yeah, but I'm not quite sure we're there yet,

Shawn. I, um, it's hard, some of that stuff. Things I left behind that I'd rather leave back there. I'm happy now, though, that's what matters. I have a family, a home. And this is nice."

"Sure, sure," Shawn said, lifting his hands up. "I won't push."

He grabbed another slice of apple and chewed it, looking off to the side thoughtfully. He swallowed and turned back to her, his eyes once again intense, this time bright with curiosity.

"Okay, I have to ask, though, do you ever think about, you know, *them*?" he asked. "I feel like I would."

Oh hell no.

That question.

He had to go and ask that question, in that way.

"What do you mean, *them*?" Leila asked, even though she knew fully well who he meant. He was officially prying. It was *them* that everyone always asked about. She knew what *them* implied. Every adopted kid or foster kid knew exactly what that meant. She didn't need an explanation.

But she wanted to hear him say it.

"You know, your, like, real parents or whatever," Shawn said, starting to look noticeably uncomfortable.

Leila smiled.

He was uncomfortable.

Good.

"First of all," she started, leaning on the picnic table, the splintering, old wood pushing into her arms, "don't say that. Don't say 'real parents.' That implies my current parents aren't real."

"Oh God, Leila, well no, obviously that's not what—"

"I'm sorry, was I finished?" Leila asked, holding a hand up. "It implies my current parents aren't real. If you were raised by someone else in your family, a grandmother or a close uncle or aunt, would you ever use the phrase 'real parents' around family that's taken care of you your whole life? Don't you think that would devastate the person you're calling *unreal*?"

"Well, yeah. Okay, I see your point."

"You can't quantify real or not-real in relationships, particularly family, Shawn. This isn't *The Hunger Games*."

Shawn stared at her.

"Never mind. It's a book." She swiped a piece of cheese off the picnic table and flicked it into her mouth. She nibbled away in silence as Shawn sat there awkwardly. Suddenly, this wasn't going as well as she had hoped. Thanks to Shawn's insensitive prying, the day was taking an epic downward spiral. The swoon-filled moment of meeting him in the café, the way he stared at her during the first meeting of B.E.A.C., all of those feelings that had swirled around inside her chest were quickly dissipating, replaced by the same disappointment she'd felt from every other boy she'd met. And not just every boy, but most people.

"I know *The Hunger Games*," Shawn said, his tone upset. "Look, I'm sorry if I don't understand your . . ." he motioned around with his hands, looking frustrated. "I don't know your world, or whatever, but I'm asking questions, aren't I? To get to know it? I'm trying, is that so terribly wrong?"

"It's the way you're asking," Leila said glancing over at her bike. "Look, maybe we should—"

"It's cute when you're all worked up, you know," Shawn said with a sudden grin. He put his head in his hands, his elbows up on the table, and peered at her like he was trying to be cute.

Leila scowled at him, and he smiled more.

"See?" He grinned. "That little patch of skin over there, on your cheek, changes color a little, gets all red. What is that, anyway? Is there a story? Is it a scar? Have you ever thought about maybe putting some makeup over that?" He reached out to touch her cheek and she smacked his hand away.

"I'm going home," Leila said, standing up and walking away from the picnic table, picking up Marigold.

"Wait, what?" Shawn said, walking towards her. "Why? What did I—"

"Take. Me. Home." Leila stressed. "Oh, fuck it, fuck this, fuck you, I'll just find my way. The road is closed off, right?" She swung her leg over the bike and unclipped her helmet from the frame, fastening it on her head and pressing it down on her hair. The road from the bridge continued forward a bit, and then curled off onto what looked like a main street.

"Yeah, sure, but, come on, Leila," Shawn pleaded. He grabbed his bike and hustled over towards her as she began to pedal away.

"Wait!" he shouted as he biked behind her. She pressed down on her pedals, hard, standing up, getting faster and faster. The street was clear of cars, entirely closed off, and just a few other cyclists joined them on the road, including a couple riding a tandem bicycle that wobbled precariously despite their beaming smiles.

She glared at them, and then tore her gaze away from the happy couple to focus on the trees around her, the bright colors and summer smells. She pushed away the shouts from Shawn and blinked at the angry tears that kept threatening to stream out as the wind buffeted her face and her bike. Shawn pedaled behind her, pleading for her to slow down, to stop, to listen to him.

She'd listened enough, heard his inappropriate questions and horrible suggestions. A few small buildings started to pop up in the middle of the trees. She recognized a handful as park cafés and facilities, the old stone structures more like cottages than anything else, and she squinted, trying to make them out as she rode by.

"Wait, is that . . ." she murmured, staring hard at a small, gray building with a number of old-looking wooden structures dotted around it.

She slowed down.

A young man stood near the wooden boxes and was reaching inside with a gloved arm. He pulled his arm out of the box, and a small owl sat on it.

Leila gasped as the man tossed something up in the air, and the owl took off, or at least attempted to. It shot up into the air awkwardly, one of its wings a different color and shape than the other, and fell back to the ground. The man rushed to where the owl fell and scooped it up, holding it tenderly, muttering something she couldn't hear as he cradled the creature in his arms.

The wind picked up, hard and fast. Leaves rustled by, tickling her ears and neck. She swayed on her bicycle.

He's the one.

The whispers. They were loud. Clear. And they were speaking to her about something.

He can help.

She could hear entire sentences, each word clear, as if someone was speaking right next to her, whispering in her ear.

Go. Speak to him.

She couldn't close her eyes, not while she was riding. She slowed down a little, taking in deep breaths. She whispered to herself.

"Bike. Park. Trees. Street."

The voices pressed, and she looked back towards the man with the owl. He looked up abruptly, right at her, and she gasped as he made eye contact.

She reflexively squeezed the brakes on her bicycle. Hard.

Too hard.

She lurched forward, the back wheel rising up and sending Leila hurtling over the handlebars and onto the black asphalt. She held out her hands and arms as she made impact, skidding across the pavement, and her head hit the hard ground and rattled around inside her helmet.

She pushed herself onto her back and looked up at the summer sky. The cool wind circled around her, as if trying to wrap her into a hug. Bike tires screeched against the road, pebbles kicked up and smattered against her, and she heard the sound of feet hitting the ground. A few faces peered over her, blocking her view of the tree canopy that hung over the road and the clouds above them. Their voices blended together with the whispering on the wind.

"Hey, are you okay?"

Go to him.

"Someone call somebody, who has a cell phone?"

He'll know. He cares.

"What's your name?"

He can help save us. All of us. All of you.

"It doesn't look like she's bleeding or anything."

He wears the chosen colors of the caretakers.

"Oh my God, Leila!" Shawn's face appeared over the skidding of his bicycle. He loomed over her, as strange and unfamiliar as the rest of them. He was sweating profusely, to the point that droplets of sweat trickled off his face and dripped onto her. She tried to move her head away, but the pain thundered in her skull.

I've been here, all this time.

"Say something, please?" Shawn pleaded. He started fumbling with his jacket and pulled out a phone.

And now, at last, you've returned.

Leila felt tired, dizzy. She felt like she was struggling to keep her eyes open.

I'll be waiting.

"Leila? Leila!" Shawn shouted. She felt someone grab her shoulders. "No, no, don't close your eyes, don't go to sleep. Yes? Hello? There's been an accident. Kelly Drive. Bicycle. I don't know just, send someone, anyone—"

You're so close, so very close.

Leila closed her eyes, and let the world go dark.

See you soon.

Get Well Soon WithouttheY!
Posted by A Dash of Paprika
AUGUST 14th, 2017 | 1:02PM
As some of you may have heard, WithouttheY was involved in an accident. She's fine and recovering, has a slight concussion, but could use some help. I made a lil' GoFundMe page. And if you can't give, just send some well wishes here. She'll be on here again soon, no doubt about that.

RE: Get Well Soon WithouttheY!
Posted by Jill the Birder
AUGUST 14th, 2017 | 6:45PM
Oh no! Sorry to hear about that. I pledged a couple dollars. Wish I could do more. Hang in there!

RE: Get Well Soon WithouttheY!
Posted by Shannon Christopher
AUGUST 14th, 2017 | 7:00PM
I always appreciate her insightful comments on local developments and environmental policies. Get well soon, WithouttheY! We'll miss you on the board! Come back to us ASAP!

RE: Get Well Soon WithouttheY!
Posted by Casually Weird
AUGUST 14th, 2017 | 7:09PM

I pledged! Feel better! And here, I made you a play-list to get you through things. bit.ly/2yNS770

> RE: Get Well Soon WithouttheY!
> *Posted by a Dash of Paprika*
> AUGUST 14th, 2017 | 7:11PM
> Girl that mixtape is FIRE. Nice work. Thank you.

RE: Get Well Soon WithouttheY!
Posted by Toothless
AUGUST 14th, 2017 | 7:15PM
Pledged. Sent you a DM, WithouttheY.

> RE: Get Well Soon WithouttheY!
> *Posted by A Dash of Paprika*
> AUGUST 14th, 2017 | 7:16PM
> If you were mean to her, I will strike you down with the force of a thousand suns.

FROM	SUBJECT	DATE
TOOTHLESS	FEEL BETTER, A QUICK NOTE Hey WithouttheY. I know most of our communication on this board circles around me saying something snippy and you responding in turn, and going back and forth picking on one another, but I have always thought of you as, you know, like an Internet friend or something. I'm actually not a monster, you know. Anyhow, I hope you feel better. I'll be thinking of you over on my side of the computer, and if you ever want to get coffee and pick on each other in person, I'm always around. We are in the same city, after all.	8/16

FROM	SUBJECT	DATE
WITHOUTTHEY	RE: FEEL BETTER, A QUICK NOTE Thanks, Toothless. That was a surprisingly sweet message. ;-) And thanks for your insanely generous pledge on Paprika's page. The fact that she launched that was a surprise as well, and I'm stunned by everyone that's come through on that.	8/17
TOOTHLESS	RE: FEEL BETTER, A QUICK NOTE Cool, yeah. And be careful with your emoticons. Winks imply, like, flirting. You probably meant a smiley face there. Probably. Right? Right. I am awkward and now hate myself.	8/17
WITHOUTTHEY	RE: FEEL BETTER, A QUICK NOTE ;-)	8/17

IX

Leila stared at herself in the mirror, a plush, beige towel snuggly around her, and scowled.

A bandage was wrapped around her forehead, tied off in the back, that pushed her hair up and over the white-tan strip. A bit of dried blood flecked the left side, a cut where her helmet had impacted her head. She thought of Shawn and the terrible date, and shook her head to rid her mind of the memory, then winced at the dull ache that pushed itself against the front of her skull.

"Damn it," she muttered, rubbing the sore part of her head. She pulled her hand away and looked at her fingers, rubbing them together to get the dried blood off them. She wiped her hand on her towel, and fished around in her dresser for an outfit and a decent head scarf to cover up all this nonsense.

For the field trip.

Over a flurry of text messages, not a single one from Shawn, Sarika had somehow convinced her to still go. She'd go despite the fact that she'd have to see Shawn and return to the park where the voices had suddenly come in full blast, to the place where she saw the guy with the bird, and where the whispered voices had tried to direct her someplace. Those voices. This time, they'd had instructions.

And apparently, they were in trouble.

As Leila wrangled up an outfit for the day, her mind reeled over the whispers' pleading. Was she really thinking of going back there? All because of . . . what? Voices she'd heard dozens of times throughout her life? And some guy trying to fly an owl like he was a falconer or something? What had the voices ever done for her, besides distract her, scare her, and make her feel crazy? They'd given her a dark secret that she had to hide from everyone except Sarika. She shook her head again, wincing and cursing under her breath.

She pulled on a pair of distressed-wash, dark-blue jeans and her favorite David Bowie t-shirt and made her way downstairs.

"There is no way you're still going on that"–Jon used air quotes–"field trip." He turned and talked to Lisabeth as Leila fussed with her light box, pulling it up onto the kitchen table. "Field trip," he grumbled. "Come on. If I walk a few blocks down the road, I can see the Fairmount Park trees. Field trips are for, like, Washington, DC, or going to a museum. Or you know, something interesting, like a Broadway show. You're sixteen. Trips like this are just a waste of time."

"We are kind of going to some special places in the park, it's not like we're holding hands and checking out the swings," Leila stressed as she turned on the light box and looked away from its glow, keeping her voice down. She'd quickly discovered that speaking too loudly made her head hurt. "There's this Japanese teahouse in the middle of the park—"

"Ugh, that's just a tourist trap," Jon mumbled.

"And," Leila interjected, "we're getting a tour of the park from some of the rangers there, and doing some community service around the gardens and pond. You can't really just do that any time you like." Leila stopped. "Okay, well maybe you can just do that at any time, but come on. Sarika is going, and the rest of the B.E.A.C. crew. You guys told me to make friends. I'm not about to let some stupid bike accident halt my life."

"Yeah, I don't know, I'm inclined to agree with your fa—Jon," Lisabeth said with a wince, quickly correcting herself. She took a long sip of her coffee, the silence awkward, the slip of Lisabeth's word hanging in the air.

"So, how bad is it?" Jon asked, interrupting the quiet. Leila shrugged.

"It hurts, and I can't like, yell or move too quick, but this afternoon is *literally* a walk in the park. And my bike is still getting repaired. I can just like, walk there with Sarika. Or take the bus. Or you guys can drive me. There are so many options that don't end in me staying home with Netflix."

"There aren't any, like, obstacle courses or anything?" Jon asked. Leila laughed as Lisabeth gave Jon a look. "What? It's a field trip to a park. It's a valid question. There might be monkey bars or those awkward summer camp ice breakers."

"This isn't one of those bonding retreats or something, Jon," Lisabeth said, shaking her head. "No trust falls or anything. Right, darling?"

"Right," Leila said, a swell of hope in her chest. "Just walking around, taking pictures, learning about trees and koi and what-not."

"Hah! Learning about trees," Lisabeth jeered. "Like they can teach you anything you don't already know. Okay, you can go—"

"Hey!" Jon protested.

"But make sure you check in with us every hour or so," Lisabeth said. "Just a text or something, alright? Keep us from worrying?"

"I think I can manage that," Leila smiled.

"Fine, fine." Jon grumbled. "But no more falls like that, please."

"Deal."

"And you have to tell us how that date went!" Lisabeth exclaimed, clasping her hands together, her eyes brightening. "Oh, you should have heard that boy in the waiting room in the hospital. He sat with us the whole time and asked a ton of questions, didn't he, Jon?"

"He did, he did," Jon said, nodding. "Seemed decent enough."

"Yeah, well," Leila started, feeling a bit surprised. She had no idea he'd come to the hospital and waited around for her. Where was he when she got out? "Don't be tricked into thinking he was some hero or something, you guys. He hasn't texted or anything since I got home. And I was riding my bike *away* from him when the whole thing happened. It's not technically his fault, but, well, you know. I was trying to get away."

"Get away?" Lisabeth asked with a glance towards Jon, her eyes awash in concern. "Why? What was he doing? What did he do?"

Jon stood up.

"Is it shotgun time?" he asked.

"No, he—" Leila started

"I have been waiting for this moment all my life."

"Oh my God, Liz, please get him to stop."

"Jon, please," Lisabeth said. "So what happened, exactly?"

"He just . . ." Leila paused. "He's a bit tactless, is all. Asked some too-personal questions too soon, brought up," she gestured awkwardly at everyone at the table, "you know, *this* stuff. And he asked if I'd ever thought about using makeup to cover up."

Jon stood back up.

"So. It *is* time," he said resolutely.

"Jon, I swear—"

"Sit down," Lisabeth said sternly. Jon dropped back into his seat like a scolded kid as Lisabeth turned and looked at Leila, her eyes intense. "You told that boy to go fuck himself, yes?"

"Liz!" Leila exclaimed with a laugh, and then winced, placing a hand on her head. Jon chuckled.

"Oh, darling." Lisabeth reached out and ran her hand gently over Leila's forehead, then palmed her cheek. "How bad is it really?"

"I'll be fine, it'll be fine," Leila said, pulling away from

Liz's touch. "Really, don't worry about me. We'll just be walking, and I promise, if I start to feel sick or woozy, I'll come right home."

"You call us," Lisabeth said. "We'll come get you. And Leila, that, um, that looks good on you."

"Hm?" Leila looked at Jon and back to Liz. "What does?"

"The scarf." Liz nodded at Leila. "That's one of mine." She smiled, her face full of warmth. Heat rushed to Leila's cheeks, and she moved to unwrap it. "No, no. Please keep it. Wear it. What's mine is yours, you know."

"Okay," Leila said, nodding softly, testing herself to see if she felt anything. The warmth of Liz's hand against her cheek flitted across her memory, and Liz smiled at her from across the table.

Leila surveyed the parking lot as Jon and Lisabeth drove away. Their electric car barely made a soft hum over the rumble of its tires over the loose rocks.

A handful of students from B.E.A.C. milled about, a few talking excitedly while others fiddled with their smartphones, snapping photos of one another or the surrounding trees. Some just stared at the screens, fingers making quick work of whatever was glowing back at them. So Leila pulled out her own phone, checking for texts from Sarika or anything from her on social media. There was just a quick text from Sarika saying she was running late, but nothing from Shawn. She wasn't quite sure what to expect from him.

"You guys see Shawn?" Leila asked two B.E.A.C. members that had been chatting with one another: a girl with bright auburn hair and fierce green eyes, and a slightly shorter Filipino guy with really long, thick, black hair. She recognized them. They'd been in that first meeting, cheering on Shawn as he spoke. They turned to her and both shrugged.

"Haven't seen him yet," the guy said. "You're that new girl, right? Leila? Always hanging out with that cute Indian chick? What's her deal? Also, her name?"

"Mikey," the girl said, nudging him. "Maybe get to know her first before trying to hit on all her friends? Sorry. He's just all girls, all the time. I'm Britt." She held out her hand, smiling with shockingly white teeth. Leila shook her hand and grinned. "You've already had the pleasure of meeting this one." Britt nudged him again, a little too hard this time, and he stumbled a little.

"Hey," Mikey said, laughing. He reached out and shook Leila's hand. "Normally I'm a hugger, but we did just run all the way here."

"You *ran* here?" Leila asked, curious and at the same time relieved he didn't lean in for a hug, due to the fact that she didn't know the guy and he was absolutely dripping with sweat. What was it with every new guy she met at this enrichment thing being positively drenched? "From where?"

"Well, my family lives down in South Philly, about," he drew out the "about" as he turned and looked towards the road leading away from the parking lot. "Oh, maybe five miles or so? Probably a little more, maybe a little less. I don't know, I don't really keep track of—"

"You're full of it," Britt snapped. She turned to Leila. "He has an app on his phone that tracks how far he walks, never mind how far he runs."

"One, stop hurling me under the bus. Two, you don't get calves like these by sitting around all day." He struck a pose and bent down a little, flexing the muscles in his legs. "Boom!"

"And what about you?" Leila asked Britt, laughing at Mikey's antics.

"Not nearly as far as this one," she said. "My house isn't too far from the Art Museum. You're new to town, right? Have you been there yet? You should run up the stairs. It's like, tradition."

"Ha!" Leila shouted. "Yeah, no, I've done that. Bad date."

"Say no more," Mikey said. "We've all been there."

"Sure you have," Britt grinned.

Leila smiled as the two of them bickered with one another. They reminded her of the way she and Sarika always jokingly went at it, playfully mocking each other the way only the truest of friends can. She wondered what their history was like, how long they'd been friends, what they'd seen together. She and Sarika, they'd been through more than most.

"I wonder where Shawn is?" Britt said to no one in particular, surveying the still-milling crowd of students. "He should have been here, like, hours ago. That guy is always insanely punctual."

"I half expected him to be waiting in the parking lot, composting the remainder of his breakfast and making us feel guilty," Mikey said, and then waved his hands about in an exaggerated fashion. "I'm Shawn. Oh no, you guys, don't sneeze, you'll murder innocent bacteria floating in the air."

Britt nudged Mikey again, and Leila laughed.

"I guess we can take the tour without him, right?" Leila didn't so much as ask as she suggested. Leaving him behind would be great. She wasn't eager to have any conversations with him, about the date or anything else. His offensive conversation, his prying questions, the bicycle accident, his lack of follow through. Not even a text, ugh. Her head hurt just thinking about all of it, never mind the concussion.

"I'm down," Mikey said, almost a little too quickly. Leila gave him a look, and he shrugged. "I'd just maybe like to enjoy the outdoors, hang out with my friends, new and old." He grinned at Leila and she rolled her eyes. "And maybe not be made to feel so terrible about being a human being."

Leila laughed with Mikey and Britt until Mikey's eyes widened, and he nodded over her shoulder.

"Incoming," he muttered, crossing his arms. "Looks like he's back taking the chariot."

"The what?" Leila asked, turning around. A dark-black SUV with tinted windows and thick, oversized tires pulled up into the dirt parking lot, pushing up clouds of dust in its wake. A couple of students coughed as the truck braked near them and a plume of dirt washed over everyone. Leila rubbed her eyes and glared.

The passenger-side door opened, and out popped Shawn, his weathered backpack slung over his shoulder, his usual sunny disposition turned way down. He walked around the front of the car to the driver's side door, and stood up on his tip-toes as the window lowered.

"Later, babe," Jessica said, leaning out the window.

"Later," Shawn said, pushing himself up on his toes a little bit more to kiss her quickly on the mouth, a sharp peck.

The SUV backed up, kicking up more dirt, as Shawn walked towards everyone. Leila stared at him, and when his eyes met with hers, he quickly turned away.

"Sorry I'm late, all," Shawn said, adjusting the backpack on his shoulder. "Dad had some things going on down at the office, and I, um," he cleared his throat. "Well, I'm here." He turned and watched the SUV as it sped out of the parking lot. A couple of half-hearted grumbles rose up from the students as he turned back and walked towards Leila, Mikey, and Britt.

"Hey," he said, as Britt and Mikey stepped away. Leila caught the two of them looking at each other with curious glances, and Leila knew she was already busted. They could clearly tell something had happened, even if nothing really had.

"Hey," she said back, shrugging.

"Look, I'm sorry about the other day. I wasn't thinking before I spoke. I do that a lot. Sometimes I really only hear myself, you know?"

"I guess?" Leila ventured. She didn't know. She didn't do that. "Were you thinking before you went out with me, when all that was clearly going on?" Leila nodded at the dust cloud that still hovered around the parking lot.

Shawn's face turned red.

"It's more complicated than . . . You know what, it's fine. I'm sorry. I'll give you your space," Shawn said, lifting up his hands. "But if you want to talk, maybe hang out again sometime, I'd like that. I'd, you know, like to do better, if that makes sense. Be friends?"

"Yeah, I don't know about that," Leila said. "I'm not promising anything. That was an unpleasant way to spend an afternoon. At least the end of it and all. Especially the whole leaving-me-alone-at-the-hospital thing."

"Oh God, Leila, it's . . . I didn't want to bail, but . . . I was there for a while. Did your mom tell you? I was—"

"Yeah, she did. I shouldn't have expected you to stay the whole time but—"

"I wanted to!" Shawn said, looking frustrated. "I'll explain one of these days. Is your head okay?" Shawn asked, looking up at her forehead. His face was awash in disappointment, his mouth a thin line, like he was holding something back.

"It's fine. Are you still worried about how my face looks?" she snapped back.

Shawn completely deflated. "Okay. I'll go get things ready, but if you start to feel like, I don't know, dizzy or anything, let me know."

"Sure, Shawn," Leila said, eager for this conversation to be over.

Shawn sighed, and walked away towards the other B.E.A.C. students. He started to do his smile-point-click thing to a few of them as he made his way to the front of the group.

"Wow, that is annoying," Mikey muttered, walking back up to Leila with Britt.

"Yeah," Leila said. "Yeah it is."

"So, the two of you?" Mikey started, making some entirely inappropriate hand gestures.

"Mikey!" Britt shouted, slapping him upside the head.

"Ow!" he said through the laughter.

Leila smiled, fighting the urge to scowl.

"No. We just went on a sorta-date the other day." Leila shrugged. "Not a good one." She pointed at her forehead and lifted her scarf up a little, revealing the bandage. Britt gasped. "I fell off my bike. It was bad. And now here he is with that other girl." She shrugged.

"Death to men," Britt said, crossing her arms. "Except you, pal." She punched Mikey in the shoulder. "You can stay."

Leila smiled. She liked these two.

"Hey everyone!" Shawn exclaimed, a bit of disappointment still lingering in his voice. "We're going to meet our tour guide over at the Japanese tea house, and then we'll take a stroll of the grounds, maybe explore some of the area before we get to work fixing—"

"Are you guys my group for the day?"

A young man sidestepped out of the woods, down one of the trails, right up behind Shawn, and patted him on the shoulder. He stood a few inches taller than him, and wore a uniform consisting of dark-green pants and a beige dress shirt, topped with a brown, thick-brimmed hat. A black belt wrapped around his waist with a number of things tucked away inside, notably a container that looked a lot like mace and a ridiculously long, black flashlight which swung about as he walked. Looking at him in profile, Leila noticed his meticulously kept beard, which was cut in strong, almost impossibly straight lines. Shawn spun around, and the man stuck out a hand.

"Landon Johnson," he said as he shook Shawn's hand vigorously. He let go and slapped Shawn on the back, and Shawn took a few steps away. For a moment, Leila felt a little bad for him, losing the spotlight he seemed so fond of. She shook it off.

Landon turned to look at everyone, and Leila gasped as he faced the group. The pounding in her head suddenly matched the thundering of her heart.

"I'm your guide for the day," he said, putting his hands on his hips.

On his shoulder.

"I'm a park ranger here in Fairmount Park, or, at least a soon-to-be ranger," he continued.

The owl.

"I'm still in training and all." He shrugged.

The owl from yesterday's bike ride. It jostled about with Landon's casual shrug, and Landon lifted his hand up to scratch the bird under its chin. It was the same one. It had to be. The one she saw after racing away from Shawn and his idiotic, heartless comments. The one that made her crash her bicycle. It was here. Staring at her with its bright-yellow eyes.

The bird swayed with the young park ranger as he talked to the group, cocking its head to the side as it looked at Leila. Its gaze quickly darted about from person to person, and then up to nothing in particular.

"Is there a problem?" Landon asked, looking to Leila. He squinted at her for a moment and her heart raced. Did he recognize her from the other day? She felt a wave of awkwardness wash over her. That whole ordeal had been so embarrassing.

"No," Leila said, and then, as if a bolt of realization hit him, Landon laughed.

"You must be curious about this guy." He lifted his arm, which was wrapped up in some fraying leather, and the small owl hopped onto it, flapping one large wing. The other was just a small nub. Leila exhaled. Maybe he really didn't realize who she was. Maybe she'd be spared the awkward conversation.

"This here is Milford." He gave the owl a small scratch under its chin with his free hand, and it closed its eyes, clearly enjoying it.

"What's, uh, what's up with his wing there?" Mikey asked.

"Well, Milford was found here in Fairmount Park as a fledgling, and his wing was broken and deformed." He kept scratching the little owl, the bird's head pushing back even farther, lost in joy, as though he might fall off Landon's arm at any moment. "It was starting to grow at an odd angle as he grew older, and they had to remove it to save him. Because of this, he's not releasable into the wild."

He stopped scratching the owl, and Milford's head shot forward, eyes darting about as if trying to figure out why the scratching had stopped.

"He shuffles between live animal exhibits and lessons at the Academy of Natural Sciences and the Philadelphia Zoo for classroom visits." He placed Milford back on his shoulder, and the owl nibbled at his ear. "Ow, come on, man. But for the most part, he's here, in our raptor conservatory. Any other questions?"

"Does he have a fake wing?" Leila asked. She had to make sure. It had to have been him yesterday. "A prosthetic?"

"No, Milford doesn't have a fake wing or a prosthetic," he said drily. He was clearly lying. "Those wouldn't work on an owl. Hell, they only work on people after lots of physical therapy. This isn't *How to Train Your Owl*, you know?" he scoffed. "Anyway, I'm part of the Park Ranger Adolescent Training program, or P.R.A.T., a rather unfortunate acronym. Today we'll be . . ."

Leila squinted, staring at him and back up at the owl, ignoring whatever he was going on about. She'd seen him yesterday. She was sure of it. It was the same owl, flying up and crashing down to the ground. He was the guy the voices were pointing her towards, and she had to figure out why.

"What's *How to Train Your Owl*?" Mikey asked.

"It's a movie reference." Britt said, giving him a shove.

"Well, a book and a movie. And a TV series, too. How did you get this far in life?"

"Oh, shut up," Mikey muttered.

Leila turned to Britt and Mikey, who were smiling at each other.

"I'll be taking you on your tour of the, the . . . Wait, where are we going today, anyway?" Landon asked, and pulled a small, black notepad out of his pocket. He flipped it open. His face scrunched up in irritation. He ripped out the piece of paper, crumpled it up, and lifted it up to the owl, who took it in his beak and tossed it away. The bit of paper fell on the ground, and Shawn scrambled to pick it back up. Landon flipped the notepad shut with an audible slap.

"The Shofuso house." He sighed and shook his head. "Can I make some recommendations? Specifically one? Who wants to see more little guys like this one?" He nodded his head towards Milford, and a few hands shot up in the air amongst the group.

"Can we see more guys like *him*?" Sarika asked, whispering in Leila's ear. Leila jumped. Sarika had appeared seemingly out of nowhere, a cup of coffee in her hand, steam still rising from the holes in the lid.

"Where did you even come from?" Leila whispered back.

"I walked." Sarika shrugged. "There's a place called Mugshots not far from here. Hopped the bus, hung out there for a while, and strolled over. You have *got* to log on to the board, by the way. There's all this drama—"

"So does that sound good to everyone?" Landon asked,

a little too loudly. Leila looked up, and he was staring straight at her. She gulped and looked at Sarika, who in turn just kicked her.

"Yeah, sounds fine?" Leila ventured.

"Mm. *Fine* is right." Sarika poked Leila, who nudged her away.

"Great!" Landon exclaimed, clapping his hands together. "Then let's go."

They started walking away from the parking lot and into the woods. Leila looked around for Britt and Mikey, spotting them at the head of the swell of students. They were chatting to one another excitedly. She made a note to introduce Sarika to them later. Jon had said to try to meet some new people, make some new friends. Shawn was definitely out of the running, and there was obviously something else going on with him. She didn't need that drama.

"So?" Sarika asked, nudging Leila as the two of them walked, taking small sips from her coffee. "Who is that? Catch me up."

Leila shrugged. There were still some things she couldn't tell Sarika. Not yet. The voices, their instructions. For now, Landon was just some guy with a bird.

"Some park ranger in training," she whispered back. "I'm pretty sure he's the guy I saw when I crashed my bike."

"Really?"

"I mean, unless there's some other local park ranger trying to teach an owl to fly."

Landon turned and looked back at her again, wearing the expression of a teacher who was waiting for his class to be quiet. Leila looked away, pretending to stare at nothing in the trees around her, though it was hard to keep her eyes away from him. He obviously took a lot of care in his appearance, his uniform was crisp and well ironed. She stared at him as he spoke to the students up front and frowned as the students fiddled with their smartphones and took selfies. He looked up from the students and made eye contact with Leila again, and she jumped back with a jolt before realizing he was looking at someone behind her. He stopped and crossed his arms as Shawn angrily bounded up the trail, brushing by Sarika and Leila.

"I'm sorry, but this isn't what we had planned today," Shawn said, standing next to Landon. "We have plans at the Shofuso house, and they are going to be waiting for us."

"This is better, trust me," Landon said, turning back around.

Shawn reached out and grabbed Landon's shoulder. Landon spun back around, his eyes boring into Shawn. He stood practically a foot taller than him, and Milford fluttered his single wing angrily.

"Don't touch me again," Landon said. "You don't know me."

"What, are you going to hit me?" Shawn smirked. "We have plans. You can't just take everyone away and—"

Landon ignored him and headed back up the trail. Shawn reached out and grabbed his shoulder again, and Landon spun around, glaring down at Shawn.

"I'm not going to hit you. But if you touch me again, we'll certainly have some words." Landon crossed his arms.

"Oh please," Shawn said. "My dad could get you fired."

Landon took a step forward.

"Your dad? How cute. Look, I don't get paid," Landon grinned. "So, go ahead. Run to your pops. Say what you want to say. I'm not here for the money. I'm here for the park. For the animals. For the trees. What are *you* here for?"

"For the trees?" Shawn spat. "Who the hell are you, the Lorax?"

"Seriously? Is that really all you've got? That's your comeback?"

A beat of silence followed, interrupted only by the sounds of the neighboring trees. A soft rustling whispered through the leaves, and a cool breeze danced around Leila's neck.

Now you see?

Leila jumped, and looked at Sarika.

He's here. For us. For you.

"It's happening." Leila whispered, closing her eyes. She felt Sarika grab her hand, and she closed her eyes and started to whisper to herself as the voices pressed. She pushed herself to get centered. To be here. To focus.

"Outside. Trees. Rocks."

You can trust him. Go to him. Tell him of what you hear.

"Ground. Soil. Wind."

"Leila," Shawn's voice said.

Leila opened her eyes, and Shawn was standing right in front of her with Landon behind him. "You understand, right?" Shawn asked. "You still up for the tea house? I think you'll–"

"Get away from me," Leila snapped, pushing Shawn out of the way. She stumbled a little into the brush, her head hammering as the voices grew louder.

He wears the colors of the caretakers.

An arm quickly wrapped around her, and she glanced up to see Sarika helping her gain her balance again.

"Are you okay?" Shawn burst in.

"Alright, what's happening over here?" Landon walked over and looked over at Shawn, his eyes narrowing. "Is he bothering you two?" He reached for a walkie-talkie on his belt. "Do I need to call someone?"

"No," Shawn said, walking away. "No, it's fine. Go look at your old bird cages that should have been torn down a long time ago."

"Wait, are we seeing the Raptor Trust?" Leila asked, looking up at Landon. As the voices faded away, she remembered what Jon had been rambling about in the kitchen the day before. Apparently, Fairmount Park had a raptor habitat that was in danger of losing funding. If Landon was taking the group there, the place that she'd rode by when she saw him flying that owl around, maybe he could answer some questions for her. Maybe she could even help Jon out with a bit more background for his future articles. "That actually sounds kind of awesome."

She exhaled and gave a reassuring nod to Sarika. The voices had faded.

"I wouldn't trust them with a parakeet!" Shawn

shouted, his back still turned as he walked away. "You all do you. I'm out of here."

Leila steadied herself and pushed forward with Sarika as Landon walked back up to lead the group down the trail. The path pushed on through some lazy, low-hanging trees and brambles that shoved their way into the legs of passersby, until it opened up on a ramshackle bundle of small, cabin-like buildings. All that remained of the B.E.A.C. group was Sarika, Leila, and Leila's two possible-new-friends Mikey and Britt. Leila shrugged at the small group. The dozen or so members who'd been milling around the parking lot earlier either went off with Shawn or had split off during all the drama.

Landon stopped the group in front of a large, barn-like building that stood taller than the rest of the smaller shed-like structures. He turned around to face everyone, hands on his hips, a smile on his face.

"Welcome to Philadelphia's branch of the Raptor Trust," he said with a proud smile. He turned to look at the buildings. "The original Trust was founded in Millington, New Jersey, and this branch opened a few years ago." Leila pulled out her phone and began taking notes while Landon went on. "Feel free to explore the grounds. We've got a few hawks and kestrels, a couple of owls here and there. Some are in the middle of rehabilitation, others are un-releasable, and we care for them here thanks to our staff of volunteers. We work with different institutions in the city to educate people about them as much as possible."

"Staff?" Sarika asked. Everyone turned and looked at her.

"Sarika," Leila said, giving her a look.

"What?" Sarika asked. "There's like, no one here."

"Well, there's one other caretaker here today," Landon continued sadly. "But you're right, staff is light. We're likely to be closed down in the coming months if funding doesn't go through, as the Fairmount Park system makes room for renovations and new construction. This site is poised to go. Rumor has it there will be a greenhouse or something. And then there's the old Thomas Mansion, the gardens, and groves. It kind of sucks, all that history with no place in the future. People just don't care."

Leila.

Leila winced, moving her hand up to the pressure in her forehead. Sarika grabbed her arm and pulled her close.

He can help me. He can help us.

The voices. So much for the break, the distraction. Here they were, and they were being direct again, whispering on the wind, pushing against the inside of her head.

Come.

Leila shook her head, the pain rattling against her skull.

Come to the mansion. Come to me.

"Road. Path. Bushes. Grass," Leila muttered. Sarika looked at her, and Leila returned the glance, her eyes wide, hoping she'd understand in the way that best friends do what was going on without her having to say anything. Sarika nodded. Of course she did.

"But, we'll see!" Landon perked up. "Might save this

place, might save the mansion and the grounds. Maybe someone cares. So go on, explore, and meet back here in, say, an hour or so? I'm pretty sure I can set up a showing of some of the raptors while you all look around."

The students dispersed, but Sarika stayed by Leila's side as they started to walk towards one of the big cages. They kicked up dirt and pebbles as they walked together; the area surrounding the Trust was a bit unkempt. Inside, a bronze-colored, large bird sat on a high perch, with an enormous branch twisting and turning its way up inside the cage. It looked like a huge piece of driftwood, plucked from the ocean and hammered into the ground, sticking up in the air, with holes throughout the trunk.

"That's Liberty, our golden eagle," Landon said, walking up behind Leila and Sarika. The little owl was still on his shoulder, eyes darting about curiously. "You know, because he's bronze and rusty, kinda like the Liberty Bell, but not really. Tourists get a kick out of it, though."

"What's his story?" Leila asked.

"Well," Landon began as he moved next to her. He glanced at her from the side, peering over the owl on his shoulder. The thin black beard on his face, shaved so close to his cheeks, chin, and upper lip, brought out the white of his teeth. "Someone was trying to keep her as a pet, and they ended up cutting the tips of her wings too short. Wing clipping, they call it. Sometimes people do that with small birds like parakeets, parrots, or lovebirds.

"It's better than pinioning, at least, where they remove the wing joint. This way they just can't fly away for a while, as opposed to leaving them grounded forever."

He looked up at the eagle, and his eyes seemed to light up when he talked about the bird.

"Unfortunately, whoever did the work on her cut way too much. We had to bandage them up when they dropped her off here. One had gotten a little infected. She'll never fly again." He sighed heavily.

"You can't keep a creature like this as a pet," he continued, his eyes wide and sad.

"Aren't you kinda doing that, though?" Sarika asked.

"This is different. We're keeping her safe," Landon said, looking back at Sarika and Leila with noticeable irritation before he focused his attention back on the eagle. "Before they clipped her wings, the person was trying to use her like a falcon. You know, for sport and all that, training them to hunt. You can't really do that with eagles. I mean, you *can*. People in the Middle East do that, nomadic people. It's a symbiotic existence. But here? As a pet and a hobby, out in the suburbs of Philadelphia?"

He stared at the eagle for a while, a beat of silence passing between him, Sarika, and Leila, and then turned back to them.

"Hey, so, I don't think I got your name?" He nodded, looking past the little owl again, who continued to look about before finally focusing on Sarika.

"Sarika," she said, reaching a hand past Leila.

"Great to meet you," he said, shaking her hand. He looked at Leila and then back at Sarika. "And it's Leila, yes? Can I, um, can I talk to you for a moment? Alone?"

Leila looked over at Sarika, who raised her eyebrows,

163

giving her a thoughtful look. She knew that look. It asked if she was going to be okay, despite what had just happened.

Leila gave her a quick nod, and Sarika smiled back at Landon.

"Well, I'm going to go look at . . . some birds . . . or something," Sarika said. She gave Leila's hand a reassuring squeeze and strolled off, turning behind the building.

"So," Leila said, her heart quickening.

"So." Landon nodded and then exhaled. "Look, I, um, I would like to apologize."

"Oh?"

"Yeah, listen." Landon looked around, the little owl swaying with him as he did so, and then he turned to Leila, speaking in a soft voice. "I'm not supposed to be out, well, trying to fly Milford out here. Or, um, anywhere, really." He scratched the back of the owl's head and sighed. "What you saw the other day . . . I wanted to run over and help you, but by the time I wrangled Milford up here and he'd calmed down enough for me to move anywhere, your boyfriend—"

"Ha!" Leila interrupted.

"Okay, so your friend from this club of yours," Landon continued, shrugging. "It seemed pretty under control and all, with a couple of people huddled around you, and the ambulance down the block. It doesn't excuse me just standing on the sidelines like that, I know, but—"

"So, essentially you chose the owl over a human?" Leila interrupted, arching an eyebrow and crossing her arms.

"Uh, well," Landon squirmed, all that confidence just

falling off him. "When you put it that way, I guess I did. I'm sorry."

"It's okay. I think I get it," Leila said, nodding.

"Thanks," Landon said, rubbing at the back of his neck. Leila stood there in awkward silence with him for a moment, looking from him to Milford to the eagle in the cage. The sounds of the remaining members of B.E.A.C. wandering the Trust filtered in, soft voices muttering from not too far off.

"So, is this the part where you tell me his real story?" Leila asked, looking back at Milford.

"Story?"

"With the flying and whatever it was you had on him?"

"Ah." Landon nodded, and then fished around inside a leather satchel wrapped around his arm. He pulled out a piece of strappy black cloth with bits of metal on it, shaped like the wing of one of those old-timey airplanes Leila had seen in history books and in black-and-white footage on television, when people rushed ill-fated contraptions madly off cliffs in hopes they would fly. "I'm the one who found Milford all those years ago. Parents' backyard. I kept him in a shoebox until my father caught me and made me bring him up here." Landon looked up, his eyes set on the eagle and the enclosure, and then spun around, leaning his back against it.

"It's been, what, seven years, Milford?" He looked at the owl, cocking his head, and the owl in turn did the same, as if questioning him in return. "And I don't know, he never really seemed happy in any of those cages. Missing a wing, hopping everywhere. So I take him out now and again, and keep trying with these things." He shook the cloth wing out before handing it to her. "I hope it'll work one day."

"No luck?" Leila asked, looking over the cloth.

"Not really." He shrugged. "Sometimes he gets up into the air for a few seconds, other times, comes crashing right back down. I mean really, there's only so much I can do, armed only with Google and my math and engineering classes at CCP."

"You're at the county college?" Leila asked, handing him back the wing. Leila and Sarika had been to the Community College of Philadelphia a handful of times, for skills workshops and other outreach programs that wrangled up foster kids and kids in group homes. A handful of the professors hung around at Adam's Café, often roping kids into the events.

"Yeah," Landon said, looking down at the wing, suddenly sad. "It works for now, at least until my parents catch on."

"Catch on?" Leila asked. "What, they don't want you in college?"

"Hm?" Landon shook his head. "Yeah, no, it's just . . . You know, we should really keep exploring the grounds, I think you'll like it here," Landon said, bottling himself back up.

"Yeah, okay," Leila nodded as he started to walk away. "Oh! Wait!"

Landon turned around.

"Why?" Leila asked.

"Why what?" He cocked his head to the side, and Milford did the same.

"The flying?" Leila asked with a shrug, pointing at the owl. "Doing it again and again, making him the wings and all. Why do it?"

Landon looked over at the owl, and scratched under its head. Milford lifted his chin up, eyes shut, lost in being petted.

"It's not about that. It's about giving him the chance to try."

The wind rustled.

Go.

The voice circled back, as the cool breeze brushed at Leila's face and neck.

He bears the colors of the caretakers. He will understand.

Leila closed her eyes and shook her head a little, trying to ignore the pounding in her temples and the voices that were coming in way too clearly.

"Hey, are you okay?" Landon asked.

She opened her eyes, and the voices faded.

"Yeah, yeah, no, I'm fine," Leila said, feeling flushed. "I'm, um, I'm going to go find Sarika."

"Okay, well, if you need anything, I'll be here," Landon nodded, walking back over. "Here's my number, text me if you're not feeling too great, and I can call a ranger to come drive you out."

And with that, Landon turned and walked towards the rest of the students, leaving Leila with her heart feeling strangely full.

OMG THANKS YOU GUYS
Posted by WithouttheY
AUGUST 19th, 2017 | 1:02PM
I mean, seriously, what do I even say right now?
I'm still not feeling great, but the outpouring of
support is no doubt speeding up the recovery pro-
cess. I think I read something about that. Because
you know, science or whatever.
Debating what to do with the extra funds, but I'll
likely make some donations to the youth centers
in my area. The Attic, maybe? I dunno. Something
good. You're all wonderful.

RE: OMG THANKS YOU GUYS
Posted by Toothless
AUGUST 19th, 2017 | 2:09PM
Awesome, glad you're feeling better. Let's make
those plans soon.

> RE: OMG THANKS YOU GUYS
> *Posted by WithouttheY*
> AUGUST 19th, 2017 | 3:02PM
> Yes please ;-)

> RE: OMG THANKS YOU GUYS
> *Posted by A Dash of Paprika*
> AUGUST 19th, 2017 | 3:22PM
> . . . THE HELL IS THIS?

X

"So," Sarika said, dropping her backpack and leaning into the lockers. "We need to talk, Miss Flirting-with-the-enemy-on-our-message-board."

"Okay, that's nothing, I've never even met him and we've swapped like a handful of messages. And he's not that bad. Maybe I'll grab coffee with him and report back–"

"If he hasn't slain you because he turns out to be a crazy Internet person! Have you even been paying attention during our Lifetime movie marathons?" Sarika said, looking at Leila with wide, doubtful eyes. "Just saying. At least bring him into Adam's for coffee, so I can protect you from afar. Maybe I'll perch on the espresso machine. With a crossbow."

"You watch too many of the *wrong* Lifetime movies," Leila laughed as she swung open her locker. "Those definitely . . . oh."

She stopped mid-sentence, staring inside her locker.

"What is it?" Sarika asked, peering inside her locker. "Oh shit."

"Yeah."

"That's . . . that's a ballsy move," Sarika said.

"I'll say."

Inside her locker sat a dozen flowers, multiple colors

and kinds, bound together in soft, white paper. A card was stuck to the front of the bouquet.

I'm sorry. – Shawn.

"I mean, what do you even say to something like that?" Leila asked. "'Kay? Thanks? Good luck with all your future endeavors? Have a nice life with your awful girlfriend?"

"Hell if I know," Sarika said, shrugging. "How did he even get into your locker?"

"Dr. Rich, maybe?" Leila wondered. "He seems like the sad-romantic sort."

Leila reached in and plucked the bouquet out. The smell of the fresh flowers was overwhelming and intense. With her hand around the thick, green stems, still wet from wherever they were before, she breathed in, and then fought the urge to gasp as she felt the flowers rustle about. It was as if they were trying to stretch in the tied-up bouquet, their leaves bending, and the petals blooming out ever so slightly.

It felt like the little tree in her yard all over again. Growing too fast, stretching out as if they wanted to touch her when she got close.

She moved to put the flowers back in the locker when they abruptly shot out of her hand with a loud slap against the paper. They hit the hard floor of the school hallway, and the voices in Leila's head came screaming back, loud and shrill, like they'd been the day the willow was cracked in half. She pressed her hands against her head and leaned against the locker, gritting her teeth and muttering to herself.

"Hallway. Locker. School."

"Hey!" a familiar voice shouted.

"Leave her alone!" Sarika yelled, her voice booming in the hall.

"What's wrong with her?" another said. "Hey, what's the matter with you?"

"I said, leave her alone!" Sarika roared.

Leila shook her head gently and turned to spot Jessica, Rebekah, and Gwen standing right there in the hall. Jessica was laughing with Rebekah, practically falling over. Gwen, the girl with the brown hair and freckles, stood away from the other two, her mouth turned down into a frown, shaking her head.

"Come on, guys," Gwen muttered, bending down to pick up some of the flowers.

"Get out of here!" Sarika shouted. She went to push past Leila, who grabbed her and held on to her. Sarika was a ball of fury. "Are you okay?" she whispered.

"I'll be fine," Leila said, the voices now faded.

"You stay away from my man," Jessica snapped. "I own him." She bent down and picked up the card, holding it between two well-manicured fingers like a playing card, and promptly flicked it at Leila. Then she turned on her heels and kept walking down the hall with Rebekah. Leila let go of Sarika, and the two of them began plucking the flowers from the hard floor.

"Sorry about all that," Gwen said, softly, handing the flowers over to Leila. "They, um, get carried away sometimes."

"You think?" spat Sarika, snatching the flowers out of Gwen's hands.

Leila took the flowers gently from Sarika, focusing on them, her hand gripping the stems tight. They didn't rustle or stretch or show any signs of movement, which gave Leila an odd, sinking feeling in her chest. She sifted the non-broken flowers back into the paper bouquet. A majority of the flowers had snapped their stems, hanging off by green threads like the lowered heads of sad people. Leila lifted the bouquet up and looked at it, shaking her head, and then plucked the "I'm sorry" card off the floor, where it had slid across the smooth linoleum to the opposite side of the hall.

"You know, forget all this," Leila said, marching back over to her locker, cramming the flowers and card inside and slamming the door. The force sent a small blossom of pain against her still-wounded head, pressing against the new head scarf Lisabeth had given her this morning. "I don't need this today. Or any day for that matter."

Leila snatched her bicycle helmet from off the ground and tossed on her jacket. Jon and Liz weren't thrilled about her getting back on a bike so soon, but the headaches hadn't been bad. And besides, she was going to do it anyway, with or without the okay. And Lisabeth's bike was good enough to ride, despite being a little too tall.

"Cover for me?" Leila asked Sarika, who responded with a sneaky grin.

"Don't I always?" Sarika shrugged. "And besides, it's enrichment, remember? You could cut the rest of the summer. But don't. We're supposed to be having fun." Sarika glared at Gwen, who shied away from her gaze.

"Let's meet up at Adam's later," Leila said. "I'll ride over there around the time you're getting out."

"Perfect."

Leila hugged Sarika softly and turned to see Gwen still standing there, shifting her feet about on the floor awkwardly. She was trying to stare at anything but the two of them.

"You can, you know, go fuck off now or something," Sarika said, waving at Gwen.

"Oh, come on, Sarika," Leila said, giving her a playful shove. "Thanks for, you know, trying, Gwen. I think you're probably better than all them, you know?"

Gwen nodded, and turned away to walk down the hall. Something about the way she carried herself, her head down, not looking at anything around her in particular, felt incredibly sad. Like she was lost.

It weighed heavy on Leila's heart.

She knew the feeling all too well.

Leila pushed forward on Lisabeth's bicycle, the frame a bit high and bulky for her tastes. It was thick and made more for mountain biking and difficult trails than the city streets. The end-of-summer Philadelphia breeze tickled her face. She exhaled, fighting the urge to close her eyes and just let her other senses take over as the sidewalks, trees, and people whooshed by her as she sped through the city streets. She sighed as a feeling of warmth rushed to her chest, enjoying the moment, welcoming the long ride back home.

Home.

The word stirred up feelings inside her, but it actually was a home this time, wasn't it? For once she wasn't pedaling towards a group home she'd grown weary of spending the night in, or speeding towards another lame job fair or skill-building workshop thrown together by well-meaning and concerned adults. She was going towards something good. It felt nice.

Leila.

Her body stiffened, and she fought the urge to slam on the brakes again as the memories of the last time this happened up on Kelly Drive came surging back. The whispering. The voices. They were louder than ever, resounding in a single voice instead of feeling like a few dozen. No longer did the whispering feel like a quiet breath against the back of her neck. Now, it was as if the faceless voice was next to her, singing in her ear.

Come to the forest.

"Bike. Wind," she started muttering to herself softly as she rode.

The forest. Come to me.

"Road. Trees."

Leila.

Her name.

The voices used her name.

Suddenly, everything felt as though it had piled up too high, and something in Leila snapped.

Shawn being a tool, asking his inappropriate questions. The damn girls in the hallway at summer enrichment. Her parents, and their sad, pleading eyes, how she couldn't give them what they seemed to desperately want. Landon, and whatever that park ranger had to do with the voices in the wind.

That was it.

Time to talk back.

"There isn't a fucking forest around here," Leila growled, her eyes darting about as she pressed on, pedaling fast and feeling angry. It was just another thirty or forty minutes on this bicycle and she'd be home, where she could hide in her room and not worry about some disembodied voices causing her to crash. She could hide out in the living room, maybe tool around with fixing Marigold in the yard. She'd check out Major Willow and see how she was doing, if she somehow had magically grown a little more in the past few days.

"This is a city," Leila said, resolutely. "There are parks. Nothing that resembles wilderness—"

There was once a great forest.

"Stop it," Leila muttered, shaking her head a little. "Just stop it. I'm not here for you. You aren't real."

But then men came, with axes and saws, killing many, leaving few.

Leila slowed down and pulled over to the sidewalk. She was in the Eraserhood, a section of Philadelphia affectionately named after a David Lynch movie she thought was weird and unwatchable. She stopped. The single voice was loud and clear, with the hint of others still whispering around it, circling like a small breeze.

She took a deep breath.

If this was the game the voices wanted to play, then fine.

She'd play.

"Where do you want me to go? Huh?" Leila asked, closing her eyes. All these years she'd pushed the voices away, shoving them down, down, down, as far from her as she could. She'd said words that grounded her to push them back. "What do you want me to do?"

The old mansion, made of stone and our fallen sisters.

Leila shook her head, the nonsensical words starting to press against the wound on her forehead.

"I don't understand. I . . . you're not real. I can't help you. G-go away."

He will know. He who has walked among us. His brothers once sought to save us.

"Who?"

The boy with the one-winged bird.

Leila dropped the bicycle, grabbed at her head, and cried. She sat on the warm sidewalk, heated by the late summer sun, with large, looming buildings surrounding her. The Eraserhood was a mixture of old, decaying structures and repurposed warehouses made into condos and offices. The shattered, abandoned buildings looked like blackened teeth next to the brand-new ones. She took a few deep breaths, trying to focus, trying to push the voices—and the dark feelings brewing in her chest—away.

Leila.

"GO AWAY!" she screamed, her head pounding.

We need you. I need you.

"What do you want me to do? If I listen, will you just leave me alone?"

The forest. The mansion. The boy. And the bird.

"That doesn't tell me anything!"

Leila listened. She waited. The neighborhood around her was quiet, save for the rumble of cars as they drove by her, some slowing down to peek at her before driving off. The wind rustled bits of trash on the streets, howling gently in the nearby alleys and empty buildings.

She listened.

And no one spoke.

With a huff, she stood up, lifted Liz's bike off the sidewalk and swung her leg over it. She breathed in and pulled her phone out of her pocket before clicking it on. She scrolled through the contact list, scrolling past Home, Jon, Lisabeth, and stopping on Sarika, her mind running on autopilot. Sarika was always the first person she messaged, but this time . . .

She scrolled back.

Landon.

The boy with the bird.

He wasn't really a boy. He had to be what, nineteen? Maybe twenty? He had all that stubble on his face. And the uniform made it hard to figure out. It was hard to tell, they hadn't really spoken all that much save for that run-in at the Raptor Trust, with his quiet confession about his owl, and his flirty, dark-brown eyes. He'd said he was at the Community College of Philadelphia in his first year, and he certainly had that younger look about him, despite the scruffy beard that Leila had to admit she really liked.

The voices said he had answers.

"Forest. Mansion. Boy. Bird," she muttered to herself.

And if he thought she was out of her mind, at least she never had to see him again.

She exhaled, clicked on his name, and held the phone up to her ear.

FROM	SUBJECT	DATE
TOOTHLESS	FREE TONIGHT? Maybe grab that coffee? How'd you explain that board message to your pal Paprika? I mean, if you guys are really besties IRL, I don't want to like, come between all that. I'm just some guy on the Internet that thinks you're really interesting and likely super cute.	8/20
WITHOUTTHEY	RE: FREE TONIGHT? Ah, I wish. I'm busy with some personal things. Another day? And she took it well. Just lots of busting chops. Also I am blushing.	8/20
TOOTHLESS	RE: FREE TONIGHT? Busting chops, surprise surprise. Alright, I'll pester you another day. ;-)	8/20

XI

"Voices," Landon said, deadpan.

"Yes," Leila said.

"On the wind," Landon continued. Milford sat perched on his shoulder, his head moving just a little, a nudge to the left, a nudge to the right, his bold, yellow eyes fixed on something in the trees. He wasn't wearing one of Landon's faux-wings, but with his other wing pressed against his body it was kind of hard to tell he was missing one in the first place.

"That's what I said."

"Were they singing?" He grinned, and Leila glared at him. "Sorry, it sounds so very . . . Disney movie princess-ish?" Landon ventured, his tone rising.

"You know what," Leila muttered, resisting the urge to tell him off. "Just take me to this house or whatever, and I'll never tell a soul about Milly there, otherwise—"

"Wow, you will call him Milford or nothing at all," Landon said, looking at the owl and giving it a scratch under the chin. "Give the old man some dignity." Milford nibbled at Landon's finger.

"Look, are you going to help me or not?"

Landon turned his attention back to Leila, this time scratching his own chin with a curious expression. His fingers made an audible *scritch-scritch-scritch* against his rough, short beard. He looked down at the ground and then back up at her, nodding his head.

"I'll be honest," Landon said seriously. "If you'd come in here babbling about these voices of yours saying anything else, I would have probably left, or better yet, called someone. 'Cause no offense, but if someone came after me about Milford and the wing because you said something, which by the way I don't think you would, you don't seem the type." He paused for just enough time to let Leila roll her eyes.

He was right. She wouldn't have turned in that owl.

Landon turned to the small, shed-like building behind him and opened the door, the old wood letting out a loud squeak as it swung. Milford swayed about as he moved.

"I'd just deny it up and down. But there's something in what you said."

He grew quiet and sighed.

"I actually think I know what you're talking about, oddly enough." Something clattered inside the shed. "But you should still probably talk to someone. I mean, hearing voices? That's not really, you know, a normal thing."

"Yeah, um," Leila started. "I've ignored it all for a long time. The voices. I have a system. I don't want to get into it. It's complicated."

"I'm sure it is," he said after a beat. "I won't pry. Not my business."

Landon stepped out of the shed with a small map and two park ranger jackets. He placed Milford on the ground, and the owl looked up at him in confusion as Landon swung one of the jackets on. It was the same coat Leila had seen him wearing the day before, bits of dirt here, a soft tear in the leather there. He tossed the other jacket to her. It was thick and heavy.

"It's a little cold today," he said, shrugging as he picked up Milford, placing the owl back on his shoulder. The owl dug its talons into the leather, kneading the fabric like a cat getting comfortable on a blanket. "And if we're going deeper into the park, you'll need that. Shade is nice, but not when it's chilly. Besides, fewer people will ask questions if they spot two park rangers digging around back there. People aren't really supposed to trespass in that section."

He took a step forward and Leila pushed her hand against his chest. He stopped and took a step back, looking at her, and she felt herself blush. She'd brushed against what were no doubt pecs under his open jacket and thin t-shirt.

"I, um," Leila started. "You haven't said where we're going."

"Oh," Landon said. "You mentioned these, er, voices saying something about an old mansion that I've supposedly been trying to keep safe?"

"Yes, with your brothers or something."

"Yeah, whatever that's all about," Landon said dismissively. "The day my brothers actually come outside and experience the fresh air is the day I set this whole forest on fire." He sighed, and Leila took in the new information. So he had brothers, a family. "Look, there's this mansion deep in the park. The Thomas Mansion. I think I brought it up when I met your group. It's a bit of a hike, but you're up to it, right?"

"Sure." Leila shrugged as Landon started walking, clearly keeping his pace slow as he stepped alongside her.

"Are you sure, though? Your head."

"I'll be fine," Leila scowled.

"Okay, okay. I mean, it isn't that far, but still," Landon said, his hands going into his pockets. "Whenever anyone in my family, or any of my hometown friends, decide to visit and I take them on a walk like this, I have to be very clear about distance. They aren't walkers. For me, around the corner means like, a mile away. For them, it actually means around the corner. Whatever corner is nearest. Even if it's the corner of like, a table."

"I actually think my . . ." Leila searched for a word that would work but came up short. "Parents," she winced and kept going, "my parents said something about the mansion."

"Oh yeah?" Landon asked as they walked forward, heading down a small trail surrounded by brush.

"Yeah my, my da–" Leila struggled again. "Ah, hell. So, look, I'm adopted, okay?"

"Okay," Landon said, his tone indifferent.

"It's just, it's new, and talking about the two of them, my parents, it's hard without using those kind of words. Like the D word and M word, without going into all that backstory nonsense."

"D and M?" Landon questioned.

"Rhymes with 'rad' and 'bomb.'"

"Ah." Landon nodded. "I understand. I think. I won't ask, unless you want me to."

"I don't," Leila said curtly, silently cursing herself in her head for immediately closing up with Landon. At the same time, it felt good to keep that bit hidden, especially after the drama with Shawn. "And I just wanted to put it all out there before you start asking who this person is and that person is, and what was it like, or if I've ever thought–"

"Leila, I'm not gonna bother you about it," Landon said, his tone final. "It's obviously not my place. I'm not even sure I know your last name yet."

"Oh," Leila said. "Uh, it's Hetter. Well, I guess Hetter-Kline, now."

"Great. Mine is Johnson, though I may have brought that up before. I'm sorry, I just give a lot of those welcome-to-the-park type of talks. Now, what is your social security number? And where are you from? Not like, from, but you know, *from*, from?" Landon turned around and grinned at her. She smirked, and he turned back. "See? I get it. It's okay. You're not the only one with some family stuff, or who gets asked those kind of questions. Here, I'll put some of mine out there. My parents? Doctors. And they would kill me if they knew I was studying environmental science and not preparing to pursue some Ivy League education post-community college. They think this," he waved around at the trees, "is just a hobby."

He sighed.

"Basically, I'm saying I get the family issues and share

a mutual loathing of people who ask too many questions. You share when you want to. Or don't."

They walked on. Leila trailed a little bit behind him, small sticks and branches crunching under her feet as they pushed farther and farther into the park. Milford's head swung about as they walked, his eyes seeming to take in everything. It was as though the more they pressed forward, the denser and thicker the entire place got. Less like a park, and more like a small patch of wilderness that had been slightly swallowed up by the city, tucked away like a secret and forgotten by time.

She closed her eyes for a moment and breathed in deep, half expecting to hear something on the wind. A whisper. A voice. A suggestion.

Nothing.

"You okay?" Landon asked. Leila opened her eyes and took in a quick breath, surprised to see him right in front of her, his light-brown eyes alight with concern. "Was it, you know? The voices or whispers or whatever? Are you tired? Are you—"

"You don't have to fuss over me," Leila grunted, walking past him, trying to shed herself of the momentary flush of embarrassment. How long had she been standing there with her eyes shut for him to notice, stop, and walk over and nudge her out of whatever moment she was having? "I'm okay, I'm . . ."

She stopped, looking at the trail, which split into several smaller trails.

"Uh," she said as she looked at them, each as identical

and leading-to-nowhere as the last. Landon stepped up next to her, his boots crunching against the trail.

"We're going right," Landon said, leaning down a little to talk to her. Leila felt her heartbeat quicken as a gust of wind pushed through the trees, carrying the smell of the forest and Landon. A mixture of sandalwood and sawdust, an earthy smell.

"Right. Got it," Leila said.

Landon shrugged and walked forward, the trail narrowing to the point that only one person could fit, shrubs and trees pushing their branches and twigs at Leila. She dodged them as they walked, and a few scratched at the thick jacket Landon had let her borrow.

A small branch sliced across her face and she winced, taking a step back, only to open her eyes and see a number of the branches and brambles pushing themselves back, inching ever-so-slightly away from the trail in front of her and behind Landon. She continued to walk, listening for anything on the wind, as the gnarled, thorny vines and shrubs seemed to bend away from her.

She shook her head lightly, ignoring it all. Was Landon seeing this? This wasn't happening. This couldn't be happening.

They approached a cleared section of the path where the thorns and vines weren't as close to the trail. Tired of the silence as they walked, Leila stared at Landon's shoulder and down to his arm, the jacket worn away a little where Milford no doubt landed and scratched. His talons were gripping into the leather hard.

"So, why Milford?"

"What?" Landon asked, his head quickly turning to Leila and then back to the path in front of him.

"Milford. The owl. Why that name?"

"Ah," Landon said. "I always felt like owls need old man names. Names that sound wise beyond their years, no matter how old they are or what they've done with their lives. Milford just felt, I don't know, right."

"What other names did you consider?"

"A handful. Wallace. Barnabas. Engelbert. Percival. Humperdinck."

Leila laughed, surprised. "Those are good. Bonus points for *The Princess Bride* references there."

"You like that movie?" Landon asked, turning around for a moment in surprise.

"Um, I like that *book*. The movie is great, too. Why shouldn't I?"

"It's just an old movie, is all," Landon said, and she could see his broad shoulders shrug as he pushed a large branch out of the way on the path, carefully navigating around the plants. He looked back towards her, his hand still clutching the tree. "Watch out. Here, walk on by."

Leila squeezed by Landon on the narrow bit of trail, brushing against him as she did. The smell of sawdust and sandalwood mixed with the scent of the urban forest: wet leaves, dried wood, the cold, crisp air. She felt herself blush again, though she didn't know why, considering how relatively cold Landon was about everything. He seemed closed off, but a warmth swirled in her chest, and the trail suddenly opened up to a clearing.

She gasped.

"I know," Landon said, walking up next to her. "Welcome to the Thomas Mansion."

The wind picked up and rustled around her. Milford suddenly sprung to life, flapping his one wing wildly. He started hooting loudly, something Leila hadn't heard once since she'd been around the bird.

"Whoa, calm down, buddy," Landon said, brushing a hand over the owl, who angrily shook his one wing. "Sorry, he's never like this."

You are here.

The voices.

Leila closed her eyes, speaking to herself, hoping Landon wouldn't hear her.

"Trees. Forest."

The voice. It was here. Carrying itself on the wind.

"Wind. Soil."

And it spoke loud and clear.

My daughter, welcome home.

Fairmount Park

♥ 47 Likes

WithouttheY Taking the road not taken. #nofilter #trees #forests

sarikathepaprika Whoa where IS that even?

XII

Leila froze, her heart beating madly.

Those words. The voices. *The* voice. Why would it say that?

"What is it?" Landon asked. He looked at Leila, and then up and around at the trees. Milford seemed to have calmed down a bit, though he was still looking about, his eyes wild and wide. "Are you . . . are you hearing them right now?"

"Shh!" Leila shushed, closing her eyes.

In the grove. Beyond the house.

Leila opened her eyes to see Landon bending over a little and looking at her intently. Milford sat quietly on his shoulder. Landon's hands were out and open, as though he was about to grab her.

"What are you doing?" Leila asked, taking a step back.

"Sorry, you just," Landon stood up and brushed his hands on his pants, as though they hadn't just been stretched out to shake her. "You zoned out for a minute there. Is everything okay?" He reached for the little walkie-talkie on his belt. "Did you . . . should I call someone? Or are they saying anything?"

"Yeah, it . . . *she*," Leila stammered, shaking her head. The headache pounded where her scarf wrapped around her forehead. The realization there, that . . . that pronoun she suddenly felt like saying, that felt like it fit with the voice. She. There was more to the voice. It belonged to someone, someone who sounded like a woman.

And daughter?

Home?

"She said something about welcoming me here," Leila said. "The voice. It, it sounds like an older lady."

"Did it, she, say where she is?" Landon asked. Milford looked at Leila as if he was just as curious.

"No," Leila said, shaking her head. She closed her eyes, hoping to hear something, anything. "Wait! Yes. A grove beyond the home?"

"Hm," Landon huffed, nodding, and looked up at the decaying house in the woods. "You sure you've never actually been here before?"

"Yes, why?"

"It's just, sorry, but you just keep talking about things only a few people even know about." Landon shook his head. "Like, the rangers make it a point to keep people away from here, with the building falling apart and all. This voice of yours say anything else?"

"Not yet." Leila shrugged. Landon stared at her, his eyes set and focused. It wasn't the sort of look she'd expected to get after admitting to all this. She'd expected . . . well, she wasn't sure what, exactly. She'd only spent a little time with him at the Trust, and now this hike, and all along he'd been mostly standoffish, a bit cold. She thought he would be afraid of her. Stare at her like something was wrong.

The way she feared Jon and Lisabeth would look at her.

But here was this boy who she hardly knew, looking at her as though he believed and understood her. Maybe she didn't need to hide anymore.

"Let's keep going," Landon said, nodding ahead.

Stretched out in front of them were the remains of the Thomas Mansion, a tall, once-beautiful, old building that resembled a lot of the older, larger homes found in the historic district of Philadelphia. It was made of large blocks of stone stacked together, sealed up with plaster and concrete, the lines since aging into brown and black. The stones were dark gray, and all the spaces where doors and windows had once swung open and closed were just empty, hollow spaces.

Leila squinted, spotting holes in the roof, and what looked like branches starting to peek out the top. Thick coats of ivy curled up the stone façade in a way that made it seem like they were the only thing holding the building up.

"Any ideas?" Leila asked.

"One," Landon said, still staring at the house. "Here, let's walk around."

Leila followed Landon as they skirted about the side of the giant home. When she peeked inside, Leila spotted the ruin of the interior: Floorboards with gaping holes, a break in the second floor that let you see straight up through the roof, plants and moss growing out of everything. Beams of sunlight shone in through the breaks, and dust particles danced in the light.

"I can see why they want to tear this place down, I

guess," Leila said, shrugging and shaking her head. "It was probably really lovely a long time ago."

"That's where you're wrong. It's *still* lovely," Landon stressed, turning to look at her and then up at the building. He placed a hand on the hard, granite stone of the house, and bits of dirt and detritus crumbled to dust on the ground. "This was built for the World's Fair in 1876, to honor the hundred-year anniversary of the signing of the Declaration of Independence." Landon took a step back, looking around at the side of the building with his hands on his hips.

"What are you looking for?" Leila asked.

"Just a sec," he muttered, and walked back to the front of the building. Leila followed, watching Landon look about, then his eyes finally settled on something covered in branches and brambles. He darted over to it, pulling the shrubbery away to reveal a large stone with a dirty bronze plaque on it, its edges the blackish-green of years of wear.

"There we go," he said, hands back on his hips, looking at the sign proudly. "See?"

The Thomas Mansion

Built for the Centennial International Exhibition in 1876, the Thomas Mansion was famously used as a cottage for visiting dignitaries and government officials in attendance. Close to ten million people from around the world traveled to Philadelphia for the 1876 World's Fair, in celebration of the one-hundredth anniversary of the signing of the Declaration of Independence.

It was during the exhibition that inventions such as the typewriter, telephone, and sewing machine were first presented to the world. Designed by celebrated architect Herman J. Schwarzmann, the Thomas Mansion is one of five remaining structures from the 1876 World's Fair, including Memorial Hall.

"Yeah, I don't understand," Leila said, scowling at the plaque. "How does something like this end up like that?" She pointed at the mansion, and Landon walked towards it, shaking his head.

"The same reason most beautiful things get left behind. Lack of time, lack of interest. It's a bit too far out into the park for tourists, really," Landon said, sighing. "I've been trying to save it for years, ever since I was a little kid. I started some websites, posted on message boards, ran a few social media campaigns and all that. A couple of my fellow rangers and I come out here now and again to clean it up." He shrugged, and then turned to his owl. Milford gave him an empty glance.

"Wait, other rangers?" Leila asked, remembering what the voices had said.

"Sure, I'm not the only one who cares about the history of this place."

"No, I'm sure." Leila thought. "It's just, the voices. The voice. It said something about you and your brothers. Maybe it, she, whatever, thinks that you're, you know, brothers-in-saving-things, not actually brothers."

"Hm." Landon nodded. "That makes sense, I suppose. As much as whatever is happening here can make sense.

We *are* all in our uniforms whenever we come out here." He sighed. "It's just too bad. Not matter how much we do, how hard we try to make it look nice, the park commission is planning to tear it down in the next year or so. They're building some kind of amphitheater out here, with a new road tearing in through the trees from Kelly Drive and everything. So much is going to go. This place. The Trust. Huge sections of the park, just to make room for the road to get here. It kills me."

When he mentioned the Trust, Landon looked at Milford with a sadness in his eyes that was unbearable to look at. The little bird would lose his home and his most ardent protector. Leila's heart wrenched in her chest. The parallels weren't hard to see, and were certainly easy to feel.

"That's a shame," Leila said, turning away and walking back up to the building to avoid the sore subject. He wasn't prying, and she didn't want to either. She ran her hand over the rough granite stonework, bits of debris flaking off as she pressed against the grainy surface. She gazed at the long vines of ivy that dug into the rock, the purple and brown roots holding firm in the solid stone.

She brushed her hands over one of the ivy's leaves, and jolted back.

Leila!

The voice came screaming into her head, loud and clear, intense, as if it was being channeled through the plants she had just touched.

You're almost here.

Leila fell to the ground next to the broken building,

where bits of rocks and broken twigs bit into her knees. She gripped her head as pain blossomed under the head scarf.

He has led you here. Come to me, my child.

"St-stop. Rock. Ivy. St-stone." Leila chanted, the pain pounding against her skull. Landon rushed over and bent down. She could feel him hovering over her and the loud flapping of Milford's single wing.

Come to me.

"What is it?" Landon said, his voice calm and soothing. "Should I call—"

"No. No, I . . . I don't know. We're almost there, I think," Leila continued, pushing herself up. She felt an arm wrap around hers, and looked up to find Landon helping her to her feet. Her body froze up, like ice was running through her veins, and she forced herself to relax, to push back the anxiety and the fear. Landon held her up, one arm wrapped around her waist, the other steadying her shoulder. He looked at her, his eyes full of concern and worry. The glance seemed to be returned by Milford, his yellow eyes strangely sad.

"Thank you," Leila said, trying to relax, but feeling her breath pick up. There was that scent again, the sandalwood and sawdust, the earth and the trees, like someone who had sat around a campfire far too long after spending the day in the woodshop.

"Can you, um, take me to this grove?" Leila asked, reluctantly pushing herself away from him, taking a deep breath. "That's, uh, that's what she seems to want."

"Sure, yeah," Landon said, stepping back, nodding his

head a little too much. Leila tried not to smile as he looked up at her awkwardly and cleared his throat. "But look, is it, like, safe? All this? And with your head all bumped up?"

"I think so." Leila shrugged. "I can't say, not really. I've been dealing with this all my life, you know. It's not like I hit my head after seeing you with the owl and suddenly lost my mind and started hearing voices, if that's what you're implying."

"Whoa, no," Landon said, holding his hands up. "Not at all. It's just, it looks like it's taking a toll on you, is all."

"I'm ready for some answers," Leila said resolutely. "Let's go."

As they rounded the corner of the dilapidated mansion Leila fought the urge to gasp. The space opened up into a garden that had certainly seen better days, but evidence of its former glory was evident. A cobblestone walkway covered in ivy, moss, and leaves rounded from the back of the old home and through overgrown hedges and trees. Thick columns jutted out here and there amidst the shrubbery, some kind of sculpture or landmark. A small stone wall made its way all around the garden, circling the overgrown plants, low to the ground and gray like the house's old granite. There were spaces in the concrete between the stones, faded from age and weather, where ivy had found a grip.

"Ah," Landon said, nodding his head in the direction of some trees. "I think we're almost there. You sure this is okay?"

"You can stop asking that," Leila said. "I'm not okay, but I'm going anyway."

The end of the garden announced itself, not just with a waist-high wrought-iron gate that was rusted and hanging off a hinge, or with the wall of stones that led away from it and connected with the rest of the crumbling bits. But instead, the edge revealed itself with how the brush and trees had simply overtaken everything around them. Landon pushed the gate open with a loud squeak, the bars groaning against the rust and the rock, and looked up at the trees with Leila.

"You can't even see the canopy," he said, taking a step into what felt like untamed wilderness. "But this is where the grove is, see?" He pointed down at the ground, where some of the cobblestones still pushed their way through the soil and earth, popping up in-between brush and fallen branches. "There's still a path here, leading in there."

He pointed into the trees.

Leila squinted. It didn't look like any light from the sun got through this brush, and the leaves of every tree looked almost unnaturally thick. How was this still inside the city park? Landon let go of her hand and grabbed Milford, who then perched on his forearm, which Landon in turn kept close to his chest.

"Sorry, I don't want him, like, getting knocked over while we're pushing through here," Landon said, an apologetic look on his face.

"It's okay," Leila said, grinning at him. "It's just the second time you've chosen your owl over me."

"Oh, come on, that's not fair," Landon said, a small smirk on his face.

"It is what it is," Leila shrugged, as Landon moved

forward. She felt for her phone in her pants pocket, thinking of sending Sarika an update, and stopped as Landon walked forward through the thick trees. There was no way she could text and walk through all this at the same time. She'd have to dish later, particularly after they finally reached the place where the voices supposedly were telling her to go.

They walked slowly through the underbrush and in-between the trees, with Landon's owl remaining strangely silent through the ordeal. And it wasn't just his owl. The sounds of the birds in the trees or skittering squirrels in the brush were gone, replaced with the crunch of their feet against the ground.

"I think I see a clearing," Leila said, squinting in the darkening woods. "Up there?"

"That would be the grove," Landon said, turning to look at her with a grin. "It's really lovely." His expression soured and he shook his head, looking back forward. "I can't believe they want to get rid of all this."

Not too far away, a bit of golden light seemed to be breaking through some of the trees, like a wide opening was hollowed out in the middle to allow the sun to pour into one place. As they drew closer, the yellow, bright crack grew wider. Leila squinted as the opening grew near, and the sunbeams were almost blinding after all the dark shade. She stepped out of the woods and into the grove just as Landon placed Milford on his shoulder and once more took her hand.

The grove spread out over what looked like at least an acre of land. Several tall oak trees grew along the edges of the grove, opposite where she and Landon had walked in. Their trunks were thick and enormous, centuries old, if not more.

And in the middle of the grove a ring of stone, similar to the ones around the garden, circled three smaller oak trees. But unlike the tall ones that stood around the end of the grove, these three were smaller, thinner.

"That's weird," Leila said, nodding at the trees in the circle.

"What is?"

"Well, I mean, you said this place has been abandoned for a long time, right?" Leila asked, taking a step towards the ring of stone and the thinner, younger-looking trees. "Then why do those look like they were maybe planted, what, two decades ago? If that? And those guys, those huge ones on the border, have to be older than the mansion."

"I don't quite see what you're getting at," Landon said, shrugging and walking with her. "It's a grove. Someone back in the day likely planted it to use as a little getaway. A hidden garden."

Leila walked forward, looking at the trees and the ring, trying to figure it all out. She spun around.

"But even if it was planted way back when, and even if you and your—as the voice likes to say—*brothers* have been trimming things once in a while, this is like, immaculate. Someone has been taking care of all this," she said, gesturing to the trees and the ring. "Those trees in the center of the grove should be huge, not pruned down like that. If it isn't you or one of the other rangers, then who is taking the time to keep all this up, especially if no one is visiting this place?"

Leila.

Leila groaned and dropped to the ground. The soil here was soft, pliable, unlike anything near the shattered house she'd walked with Landon from. She could feel her knees sinking into it, her hands against it, soft and cushioned. Almost as though she belonged there, planted with the trees. The grass under her hands felt as though it was moving, tickling against her palms and fingers.

I am glad you are here.

"Landon," Leila muttered, looking up at him, lifting a hand to her pounding head. He was frozen in place, his mouth open and eyes wide.

We are glad you are here.

"Landon?" Leila asked, moving to stand.

"Don't!" Landon shouted, lifting a hand up. "Don't move a muscle, don't move anything, just . . . just stay there." He started taking steps towards her with his hands outstretched, his body hunched low to the ground as he walked.

"What is it?" Leila asked, moving to turn around.

"No, stop!" Landon yelled. He reached for his walkie-talkie, and his shaking hands fumbled with it. The small black plastic device tumbled out of his hands and crashed against one of the granite stones, and pieces broke off instantly. With that, Milford hopped off his shoulder and onto the ground, flapping his one wing wildly as he made his clumsy decent to the earth. "No, Mil–" Landon started, moving to scoop up the owl, and then he turned back to

Leila. He shook his head and walked towards her, still crouching.

Leila's heart pounded in her chest.

Whatever it was, it had been enough for Landon to ignore the owl.

Leila turned around.

Welcome home, my daughter.

She screamed just as Landon ran up behind her and pulled her to her feet.

"Whatever this is," he said, his voice terrified and eyes wide, "we have to run."

XIII

Leila stared into the ring of stone, her eyes wide and watering, her breath short, all while Landon tugged on her arm.

"Leila," he said quietly. "Leila, please." His tugging stopped for a moment, and after a quick rustling sound, returned. She turned to look at him. Milford was perched back on his shoulder. The owl's eyes made contact with what stood in the ring, and he started flapping his one wing wildly again, the feathers around his neck gone ruffled and fierce.

Leila turned back to the ring, the soft blasts of wind from the owl's angry wing rustling her hair and tickling her neck.

"Is it you?" Leila asked, taking a step forward.

"What are you doing?" Landon shouted. Leila turned back to him, and lifted a hand up.

"Getting answers. You can leave if you want."

"I'm not leaving you here with that, that *thing*." He shook his head and backed down, taking a step away.

"Is. It. You?" Leila pressed again, turning away from Landon and taking a step towards the ring of stone.

There, in the middle of it, stood a woman.

But she was unlike any woman Leila had ever seen.

She stood there, naked and exposed, but where one would normally have skin, she was coated in a thick, brown bark, covering her from her feet up to her face. Instead of hair, she had brilliant curls of dark- and light-green leaves blended together with streams of purple vines, almost like highlights, which danced around her face. Her eyes glimmered, bright, fiercely green irises swirling in the unusually human whites of her eyes, casting a contrast against the rest of her.

She took a step forward, and Leila gasped as flowers and moss bloomed where the tree woman's foot pressed down, wildflowers of multiple colors and hues and shapes. She extended a hand, and as she moved, bits of bark crumbled off her arm, her body creaking like an old tree in a light breeze.

"Come into the circle," she said, her voice honeyed and soft, not at all like the whispering that had echoed in the recesses of Leila's mind all these many years. It was still familiar in a strange way, as though she'd been speaking through a muffled receiver on a bad cell phone connection and now the tone was finally clear. Her voice carried on the wind, like a breeze, rustling the leaves in the trees around them.

Leila took a step, and Landon put his hand on her shoulder. She shrugged it away quickly and turned to glare at him.

"What are you doing?" he asked, his voice full of concern. "We should go."

"I can't do that. You know I can't," she said, taking a step back towards him. She surprised herself by grabbing his hand, finding it rough and calloused. She squeezed it, the hard skin pressing against her soft hands. "Wait here."

Leila turned back and walked into the circle, where the woman of ivy, branches, and leaves stood with flowers and greenery blooming around her bare, brown feet. The woman walked slowly towards her, and when she was just an arm's length away, lifted a hand up and placed her palm on Leila's cheek. Leila stiffened at the touch, which was hard and rough. The bark-like skin scratched her face, but gently, like a cat's tongue.

It was hard not to stare.

Up close, Leila took notice of the woman's features. The pointed nose, the bright-green eyes that looked far more human than the rest of her. A handful of butterflies and a hefty bumblebee flitted about in her hair of ivy and leaves, and small flowers were tucked away in the green.

"At last, you've come home to me," the woman said, and as she exhaled, soft plumes of what looked like pollen gently floated from between her lips. She pressed her hand against Leila's cheek a little more firmly, rubbing a hard thumb over her cheekbones. Leila could feel it scratching the surface of her skin, and winced. The woman let go and looked down, reaching out to grasp Leila's hands, which had been firmly at her sides.

Then the woman's hands held hers, the skin dark and brown like a tree, rough as bark.

"I'm sorry," she said, looking back up at Leila. "It has been a long time since I touched a human." She looked off to the side, wistfully, and Leila followed her gaze, seeing nothing. "Not since I last saw your father."

Leila breathed in sharply.

Her father?

The tree woman turned sharply back to Leila, and Leila could feel her heart racing, the rush of blood thundering in her head, pounding in her ears.

"I'm your mother, Leila," the woman said, smiling without opening her mouth. Her lips were a softer shade of brown than the rest of her body. "Though I suspect you know that now."

"How . . . ?" Leila stammered, looking down at the still-blooming flowers under her feet. "How is any of this possible? How . . . how are *you* possible?" She closed her eyes and shook her head, which still ached. "This can't be real." She looked up at the woman, who continued to gaze at her. Her eyes were human, but hard. "You can't be real."

Leila looked behind her to Landon, who stood outside the ring of stone, Milford perched on his shoulder. The owl shifted about, looking uncomfortable and panicked. She could try to say how unreal all of this was as much as she wanted, but there he was. A witness.

"You see all of this, yes?" Leila asked.

Landon nodded, his mouth closed tight and his eyes watering.

"Please explain," Leila said, turning back to the woman. "Please. I've heard your voice all my life. From the group homes to the foster homes, outside as a child and inside the walls of my new home. And now, louder than ever. Why? How?"

The woman closed her eyes, small flecks of brown bark and silt fluttering off her eyelids, and let out what seemed to be a sigh. It was more of a soft breeze that rippled through the leaves and vines in her hair, and it washed over Leila. It felt like the winds that came whenever the voices did, the breezes that tickled her neck. The tree woman opened her eyes again and this time her look was forlorn and sad. She turned away, taking a few steps back into the middle of the grove.

"What are you doing?" Leila asked, moving forward, heat rushing through her body. "I have questions. Why did you call me here? Why do you keep calling me?"

The woman raised her hand, her fingers like gnarled, old vines, her arm a branch. She looked back at Leila.

"We are in danger. I . . . we . . . needed someone who could speak for us."

"Us?" Leila asked. She turned to look towards Landon, who had walked up closer to the circle surrounding the grove. Milford's neck feathers were still ruffled and mad. Landon took a slow, careful step into the circle of stone and squinted, as if anticipating something.

When his foot touched the ground inside the circle, he looked immediately relieved.

"What did you think was going to happen?" Leila asked, smirking.

"I don't know," Landon muttered. "I'm new to this magic thing." He exhaled. "But I'm here with you."

Leila looked back up at the woman in the woods, who was waving a branch-like arm in the air. A soft breeze rustled in the trees, and Leila shivered.

"If something goes wrong, we run," Landon said. "I'm not going to let anything happen to you."

Leila looked up at Landon. He stared ahead, focused on the strange woman in the center of the grove.

She believed him.

"Us," the woman continued, turning back to Leila and Landon. As she slowly spun back around, the trees that bordered the large center oak that she had stepped out from began to groan. They twisted, impossibly, shifting back and forth despite their thick, heavy trunks, and each slowly split down the middle, a thin crack making its way right down the center of the trees. There were two of them, and they shook and quivered as thin cracks cut their way from the top of their green branches down to the bottom, where the roots plunged into the earth.

Leila's hand suddenly felt like it was being crushed, and when she went to move it, discovered Landon was holding her hand tightly.

The cracks in the trees opened wider, and hands plunged out: dark, brown, the texture of bark; followed by arms, and then legs, feet pressing against the earth, sending blooms and flowers wherever they stepped.

There were more of them.

Two more.

The two other . . . creatures? Tree people? Monsters? Leila wasn't sure what to call them, stepped into the center of the grove, joining the woman who'd addressed Leila. These other women bore similar features. The bark skin, rough and textured, matched the oaks they'd stepped from, with small differences. One had golden, almost yellow, eyes that shone with a brightness that rivaled even Milford's. The other's hair wasn't the tangle of ivy and leaves like the others, but instead was short, made up of what looked like firm moss, close to her head. Like she'd had a haircut recently. Leila smiled at this one, even as they grew closer.

Something seemed . . . familiar about them all.

Safe.

She moved away from Landon and took a step towards the creatures, who shifted towards the two of them slowly. Landon reached out and grabbed her hand again, and she shook it free. Milford's feathers seemed to ruffle up even more.

"It's okay," Leila said, and then looked up at Milford. She reached out and scratched under his chin.

Leila turned, facing the women, who all stared at her curiously.

"This reminds me of the last time," the one with yellow eyes said. Her voice was rough, like a bushel of sticks being pressed down into a box, crunching and twisting with each word. "Do you remember, sister?"

"I do," the one with the short, moss-like hair said. Her voice was similar, but warmed up as she spoke, slowly becoming soothing and gentle, like a passing breeze. "But this one is different. Not fully one of us."

"She's half," the golden-eyed woman said, her voice smoothing out, "and she's family."

"He wears the colors," the moss-haired woman said, taking a step forward. "He's like the last human. Your human, sister."

The creature that had been speaking to Leila all this time, with her long hair of ivy and leaves, turned to the moss-haired woman quickly, and then back to Leila and Landon, her eyes sad and far away.

"Your questions," she said, taking a step towards Leila and Landon. "Ask. Few humans come here anymore, save for the caretakers. We have time."

Leila looked at Landon, who simply nodded.

"Who are you? What are you?" Leila asked.

"We are what your people refer to as dryads, though we've had many names. The meliae, the hamadryad, the nymph, the salabhanjika." As the words grew longer and more complex, they came out more roughly on the creature's tongue, her mouth twisting to pronounce the words, shaping them slowly and with difficulty.

"That one is my favorite," the creature with the moss-hair said, a soft smile on her rough, bark-like face.

"As for the who," the woman with the leafy hair continued. She sighed, and again, the breeze picked up. "I am called Karayea. This is Tifolia." The creature with the golden eyes nodded. "And this is Shorea." The moss-haired creature followed suit.

"I . . . am your mother," the dryad said, a shy smile lighting up on her face. "And Shorea and Tifolia are, I suppose by human custom, your aunts? Yes?"

She looked to the other dryads, who shrugged in response. At least, that's what it looked like. Their leaves and branches rattled. Leila heard steps behind her as Landon moved to her side.

"You okay?" Landon asked.

"No," Leila said. "You?"

"Nope," he said, staring straight ahead. "I'm here though."

"He is just like the other one," Tifolia said, looking at Shorea. "A guardian. Brave."

"He's different," Shorea said, shaking her head and branches. "The two of them are much different."

"Still, I see—" started Tifolia.

"Sisters, please," Karayea said, her sighs becoming heavier. Leila looked at her, arching an eyebrow, as the dryad's breathing—if you could call it that—seemed to become heavier, weathered. The dryad staggered back a little, and Tifolia and Shorea walked towards her, their pace slightly quicker, but still slow and measured. The two dryads supported her, and Karayea looked up at Leila, her eyes once again sad, the bright green fading away.

"It becomes . . . difficult, when any of us stray too long from the trees. Over the years, I've been using the plants around your city to watch you, and recently, to speak with you. To beckon you here. It has taken much from me," she said, turning with her sisters and walking back towards the center of the grove. Leila's heart raced as she watched in realization. The moving flowers. The stretching tree in her yard. The brambles on the path. These things had happened, they had to be happening, because of the dryads here. She looked up at Landon, who stared straight ahead, his eyes wide and breath short. The small owl shook his head, feathers around his neck still agitated.

All three of the dryads reached their respective trees in the grove, and took steps back inside the split trunks.

The trees shook as the splits started to seal back up, and the dryads closed their eyes and tilted their heads up towards the canopy as the bark regrew along the splintered wood.

"Hey! Wait!" Leila exclaimed, darting forward. "Wait, I have questions! What's all this 'half' stuff? Why are you talking about Landon like he's," she turned and looked at him, baffled, "like he's part of all of this? I just met him!"

The two trunks holding Tifolia and Shorea sealed up, the leaves and branches of their respective trees rustling as though a gust of wind blasted through them. The center tree, with Karayea in it, remained open with the dryad inside. The tree was sealed up to her waist. She reached a hand out and motioned for the two of them to walk forward.

"There used to be many of us in these woods," Karayea said. "But our numbers have dwindled. The world around us has grown quiet. The last time we spoke to a human, we discovered we were the last, and the vast wilderness where our kind lived was long torn asunder. He was a lot like you, you know." Her eyes focused warmly on Landon.

"Me?" Landon asked, stepping forward towards the trees. Milford, as though sensing his discomfort, ruffled his feathers.

"Who?" Leila asked, looking from the baffled Landon to the dryad in the tree.

"Your father," Karayea said, matter-of-factly. "He protected these woods, wearing the same colors as you." She sighed, and the wind rustled through the trees around them. "I loved him."

Leila sat down on the ground. Twigs and leaves pressed against her jeans. She took deep breaths, resisting the urge to just curl up and disappear. Landon knelt down next to her, and she felt a tentative hand on her back. She closed her eyes, unflinching.

"Are you alright, my daughter?" Karayea asked.

Leila looked up at her and immediately shut her eyes, trying to hide the surprising, brewing anger that swirled inside her with a wealth of other emotions, confusion being at the top of the list. Who was this . . . woman? Creature? Weren't dryads mythological? How was any of this even possible? If it wasn't for Landon being here with her, if she'd been all alone, this could have been enough to drive her mad. She wouldn't have believed any of this was even happening.

And the mention of her father.

Not only had she supposedly found her birth mother, but she had some hints about her biological father.

It was information overload, mashed together with a swirl of additional questions that absolutely terrified her. Primarily, if this was her mother, a creature of myth, and her father was a human, what did that make her?

"Why?" Leila said, her eyes shut. She opened them and stared at the dryad in the tree. "After all this time, why did you bring me here? Why keep talking to me? Why not just, I don't know, speak clearly to me, like you did when I got close? What is it that you want, and why shouldn't I turn around and never come back?"

"Leila," Landon said, sounding surprised.

"What?" Leila snapped, immediately feeling sorry for

the outburst. "Where was she all this time?" She turned back to Karayea. "Hm? And if you know who my father is, where was he? Why have I been bounced around through foster homes and dealt with terrible people my whole life, if you were right here? Right here!"

"We, myself and your aunts," Karayea said, the word strange in her mouth, "we are bound to this patch of land. To this grove here. All dryads have their trees, their land that they are attached to. Speaking to you through the wind can only be done with more trees around. The farther away you are, the fewer trees connecting the wind, the harder it is to speak. It gets easier the closer you are, and the more trees nearby."

The dryad closed her green eyes and let out a sigh, rustling the leaves in her hair and on the trees nearby, a soft breeze.

"I called for you many times, when I felt you might hear me, when I felt you closest to the trees. I wondered what became of my daughter, who once ran through the moss and sang with the birds. I called with what humans often call magic, but for us it is just a part of who we are." Karayea breathed in deeply, and again, the leaves shook. "And now you are here, and we have been in trouble for quite some time, as I'm sure your friend can attest."

Leila looked up at Landon, who shrugged.

"I'm not sure what you mean?" Landon asked.

"The mansion, the home near us," Karayea said, nodding her head slowly in the direction behind Leila and Landon. "Soon men with monsters of steel and smoke will rip it down, and take our grove and neighboring trees with it. My sisters and I have heard them of late, quite often, as they walk through our woods speaking of their plans."

The dryad grew quiet, and then looked right at Leila.

"It is to happen soon. And we will all perish."

"The developers," Landon said, nodding to Leila. "Like I told you about. They want to put a concert venue in here or something, but have had a hard time because of the historic building, the gardens, and some endangered native wildlife. A mouse, if you can believe that."

Leila nodded. There were a lot of things she suddenly believed in.

"I've tried speaking up, at meetings over at City Hall and with the Fairmount Park Preservation Association, but no one comes back here. Sometimes it's hard to fight for something no one really cares about." His eyes widened and he looked back at Karayea. "No offense, er, ma'am."

"There's a reason the trees flourish around the humans here, dear children," the dryad said, her tone serious. "As the land grew more toxic from your waste and carelessness, the soil grew harsh and barren. Without us, the trees surrounding this land will perish, and with us, so go all creatures. Including you."

"I'm sorry, you control all the trees around Philadelphia?" Leila asked.

"Yes. That is the name of this place, according to what your father once told me," Karayea said, nodding. "What remains of the wilderness, what remains grounded around the humans surrounded by smoke and death, it survives because of us, here in this grove. I need you to stop what the humans are planning, and rescue them from themselves. Your home will suffocate under your own breath."

Leila looked up at Landon, who scratched the back of his head, and Milford reached around and nibbled the back of Landon's head with his beak. He stopped when Landon did.

"I see you, too, are one with nature," Karayea said, nodding softly at the owl on Landon's shoulder. Milford perked up, squinting as he gazed at the dryad.

"Oh, him?" Landon asked, laughing nervously. "I dunno, I'm pretty sure if he actually had two wings, he'd just fly away. He's here because he needs me."

"Or because you need him," Karayea said, smiling. "Or you need each other. You humans call it sym . . . bi . . . os . . . is." She spoke as though she was pushing the complicated word out, each syllable coming out rough. "I'm sorry. Some of the words your father taught me, they are still difficult to say. It's what we are, here in the woods, to the trees and you humans, even if none of you know it. Your people once did, but no longer. He taught me much about what was outside of this place, before he was taken from me."

At this, Leila felt a rush of warmth.

"Taken?" she asked.

"Indeed," the dryad said, sadly. "Shortly after you were born. No one believed him about us, about the grove. He'd told a few close to him, and was shunned. Soon, he no longer wore your colors." She nodded at Landon, who looked back at her quizzically. "Those he served had, as he said, let him go."

Landon gasped, his eyes wide.

"Wait, so he was a park ranger?" he said. "That's what you're saying. That's what you mean about my colors or whatever." He took off his jacket. "He wore something like this?"

"Much the same," Karayea responded sadly.

"When did he . . ." Landon looked down at Leila, suddenly looking just as crestfallen as the dryad. "When did he leave? Disappear?"

"When Leila was but a sapling," Karayea said with a soft smile on her face. "You took to the woods well, my child. But you needed school, he said. A life away from this small grove. Your father knew that. But at least I had two full cycles with you, here, in the woods and in my arms."

"You were two when you entered into the system?" Landon asked.

"I think so," Leila shrugged. "It's not like I have any memories of back then. Who remembers anything from when they were babies or toddlers?"

Landon put his jacket back on and stared down at the ground, his eyes hard. Milford shifted about on his shoulder, appearing as uncomfortable as the silence.

"Landon?" Leila ventured. "What is it?"

"It might just be a coincidence," Landon muttered, shaking his head. He looked down at Leila. "But I think I know who your father is."

The wind rustled madly, and Leila shielded her face from the breeze. Milford flapped his single wing intensely against it.

"I tire, sweet children," Karayea said. "Go, come back

after the sun and moon have danced a few times. I must rest. All of this," she sighed, rustling the leaves, "has taken much from me." She looked up at Leila, her bright eyes green and focused.

"I'm counting on you. I believe in you. It isn't about saving us. It's about saving them."

And with that, the bark around her sealed up, and the tall oak tree she dwelled in shook and grew still, as though nothing had even happened.

LEILA: Hey!

LEILA: So . . . I'm out with Landon, actually.

LEILA: There are . . . things to discuss.

> SARIKA: Damn it must be going good.

> SARIKA: ;-)

> SARIKA: Hello?

> SARIKA: Girl you okay, where are you?

LEILA: Hey!

LEILA: Everything's fine, he's fine, I'm fine.

LEILA: Phone is dying though.

LEILA: I'll text you when I get home.

> SARIKA: Yeah he is.

> SARIKA: Fine, that is.

> SARIKA: I can't text with italics, but "yeah" should be in italics to emphasize his hotness.

LEILA: Oh my God.

LEILA: Nothing is happening with him like that.

LEILA: Adam's tomorrow. Please.

> SARIKA: I want all the details. All of them.

LEILA: You aren't even ready.

> SARIKA: That's what he said. ;-)

LEILA: You need to stop this.

XIV

"Can I get you anything? Coffee? Soda? Hot chocolate?"

Landon fussed over Leila as she sat in his break room, a small but cozy little space tucked away in the back of the ranger station in Fairmount Park, just a forty-minute hike away from where the grove and mansion were. They'd walked in relative silence as the events replayed in Leila's head again and again. She sighed and tried to sink further into the squishy chair she'd decided to live the rest of her life in, nestling into the extra ranger jacket Landon had given her. It smelled like him, of the sawdust and crunchy leaves, sandalwood and vanilla soap.

"I'm good, thanks," Leila said. She pulled out her phone and scowled at the dead battery, the black screen blinking on just to remind her it needed to be charged.

After a moment, he returned with two steaming cups.

"I got you a hot chocolate anyway," he said, sitting down next to her and pushing the cup across the smooth wooden table. "Holding up okay?"

"I don't know. It's been a weird day. My biological mother is a magical creature from mythology. My father is, well," Leila looked up at the small plaque in the break room, her heart heavy. "How'd you figure it out?"

"Math, I guess." Landon shrugged. "The, uh," he shook

his head, "the *lady* in the woods said you'd been taken away when you were two. And almost everyone who works in the park service, at least the ones who work outside, know the story of . . . should we say your dad? Your father?"

"What?" Leila asked, her eyebrows arching up.

"It's just, you know, I know he's your biological father and all," Landon said, his words careful, as though he was walking on eggshells. "Look, I just don't want to say the wrong word here. You're adopted now, you have a father, and this other man? I just know it's a sensitive thing and want to be aware of what I'm saying. If that even makes sense."

Leila smiled, and felt a bloom of warmth in her chest. She fought the urge not to reach out and hold his hand. Why couldn't everyone be this sensitive to her situation?

"It does. And I appreciate that," Leila said. "I suppose 'biological father' is fine for now. Or just his name."

She glanced up at the plaque again.

In Memory of Jared Blackwell
June 8th, 1957 - August 17th, 2004
Service: 1979 – 1999

The Blackwell Ranger Station was built and established in June of 2005, to honor and remember Jared Blackwell, a member of the Fairmount Park Service for over twenty years.

In the photo attached to the plaque and in the bronze relief of his face outside the building, she could see it. In his features, his eyes, his cheekbones, and sharp nose. There was no mistaking it, and it shook her every single time she glanced up at that photo.

"I just wonder what happened to him," Leila said, gazing at the photo across the room.

"Yeah, well, a lot of people do," Landon said, walking over towards the plaque. "It's one of those things they talk to all the new recruits about. Don't go into the park alone, be careful at night, things like that. It isn't just visitors wandering the park at night who can end up hurt or missing. Rangers, too. People with experience."

"I just don't see how that kind of thing happens when, you know, your girlfriend is a magical creature of the forest," Leila said, shaking her head. "How do you get lost? Wouldn't some woodland creatures come to save the day or some such cartoon-movie nonsense?"

"I dunno." Landon shrugged. "Seems like they're pretty stuck where they are. Maybe he fell, hit his head or fell in the water. It happens with hikers sometimes. That's one of the theories. It's a big park, Leila."

She sat in silence with Landon, looking at the photo.

"I'm sorry, I feel like I'm being too blunt here." Landon shook his head.

"No, you're just being real. Is it weird that I'm mad?" Leila asked, still looking at the picture. She glanced over at Landon, who walked over to her and sat back down. "I mean, I dunno. All my life I thought that if I found some answers, they would be . . . different. Obviously not your-mother-is-a-tree-creature different, but, like, maybe she was a runaway who got pregnant, had to give me up, didn't know my father. Maybe they were a couple but just too young, and are now living happily someplace with a new family, and they think of me from time to time. Or my birth father was an awful man, a criminal, who forced himself on her."

She shook her head, trying not to let the tears come, but failing.

"That's what happens, you know? You dream up all these scenarios. Some are grand and ridiculous and you know that they are, like your biological parents are millionaires or celebrities or even just, like, someone in your neighborhood that you've never run into before. Or they are tragic and awful, they gave their lives for you, or died in an accident, or got murdered.

"It's messed up and I know it's messed up but I can't help it, we all do it." Leila choked back a sob and Landon tentatively moved closer to her. "But this? A tree? A missing person? It's like everything has just been taken from me and replaced with something so outrageous that no one will ever believe it."

"I believe you," Landon said, looking right into her eyes.

"Sure, because you saw it all." Leila buried her face in her hands. "Oh my God, how am I ever going to tell Sarika about this? We'd talked about the voices. About ignoring them. She's going to think I lost it. And how are we supposed to save the tree people, or whatever?"

Leila laughed.

"At least I got one cliché," she said, shaking her head.

"What's that?" Landon asked.

"My birth mother finds me, and what does she want? Help." Leila stood up, pushing her chair out. "It's one of the things everyone warns you about. There are a million Lifetime movies about it. Your biological parents could come back and end up being terrible. Maybe they'll want money or want to use you. Need an organ or something. Be careful. Blah, blah, blah. And now here we are."

"Well, it feels a little different than that, no?" Landon asked. "I mean, it's not about her or her tree pals. It's everything around them. It's you. Your new family. Your friends. She could let the city die with her, all these humans who forgot about her and the system that didn't believe your biological father, who let him just disappear. But instead here she is, reaching out."

Leila paused for a beat and took a deep breath, nodding.

"Hm," she muttered. "You might be right on that. Still. I know it's hard to understand, but it's like something was just taken from me. Now there's this responsibility. And I don't know if I want it."

Silence hung thick in the room.

"I should get home," she said, looking at Landon. "This was . . . you were great. So great." Her heart started to pound in her chest as she looked up at him. "I wish we'd met under normal circumstances. Maybe again at the Raptor Trust, or catching you trying to help Milford fly again. But, well, it is what it is."

"Eh, I've had worse," he said, shrugging with a little smirk.

"You have not."

"One time, this girl I went out with, her mother was a mermaid. Lived in the Schuylkill River, I kid you not. Her uncles were sturgeons. You're not the first mythological-creature-human I've spent an afternoon with."

"Landon."

"You sure you have to leave?" Landon asked. "I don't mind, you know, making more hot chocolate and giving you some time to collect yourself in here."

"Thanks, really, but no." She pulled her phone out and waved it about. "My phone's dead, so Jon and Lisabeth are going to be worried sick. Sarika is probably exploding by now."

"I'd say 'let's do this again sometime,' but maybe come by to just see the birds instead?" Landon suggested, smirking again.

"Sure."

"Come on," he said, standing up. "You can charge your phone in my truck. I'll take you home, and I'll be there for whatever other adventures await after today."

He reached out his hand.

Leila took it.

Sarika Paprika

@TheSarikaPaprika

Coffee lovers! I'll be at @AdamsPhillyCafe a little later today, around 11-ish. Come say hello! #SarikaTheBarista

8/23/17, 7:47AM

16 Retweets 47 Likes

> Ali @YohananAliQ   9m
> @TheSarikaPaprika @AdamsPhillyCafe yes!
>
> Leila @WithouttheY   7m
> @TheSarikaPaprika @AdamsPhillyCafe see you soon!

XV

"You sure you don't want to wait?" Mr. Hathaway asked as Leila handed him a dollar for a small coffee. He plucked the dollar from her hand, stuffed it into the already-open, totally broken cash register, and made his way over to the coffee station. He started pouring the thick, black liquid into the contrasting white mug.

"I mean, she'll be here in fifteen minutes, a half hour tops," Mr. Hathaway continued as he pulled the mug away from the coffee machine, and started filling it with an amount of sugar offensive to most coffee drinkers. Just how she liked it.

"It's not like you're in your thirties, balancing graduate school, a full-time job, and a family," he went on, talking as he stirred away, the metal spoon clinking about merrily in the cup. "I think you can live without all this extra—"

Leila interrupted, holding up a hand, "Not right now, okay? I just need to, like, clear my head."

Mr. Hathaway scowled and slid the coffee mug across the surface of the countertop.

"Fine, fine," he said, returning to the register and fussing with the door. "I'm just saying. She'll be here soon, you coulda waited for her to make it. She's the master, not me."

"It's alright. I need some 'me time' for a bit." Leila

grabbed the coffee and carried the mug over to a table in the back. She had her choice, the place was utterly barren, though it was only a matter of time before it filled up.

She sat down and the chair squeaked as she pulled it across the hard floor. She wrapped her hands around the hot mug and sighed. The warmth was comforting against her palms.

How was she going to explain all of this to Sarika?

She blew at the steam rising off the hot coffee as her thoughts wandered, playing the scenarios in her head over and over again.

Hey, so yeah, I ended up hanging out with Landon. We explored the woods, scoped out this abandoned historic mansion, and oh, I found my birth mother and biological aunts, who are trees living in the grounds behind the mansion, and they're in danger, and we need to save them in order to save the entire city.

Yeah.

That was going to go over well.

The door to the café swung open, and the small bell above it chimed out loudly in the empty place, the happy sound reverberating off the walls. Sarika bounced in, a satchel over her arm, and jumped over the coffee counter to wrangle herself into position behind the bar.

"Let's do this!" she shouted in a silly, overly deep voice, flipping on the giant espresso machine. Leila put her elbow up on the table and leaned into her hand, watching her get things set up. Sarika poured milk into the steamer and plucked old espresso beans from inside the machine. She made quick work of the thing, her movements precise and meticulous, much like the machine itself. For Leila it was a joy to watch her best friend, someone she'd been through so much with, be truly at home.

Especially now, knowing what she knew about herself. Or, at least, sort of knowing. There were so many unanswered questions. How did her father even meet her mother? Why hadn't the dryads spoken to anyone other than her? And how was she supposed to save them? No one was going to believe that there were these mythological creatures living in the woods and that the fate of the city's breathable air basically depended on them. Landon had already expressed as much, as they wandered away from the forest and mused over text messages throughout the evening.

Leila scowled at the thought.

Most boys texted with girls long into the evening about other things. Flirting. Long discussions about life. Flirting. Talking about the future. More flirting. Instead, that option had been ripped away from her, replaced with conversations about conservation, government officials, and environmental justice groups. She wasn't even sure she wanted those warm and fuzzy discussions with Landon, especially after the disaster that was Shawn. But the option would have been nice.

How was she going to tell Sarika?

And Jon? Lisabeth? Or the B.E.A.C. club or the message board? She couldn't tell them the real story, just that they had to save that section of the park. Was there a way to talk about saving the grove without giving the real reason why?

Even she'd made assumptions about the crumbling, old building. Would she have cared if it hadn't been for the dryads? How could she make anyone care about this?

Sarika looked up from what she was busy fussing with and caught Leila's eye. She smiled and waved excitedly, leaping over the coffee countertop again to hurry over.

Leila breathed. One thing at a time.

"Tell. Me. Everything," Sarika said, swinging a chair out from under another table and whipping it around to the one Leila sat at. She straddled the chair and put her elbows on the table, her head in her hands in an exaggerated fashion. "When you left enrichment, I thought it was to, like, go home and unwind, not run off into the woods with the gorgeous park ranger. Was he into you?"

"Maybe," Leila said, smirking with a shrug. "Things got a little weird, but–"

"Shawn weird?" Sarika asked, standing up and moving the chair around to sit normally.

"No, few things are Shawn weird." Leila laughed uncomfortably. She took a deep breath, and looked up at Sarika. "Look, there's something I need to talk to you about before your rush comes in, and I just . . . I don't think it can wait. There's something I have to do, and I need to know we'll be okay because it's weird, Sarika, alright? It's really weird, and if I don't have you here, I'm not sure–"

"Whoa, whoa," Sarika said, reaching out across the table and grabbing Leila's hands. Leila hadn't realized they were shaking. Her breath had gone quick, her heart hammered in her chest. "Relax. I won't go anywhere. Come on, what could be so awful that–"

"I followed the voices, Sarika," Leila said. The color seemed to drain out of Sarika's face, and she let go of Leila's hands. She blinked and took a short breath before looking around the café and facing Leila again.

"Why . . . why would you do that?" Sarika asked, sounding almost angry. "We spent, like, years trying to bury all that. What if, what if the voices, which are all in your head, led you somewhere that got you hurt? Or killed? They aren't real, we both know that, you know that, and—"

"They are real," Leila said. "Or at least, she's real. The woman who has been talking to me. It's always been only one."

Sarika blinked, her expression full of worry.

"Leila, you can't—"

"She's my mother, Sarika," Leila said. "My birth mother. All those jokes and dreams about our birth parents being millionaires or whatever are definitely thrown out the damn window."

Sarika looked around the coffee shop, her eyes wide, expression panicked. She turned back to Leila, grabbing her hands again.

"Do we need to go to the hospital or something?" Sarika asked. "Because I'll go. I'll be there all the way."

Leila squeezed Sarika's hands harder and closed her eyes, feeling the tears welling up.

"It's not like that," Leila said. She opened her eyes and looked at her friend. "I'm here. One hundred percent. And I need you to believe me."

Leila took a deep breath, and let it all pour out.

The way plants had rustled around her, the voices on the bike ride home, the phone call to Landon, the walk through the woods and down the darkened path to the bursting, brilliant light after the canopy cleared. The old mansion, the grove, the three dryads, and finally the ranger station named after her missing birth father.

Sarika stared at Leila through all of this, her eyes unwavering.

She squeezed her hands and let go to fuss with something inside her jacket. She plucked out her smartphone, her fingers nimbly jabbed away at something unseen, and then she put her phone back.

"Don't worry, I canceled on my adoring public, just for you."

Leila's phone buzzed. Sarika smirked as Leila turned hers on.

"How do you already have nine retweets?" Leila asked, turning off her phone and wiping away a stray tear.

"What can I say? I'm popular on the Internet." Sarika grinned. She stood up and pushed the chair in. "Well. I'd like to see all this for myself, so let's get out of here." Before Leila could protest, Sarika darted her way over to the barista station to grab her satchel.

"Sorry, Mr. Hathaway, something's come up!" Sarika shouted as she made her way to the front door. She looked at Leila and motioned for her with her hand, mouthing "hurry up."

"I'll be back next weekend or during the week sometime, sorry!"

"Wait, what?" Mr. Hathaway shouted from the kitchen

of the café, pans and pots clattering as he made his way out and behind the counter. "Where are you going? Sarika!"

"I'll make it up to you, I swear!" Sarika shouted as she swung the front door open, holding it for Leila, who hurried through as the bell chimed above them.

Outside, Philadelphia was already bustling, even in a neighborhood that generally didn't have a lot of people walking around or commuting here and there.

"Wait, wait," Leila said, rushing up to Sarika, who was making her way over to the bicycle rack outside Adam's. With a pang she looked at the empty spot next to Sarika's bike, where bits of yellow paint chipped against the black metal, left over from scrapes with Marigold. Her bike was still a mangled mess in the backyard, and she'd left Liz's bike at the house. It had taken forever to clean after going to the park to meet Landon and its ride in the back of his truck on the way home. She wasn't in a rush to dirty it up again.

Sarika was fussing with the locks on her bike when she looked up at Leila.

"What?" she asked, unhooking her lock, and then glanced at the empty spot where Marigold was usually locked up. "Oh, that's right. So how do you propose we get to your magical garden?"

"Are you sure you want to go?" Leila asked. "It was a lot to take in."

"I'm not going to let you face this alone, whatever it is," Sarika said, resolutely.

Leila gave Sarika a friendly nudge, and pulled out her phone. She stared at it for a beat.

"What is it?" Sarika asked, nodding at Leila's phone.

"It's just, I've already asked him for help. Landon. Like, yesterday," Leila said, looking down at the glowing screen. "And it was an intense day."

"So?" Sarika asked, shrugging.

"I just don't want to seem all 'princess' or 'damsel in distress,' you know? Is it normal to call a guy, like, the day after we first hung out?"

"Leila. There is nothing normal about this situation," Sarika said, grinning. "I don't think you can Google for advice on whether or not you should call a guy you're maybe interested in after you've seen magical mythological beings in the woods outside an abandoned historic mansion together. That would be a very niche think piece."

"Fair enough," Leila said, smiling. She scrolled down to Landon's name on her phone and hit "dial".

Sarika Paprika

@TheSarikaPaprika

Sorry #SarikaTheBarista fans! Something's come up. I'll be back to @AdamsPhillyCafe this weekend! First one to RT gets a coffee from @WithouttheY!

8/24/17, 9:47AM

38 Retweets 7 Likes

> Stallwood @WilhelmStalw00d   9m
> @TheSarikaPaprika @AdamsPhillyCafe nooooooooooooo! cc @krummali

> Allison @krummali   7m
> @wilhelmstalw00d @TheSarikaPaprika @AdamsPhillyCafe there go my plans for the afternoon! Ugh!

> Sarika @TheSarikaPaprika   5m
> @wilhelmstalw00d @krummali @AdamsPhillyCafe sorry guys! You were the first to RT this though, so coffee on @WithouttheY next time you're in! ♥

XVI

"So, where's your owl friend?" Sarika asked as they made their way down the trail towards the Thomas Mansion and the grove where the dryads lived. Landon had thankfully picked them up at the café and driven them out here. Today he wasn't dressed in his uniform, but some ripped jeans that looked as though they'd been on endless hikes, paired with a black t-shirt with Hedwig from Harry Potter in the center and the word "HERO" in fancy typeface below the illustration.

Landon smiled sadly as they walked, and moved closer to Leila. There it was again, even without his park ranger uniform on, that smell of sawdust, sweet and surprising.

"He's resting, back in the Trust. He's been a bit out of it lately, not sure why," he said with a soft shrug. "Yesterday was a good day for him despite the, uh, unusual circumstances he found himself in."

"Not used to magical tree spirits?" Sarika asked.

"It's just up ahead," Landon continued, seeming to ignore Sarika's joke and looking back towards the trail. "Some people were here a bit earlier today, some contractors. I heard it over the CB." He tapped the walkie-talkie on his hip. "I might not be at work, but it's nice to keep up with what's going on. Kinda hard to turn it off sometimes."

"I know what you mean," Sarika said, pulling out her smartphone and flipping through something on the screen. "People are not happy that I bailed on the café today."

"Sorry about that," Leila said, resisting the urge to take out her phone and look at her mentions. Ever since Sarika had said she wouldn't be at Adam's, her phone had been lighting up with alerts.

"Eh, it's just the Internet." Sarika shrugged. "They'll forget all about my horrific deed by tomorrow morning, despite the fact that I am clearly a monster. Not coming in to make them coffee, how do I live with myself, you guys? How?"

"Seriously, you should be—" Leila started, and then stopped.

The path leading towards the mansion had been widened since the day before. A number of the shrubs and trees that had blocked their way or made things awkward for them yesterday had been cleared. Off to the side of the now-widened trail were the remains of the plants and brush that had been cut from the trees or ripped from the ground, the brambles almost making a wall along the trail.

"Wow, they really have already started working up here," Landon said, looking over the trail and the bushes piled along the way. "This was all in the road just yesterday."

"The dryads," Leila said, her heart beating madly. She darted up the trail.

"Leila, wait!" Landon shouted.

"Come on!" she heard Sarika yell as she rushed

forward, her feet hitting the now-clear dirt path harder with each angry step forward. She still had too many questions. What was her father like? How did she end up in foster care in the first place? She had a chance to finally connect with a part of who she was, and she wasn't about to let some fools with axes and sheers ruin everything.

Not just for her, but for the world.

Philadelphia wasn't really the world, she knew that. But the dryads' claim that their demise would bring about the crumbling of the city shook her, even if she wasn't quite sure she believed any of it yet. It brought up too many questions. Were there other mythological creatures throughout Philadelphia, or even the world, that clung to life and subsequently supported all of ours? If there were dryads in the wilderness, were there mermaids and sirens in the sea?

The questions pounded against Leila's skull. The pain from her bike accident still thundered inside, blending with her more practical, slightly less magical concerns. She imagined Sarika's family having to leave their home, the old group home being shut down, Jon and Lisabeth having to leave their lives and their careers. Would the air became unbreathable? The soil ruined? What was it that would happen, exactly?

She ran.

For herself.

For her friends.

For the family she was just starting to feel a part of.

She stumbled to a stop against bright-yellow con- struction tape that blocked the end of the trail, crossing over it in a giant X shape, hung from two nearby trees. Leila ripped it away and flicked the frayed, yellow plastic from her as the mansion came into view. The ruined building now had the same thick, yellow tape all around it, a number of nearby trees had bright red Xs spray painted on them, and several shrubs were coated in blue spray paint.

Her eyes darted to the path behind the mansion that led out to the gardens, and she rushed down it, ducking under more yellow tape hanging from the archway. In the gardens behind the home almost everything was marked with the same bright-red spray, and she pushed forward until she came to the entrance to the grove, which was also marked with red.

She no longer had to weave her way in and out of branches or step over brush as she walked the path into the grove, so much of it had been cut and cast aside. Here, too, the trees were marked with red Xs.

"No, no, no," she muttered, moving forward, her feet hitting the hard dirt path. She could hear Sarika and Landon hustling behind her. The light from the grove was just up ahead, bright and beaming, where the canopy opened into the secret, hidden nook. She burst out into the grove and the sun flooded her eyes. And everything came into view.

The rocks that lined the grove were marked with white Xs, and a number of the trees that surrounded it were marked with the bright-red Xs. The three center oaks, the trees where Karayea, Tifolia, and Shorea dwelled, were still standing tall.

But they were marked.

Leila walked into the grove past the spray-painted stones.

"Karayea?" she asked, looking directly at the center tree. "Tifolia? Shorea?" She was surprised at the fact that these strange-sounding names were already permanently seared into her mind. It took her days, sometimes weeks, to remember the names of new kids that came into the old group homes, and sometimes by the time she had them set to memory those kids were on their way out.

She walked up to the center tree and ran her hand over the bright-red X. Bits of red paint came away on her palm. She glanced up at the tree's leaves, surprised to see they were changing, as though the autumn months were already on them. Her eyes flashed to all the dryads' trees, the trees that bordered the grove, and those down by the path. Mixed in with the greens now were pops of yellow and red, and some light brown. The leaves were changing color way too soon.

"M-mom?" Leila whispered, the word feeling heavy and foreign, full of unsaid things. Her heart was racing. Were the people who did this still here? Could they hear her?

"Leila!"

She jumped and spun around. Landon and Sarika hurried into the grove, both looking worn and exhausted.

"Sweet Jesus, girl, I had no idea you could run like that," Sarika said, huffing and trying to catch her breath. "All that bike riding has certainly paid off cardio-wise. I'm dying. I think I'm dying."

"Oh my God," Landon said, moving towards the grove.

He dropped down on one knee and put his hand against one of the spray-painted rocks, and Leila saw his hand come away with wet paint on it. Leila walked towards him, her heart sinking. The dryads weren't coming out, and there was Sarika, looking about intensely, clearly taking everything in.

"The assholes were just here," Landon stood up, balling up his hands into fists. He straightened his shoulders and narrowed his eyes, looking at the trees. He turned to Leila. "Anything?"

"No," Leila said and shook her head. "But look at the trees. The leaves."

Landon stared up at the canopy, his head turning this way and that as he walked into the grove, and he put his hand against one of the trees. He wiped off some of the wet spray paint with a finger. He poked around at the ground, and Leila turned and walked over to Sarika.

"This is really weird," he said, sucking at his teeth. "They shouldn't be changing this soon." He paused, thoughtfully. "You don't think–"

"Don't say it," Leila said, surprised to feel a sob threatening to come up.

"So this is it?" Sarika asked, looking up at the canopy. "I mean, it certainly feels like a magical place, you know. How's all this work? Are you going to like, summon them or something?" She grinned. "Is there a song?"

"Don't make fun of this," Leila said, trying to sound less hurt than she was.

"I'm just trying to lighten the mood," Sarika said, a frown on her face. She walked over and hugged Leila close, and Leila could feel herself starting to choke up. "I believe you. Whatever it is, I will always believe you."

"Last time they just came out," Leila said, her shoulders heaving against Sarika. "Landon saw the whole thing, he knows."

"It's true," Landon said.

"Maybe they're upset or something," Leila mused, letting go of Sarika and turning to the grove. Roughly cut bushes and spray paint were everywhere.

"Yeah, well, if a bunch of strangers came into my home and painted all over my things, I'd probably stay in all day, too," Sarika said. She stopped at the path leading into the ring of stones, and knelt down at one of the rocks. "Look at all this. This is, like, centuries old. Who just tears down something like this? And why wouldn't these dryads just, you know, appear and stop everything that's happening to them?"

"We only appear in the presence of our own," spoke a familiar voice.

Leila looked up as Karayea stepped out of the center oak tree. Her movements were slow, precise, not as fluid as the last time she approached her. Sarika backed away, bumping into Leila, and promptly grabbed her hand.

"It's okay," Leila said, giving her hand a reassuring squeeze. Landon peeked out from the other trees and made his way over to them, taking a wide stride around Karayea as she walked towards the edge of the circle. He gave her an awkward nod hello, and Leila grinned. It was the sort of awkward, quick greeting one gave someone familiar at a café or in the hallways of school. Not an ancient creature of myth that had existed for centuries, maybe millennia.

It was cute, in its incredibly unusual way.

Landon joined Leila and Sarika outside the circle as Karayea reached the edge of the stones.

"Oh," Leila said, catching a gasp in her throat. "Your arm."

Karayea slowly looked down at her arm, her neck creaking like a branch in the wind, and frowned. There was a bright-red mark on her right arm, a bit of spray paint from the X that marked the rest of the tree.

"It'll fade in time," she said, her words slow and measured, as she looked back up at the trio. "The poison will wash away with the rain and new growth."

"Poison?" Leila asked, her heart hammering.

"There are toxins in this color that the humans put on us. I fear it has affected my sisters more than me." She slowly turned and looked at the other two trees in the grove, which hadn't moved or opened. "They aren't as eager to talk to anyone right now, especially to the one with the bird. The one who is supposed to protect us."

"Me?" Landon asked, surprised. "What did I do?"

"It's what you failed to do. The men who came with the torches of color," Karayea continued. "They wore your colors, the ones you bore yesterday, and the ones Leila's father bore ever so long ago. You and your people, the caretakers, the ones we have trusted for so many years, have turned against us."

Landon shook his head, and turned to Leila and Sarika.

"There was a maintenance call on the CB yesterday

for a project today," he said. "It must have been this. I'll have to talk to the crew. They're just doing their jobs. They don't know about you. If they did, there's no way they would have done any of this."

"How . . . how is this happening right now?" Sarika asked, her focus on no one in particular.

"You," Karayea said, extending a gnarled hand towards her, her fingers like twigs and vines. "I know you. I know your voice from the winds. You have guarded my sapling all these years. Protected her. I have listened to you two together when I could. I thank you, young guardian."

"If I faint, please don't let me hit my head on a rock," Sarika said. Leila wrapped an arm around Sarika and hugged her close.

"What did they say?" Landon asked, taking a step forward. Leila looked up at him as he walked towards the dryad. "The men who came here, with the paint and the shears, cutting things. Did you hear them talking about anything? Their plans?"

Karayea shook her head slowly, the vines and leaves rustling on her head.

"They spoke of things unfamiliar to me," she said, speaking as though she was forcing out every single word. "A museum, a marker, a mouse, and a man." Her voice faded as she spoke, drifting with each word, and she abruptly fell to one of her knees. An audible crack echoed through the grove as she hit the hard earth. As if a massive gust of wind had hit the grove, piles of leaves fell from the neighboring trees, fluttering down and turning unnaturally quickly from green to red to yellow to brown.

"Oh, God!" Leila shouted, rushing forward as more leaves fell around her. She reached out and touched the dryad, gripping her branch-like arm, and felt the hard wood, moss, and ivy around it as she helped her back up. "Are you alright?"

"I am unsure," Karayea whispered, her head down. The leaves and vines of her hair tickled against Leila's face, but weren't as bright green as they had been. Leila gazed down, and quickly noticed a large break in Karayea's branch-like leg.

"Oh, oh no," Leila said, looking up towards Sarika and and Landon. "Help me, let's get her back into her tree."

"Will that help?" Landon asked, hustling next to the dryad.

"I don't know!" Leila said, panicking.

Landon quickly put an arm around Karayea, and Sarika joined Leila by Karayea's arm. Together they walked her towards the center oak, the split wide and maw-like. It only split halfway down; Karayea had stepped out of the center of it.

"What do we do?" Leila muttered, looking at the large space.

"I've got her," Landon said, wrapping his arms around Karayea, lifting her up. "My goodness, she's heavy." He placed her back inside the tree, and Karayea reached out to grip the sides of the oak and hold herself in place.

"I . . . I must heal or . . . or the land will suffer," she muttered. "Go . . . Give me time. Find these men if you can . . . If you cannot . . ." She looked up, her bright green eyes fading into brown, and reached out her brambled hand to run the rough, bark-like fingers over Leila's cheek. "You must go. Take your new family, your friends, and leave this city. Go where there is green. I want you to thrive, my sapling."

She pulled her arm back into the tree, and leaned against the inside, closing her eyes.

The earth rumbled softly, and Sarika grabbed onto Leila, who in turn held her close, as the oak tree began to rustle. The leaves shook above them, and the front of the tree sealed up with loud snaps and cracks until it looked as though nothing was there at all.

PROTESTING IN FAIRMOUNT PARK

Posted by WithouttheY

AUGUST 23rd, 2017 | 8:02PM

I know it's been a while since we organized to really do anything, but recently, an historic mansion and (more importantly) an ancient grove of oak trees have become the target of demolition in Fairmount Park. It's in an area that doesn't get a lot of foot traffic—in fact, it gets none. They are planning to place an amphitheater in there, and build a road into the area from Kelly Drive.

Anyhow, I'll be assembling near the Horticulture Center to do a bit of protesting, and taking to social media to tell people what's going on. I hope some of you will join! Just chime in if you're interested, and I'll send you a DM with details. It's a public board, after all.

RE: PROTESTING IN FAIRMOUNT PARK

Posted by A Dash of Paprika

AUGUST 23rd, 2017 | 2:09PM

I'm in.

> RE: PROTESTING IN FAIRMOUNT PARK
>
> *Posted by WithouttheY*
>
> AUGUST 23rd, 2017 | 2:09PM
>
> Yes obviously. :-P

RE: PROTESTING IN FAIRMOUNT PARK
Posted by D Meier
AUGUST 23rd, 2017 | 3:09PM
Same, sending a DM!

RE: PROTESTING IN FAIRMOUNT PARK
Posted by A Jimenez
AUGUST 23rd, 2017 | 3:19PM
They're tearing down part of the park, and no one knows about it? I am SO in. That's messed up. Let us know what the hashtag will be on social media.

RE: PROTESTING IN FAIRMOUNT PARK
Posted by JessDeLaCosta
AUGUST 23rd, 2017 | 4:09PM
LOL. Man fuck your park. You bitches are standing in the way of progress.

> RE: PROTESTING IN FAIRMOUNT PARK
> *Posted by A Dash of Paprika*
> AUGUST 23rd, 2017 | 4:15PM
> JESS GET OUT OF OUR BOARD. YOU ARE SO BANNED.
>
> RE: PROTESTING IN FAIRMOUNT PARK
> *Posted by PAPRIKA SUX*
> AUGUST 23rd, 2017 | 5:02PM
> OH NO PLEASE DON'T KICK ME OUT WHAT WILL I EVER DO.

FROM	SUBJECT	DATE
WITHOUTTHEY	THE PROTEST Hey Toothless! So this week we're going to do a bit of protesting in Fairmount Park to save this grove and old mansion and yada yada. You can see the message board post in the Philadelphia section. You should come. We could finally meet. I have to be honest. I might have met someone? I dunno. I know you and I been like, flirting a bit on here. I just don't want to mess up anything. Don't hate me?	8/23

WITHOUTTHEY	RE: THE PROTEST Hey, did you get my last message? I hope you're not upset with me. I'd really like for you to be there. Are you seeing the drama with Sarika and that Jessica girl? She's from our school, always starting shit.	8/24
WITHOUTTHEY	RE: THE PROTEST Silence says it all. I'm sorry. 😫	8/25

XVII

Leila stared out the window of Belmont's science lab at the trees in the distance, at the edges of Fairmount Park that were visible from the school, and the green that dotted the city landscape. Trees throughout the area had already started changing color, bursts of red and orange and yellow scattered about like paint. What she once thought of as a beautiful sight was now entirely ominous, and filled her heart with dread.

"It's happening already," Sarika said, standing next to her.

"Yeah," Leila said. She closed her eyes, and for the first time wished the voices would come to her, but they remained silent. The dryad in the woods, her mother. She stayed quiet.

"Are you sure this is the best idea?" Sarika asked, as she pulled out one of the stools in the science lab.

"I mean, there *are* a few people who are into saving the planet in this club," Leila said, shrugging. "And I know Shawn is a bit of a tactless prick, but I think he actually means well. We texted a lot last night. He's on our team."

"Yeah, we'll see about all that. You know I'm on hashtag-Team-Landon right now. Shawn fell off the leaderboard a while ago, and Toothless isn't even on it. I still don't know why you talk to that troll."

"Oh God, there's seriously not even a team to be on," Leila said, giving Sarika a shove. "Toothless stopped talking to me, and who knows what's actually going on with Landon. I feel like there's something there, but I don't know."

"Wait, Toothless isn't talking to you anymore?" Sarika asked. "Why? What happened?"

"Eh, I brought up that I kinda met someone, wasn't sure where it was going. You know, with Landon and all." Leila shrugged. "I said we could be friends, I wanted to see where that would go, but he hasn't messaged me back in days."

"Damn. Well, you're better off. Speaking of the board, though, I can't get over Jessica having the nerve to go on there," Sarika grumbled.

"Don't worry about it," Leila said, pulling Sarika in for a hug. "She's just trolling. We'll figure out how to ban her I.P. address or something."

The members of B.E.A.C. slowly filtered into the room. Several looked worn out and tired, no doubt after a busy morning of summer enrichment and/or gossiping. A flash of red caught Leila's eye, and she quickly waved to Britt, the red-headed runner she'd met on the recent field trip. She smiled and waved back, hurrying over to join them as Mikey trailed behind her. They took the two seats across from Leila and Sarika, filling their small lab table.

"Sarika, this is Britt and Mikey," Leila said.

"Great to meet you!" Britt said, reaching out and

shaking Sarika's hand, a beaming smile on her face. "Sorry I missed you saying hi on the trip and all."

"It's okay," Sarika said. She turned to Mikey and winked at him as she stuck out her hand. "And Mikey, is it?"

"You too!" Mikey said, reaching out and shaking her hand, before immediately closing his eyes and sighing loudly. "I mean, me too. Me too, sorry I missed you. Too. Ahem. I mean, hi, my name is Mikey, and I'd like the earth to open and swallow me whole right now."

"Smooth," Britt said, nudging her shoulder against Mikey.

"I like them," Sarika said, smiling at Leila.

The door to the classroom swung open and hit the wall with a loud bang, rattling the nearby tables. Everyone jumped in their stools, the seats squeaking against the science lab's hard linoleum floor. Shawn barreled in, his expression hard, his hands balled into fists. Trailing right behind him was an equally as angry looking Jessica.

"Don't you dare walk away from me!" Jessica shouted, the two of them stopping at the desk in the front of the room. Shawn sat down on it, staring ahead at the members of B.E.A.C. The look in his eyes was pained and distant. Leila frowned. His eyes were red, and there were shadows under them, like he hadn't slept in days.

"I'm fucking talking to you!" Jessica spat, and pushed a bunch of papers and books off the desk, sending them clattering against the floor. Leila moved her stool back, ready to get up, when Shawn locked eyes with her. He shook his head softly, and looked down at the floor.

He rubbed his hands together, and eventually clapped them and jumped to his feet.

"Alright!" he exclaimed. "Let's get things started." He beamed a bright, visibly forced smile at everyone, the awkwardness in the air thick enough to cut with an axe.

"The hell do you think you're doing?" Jessica yelled, walking in front of him with her back to the rest of the club. "You do not get to ignore me. You don't get to break up with me. You're mine, Shawn Kennedy. You and your whole family are mine. If you don't stop this—"

"As Leila was kind enough to point out via our email list," Shawn continued, standing up and walking around Jessica to speak to the rest of the room. Sarika shook, and Leila turned to see her holding in a laugh. Leila smiled.

Go Shawn.

"There's a protest scheduled for outside the Fairmount Horticulture Center later this week." Shawn began pacing the room, and Jessica sat on the desk, staring daggers at him. "The plan is to meet at the center promptly at 4:00 p.m., when people there are still at work, and hang in there until after 5:00 p.m. in hopes that we'll have generated enough buzz for the local news to come out and catch some of the workers there off guard as they leave the building.

"If we can call public attention to what's happening," Shawn continued, "it'll be easier to shut them down. People know that there is an amphitheater being built, but no one is talking about the fact that it's going to demolish an historic building and garden. The more outraged the public is, the harder it will be to mow down that structure and take out that grove."

"Shut them down?" Jessica spat, standing back up.

"Yes, Jessica," Shawn said coldy, turning to her. "Just because something is old and forgotten, doesn't mean it has lost its value. And there are the mice! Some of the park service tipped us off to them. They are endangered and deserve our—"

"Mice?" Jessica scoffed. "Who the fuck cares about some mice? You sound like your damn father." She crossed her arms.

"And you sound like yours." Shawn glared at her.

"Fuck your trees," Jessica said, storming away from the desk and shoving past Shawn, sending him stumbling against a lab table. "And your mice." She turned to the whole classroom as she reached the door. "That old building and crappy garden will be gone in a week."

"And you," Jessica pointed at Shawn. "Tell your dad to pack up his office. I'm going to have a little talk with mine about all this." She opened the classroom door with an angry swing and slammed it shut, rattling everything on the tables and sending a lone beaker shattering against the floor.

Leila winced. It was hard hearing someone talk about the grove so harshly, knowing what was actually in there. Sarika grabbed her hand, and she looked up at Shawn, who stared at the door, his shoulders sunk. He turned around and walked back over to the desk slowly, sitting on it with a sigh.

"As some of you know, as it isn't exactly something

secret, Jessica's father funds my father's nonprofit efforts," Shawn said, wringing his hands. "I'm not super concerned by her threats, but . . . well, who can we count on being there?" Shawn asked, a forced smile on his face again.

Leila and Sarika raised their hands, as did Mikey and Britt. The rest of the room looked around uncomfortably, and Shawn crossed his arms, flashing them all a scowl.

"Right," he said and leapt to his feet. "Then why are you even in here?"

Leila's eyes went wide and she looked over at Sarika, who nodded approvingly.

"Is it for the summer credit? Is that the deal?" Shawn asked, as the students looked increasingly more awkward. "'Cause, newsflash, you're not going to get it if you don't participate in anything we're doing. Instead of doing community service at the Japanese tea house the other day, a bunch of you walked around looking at birds. Which is fine, but I bet if I asked you to name more than two birds there, you wouldn't have an answer. Saving the world takes work. You want to play along? Put the work in."

A few of them muttered to one another. Leila glanced at Sarika, who winced. They were some of the people who had skipped out and wandered around.

"Look, I'm sorry for how I acted the other day on the field trip. Jessica's family is in charge of the construction of that amphitheater. They're handling the road construction and tearing down that Raptor Trust place, and I was . . . emotionally compromised." Shawn continued, regret tinting his voice. "I know Dr. Rich isn't in here supervising, but I'm the one who turns in the attendance.

I tell him who has been going to what. I'm the one who signs off on those final papers of yours at the end of this summer. Me." Shawn's voice grew louder and more anxious. "This is something I'm in charge of. Now, you'll go, or you won't get the credit you want from this enrichment course."

A few heads nodded.

"Am. I. Clear?" he said, angrily.

All the heads nodded.

"Good." He crossed his arms and sat back on the desk, a smirk on his tired face. He looked over at Leila and winked.

"Now, everyone is going to have a role to play in this protest," he continued. "It's early in the day still. Some of you will work on fliers to tack around the school and outside in various neighborhoods around Philadelphia. I'll need someone working on the social media aspect of things, as we definitely need an event page and a hashtag running through everything. As for me, I'll alert local media. Everything about this protest will be perfect."

Shawn walked around the room, handing out assignments to the members of the club, a majority of whom begrudgingly accepted them before walking out of the classroom to work. Social media here, fliers there.

"You four," Shawn said, pointing at Sarika, Leila, Mikey, and Britt. "I'll need you to flier up the school, which shouldn't take all that long, and get to work on some signs. You can meet us over at the center with them on Saturday. Try to come a little earlier? 3:30 would be great, so we can distribute materials."

"Sure, Shawn, but—" Leila started.

"Don't worry," Shawn said, smiling, a dimple on the corner of his mouth. "I've got this. You just worry about signs and fliers and keep an eye on your park, while I fuss over the logistics. This isn't my first rodeo." He leaned over on the table. "Look, I know this is important to you. And I, well, I fucked up. I hope this makes it up to you. I'm not totally an inconsiderate monster, I swear."

Leila smiled.

"I appreciate that, and I know," she said. "It's a good start."

LEILA: Good morning!

LEILA: Hey we're planning out the protest this afternoon, you at work?

LEILA: You around at all?

LEILA: Hey! You there? We're on our way to pass out fliers near the Trust.

LEILA: Heading to that café I told you about.

LEILA: Come on, you should come to this thing. I want you there.

LEILA: Landon, everything okay?

LANDON: Hey. Yeah sorry, won't be able to make it.

LANDON: Send me pictures, let me know how it goes.

LEILA: Sure? You okay?

LANDON: I'm fine, really. Don't worry.

LEILA: K.

XVIII

Leila wiped the sleep from her eyes and shuffled through the stack of fliers on the kitchen table. They were printed on colorful paper, each practically see through, like the recycled, brown paper towels in the school's bathroom. She made a mental note to ask Shawn where he found this kind of printer paper. It was the same as the flier she'd seen back in Adam's Café when he first walked in. He'd been nice, he was trying to fix things, trying to build some sort of friendship out of the mess he created, and he was clearly making some sacrifices to come through for her.

But Landon. Radio silence. After everything they'd been through together, he'd just gone quiet.

Leila held up a flier and angled it towards her light box for a moment. The bright light shone right through the paper, and she added it back to the stack. She took her phone out, but before she could turn it on, she blinked at the dark screen, surprised. In the vague reflection, she saw something different on the side of her face.

Her birthmark.

It seemed to have grown a little, the pale spot spread a little higher on her cheekbones. But that was impossible. She scratched her head, fussing with her scarf, and when she pulled her hand away, noticed a few strands of hair coiled around her fingers.

What was happening? She glanced out the window towards Major Willow in the yard. The soft, green sphere of leaves was turning red and yellow. Some of the bark on the thin trunk looked a bit paler, and like it was peeling. Her heart ached. It was far too soon for the little tree to be changing color. And shedding bark wasn't a good sign, either.

"Hey, Leila?"

She turned and spotted Jon standing in the door of the kitchen, his hands awkwardly clasped around one of her fliers, his eyes darting about nervously. She put down her phone.

"Can we, uh, talk about these?" He held up one of the fliers, a light-green one, and made his way over to the kitchen table. He slowly pulled out a chair and sat down next to her.

"What's up?" Leila asked, putting the sheets into a folder. She reached under the table and unplugged her light box, and then slid the folder into her backpack. "You look all . . . you don't look good."

"Ha, thanks," Jon said, smiling. "Look, Liz and I really love your spirit, Leila. We do. How you care about the environment and the world around you. Most kids your age, well, frankly they couldn't care less."

"Tell me about it," Leila groaned, thinking about the "members" of B.E.A.C. who didn't want to do a thing until their credit was threatened. "You, um, sound like you're building up to a really big 'but' moment."

"And you're also incredibly perceptive," he said, shaking his head. "What can you tell me about all this?" He placed the flier on the table and slid it across, so it sat in-between them on the polished wood surface.

"It's a project B.E.A.C. is taking on," Leila said, feeling her heart quicken and warmth pour over her skin. Did he know about the dryads? Her biological mother and father? Of course, she hadn't posted about it anywhere and barely texted anything about it with Sarika or Landon. He couldn't know, there was absolutely no way he knew. Liz either. And she wanted to keep it that way. She'd seen enough made-for-TV movies about adopted kids seeking out their birth parents to know it could hurt the adoptive parents, no matter how much they claimed it didn't bother them. And the fact that her biological mother might be a mythological being living in the woods and keeping Philadelphia's greenery alive would be a stretch way too far.

"Yes, but, why?" Jon asked. "Why this particular place?"

"Have you been there?" Leila asked, raising an eyebrow.

"Well, no, but–"

"There's this old, historic mansion on the land," Leila started, sighing. "It's gorgeous, and just needs a little TLC. Just because it's abandoned doesn't mean it isn't worth taking care of. There have got to be people out there that would appreciate it, if only they knew it was there.

"And then there is this grove of trees, Jon," Leila continued. "Oh, this grove. Once you push out past the gardens, which if they were maintained and fixed up would be gorgeous, there's a hidden nook that is just beautiful.

Old trees, ancient, thicker than anything else in that entire park. How can anyone justify cutting down what feels like an old-growth forest in the middle of a city park? It's maddening."

"Look, Leila—"

"And mice!" Leila exclaimed, pulling out anything she could that didn't make her have to say something about the magic that was actually there. "There's some kind of endangered field mouse out there. That should make it against the law, Jon. Never mind just saving the place because it's beautiful."

Jon stared at the flier. For someone who loved to tell jokes, he was unusually quiet. His mouth was in a thin line, and he nodded slowly as Leila spoke.

"What is it?" Leila asked. "Jon?"

"Look, I . . ." Jon sighed. "Leila, you know I'm on a few boards around town, leftover from my law days. And one of them is the city's Center for Horticulture, the people that are planning to build something over there. And I'm not sure how good it's going to look if my . . ." he looked up at her and sighed. "If my daughter is out there protesting what they're trying to do. It'd be cute, maybe, if you were, like, seven and trying to save some trees. But you're almost an adult. And you're on the Internet with these things and . . ."

He buried his head in his hands.

"I'm not going to ask you to not do it, but I need you to help me understand the why of it," he said, slightly muffled by his hands.

"So, if you're on the board," Leila started, sitting up a bit more, her mind spinning, "can you stop all this?"

"You still haven't given me a why," Jon said, looking back up and staring at Leila.

"Jon, you need to go there to understand," Leila said, shaking her head. "The grove, oh, it's so beautiful. And the old gardens. The ancient home. The mice! People need to know about it."

"Yes, but why? What's there that's—"

"You don't just throw stuff like that away because it's been abandoned!" Leila yelled.

"Leila," he sighed, sounded exhausted. "This is the willow tree all over again."

It felt as though all the air had been sucked out of the room.

"I'm sorry, I shouldn't have said that," Jon said, shaking his head, his eyes gone wide.

"No, no, you're probably right," Leila snapped, standing up and grabbing her backpack. "I'm just some broken girl comparing herself to other things. Oh, this house is abandoned. I'm also abandoned. I'm just like this house. Let me make things difficult for Jon. People aren't paying attention to these mice, I'm so ignored like a small woodland creature. Oh, this tree is going to get torn down because it's a little broken. Maybe I'll get thrown away too. Look at how emotionally damaged I am. I'm just like this fucking tree."

"Leila, come on, I didn't—"

"No, you said it, and you're right." Leila swung the

backpack over her shoulder. "My reasons are my own, Jon." Leila stormed for the front door.

"Yeah, well, your reasons aren't going to be good enough," Jon said, sounding a little more heated. Leila stopped and turned around.

"Listen." Jon stood up and pushed the chair out, the wood squeaking angrily against the floor. "If you want to save your grove and this old house, come back with something other than ideas about the place being pretty and supposedly having these endangered mice, and, Leila, I will help you. I want to. I want your causes to be mine. The amphitheater isn't, I don't know, evil or nefarious here. It's being built with good intentions. It'll bring people to the park. It'll help the whole park system make money, which can help fund other projects. Maintaining older sections of the park, repairing historic structures, things like that. And it's been in the works for a long time. But maybe they can build it someplace else.

"But let me be clear on all this," Jon said, walking towards her in the hallway. "This is going to happen. The permits are there, plans are being made. They're going to lay the foundation in the next week or so, which means you've really only got days. And no one has been able to find proof those mice live there. Otherwise it wouldn't be happening."

Days.

Leila held her feet firmly to the ground, fighting the feeling that she might stumble over from the revelation. She put on a face, looked at Jon and shook her head, resisting the urge to burst into tears. Days. Days to ask questions. Days to hope that Karayea recovered from the chemical-filled spray paint. Days to get answers to her questions and save the grove, and possibly, save Philadelphia.

"What do I need to do?" Leila asked, pushing the anger down and away.

"You need to find something that'll prevent them from building. If the fact that it's a historic landmark didn't help, then it needs to be something else. Something bigger than that."

"Landon, this park ranger I met over there," Leila said. "He's the one who knows about the endangered mice. I can bring him in, he can talk to your board or however all that works. It's illegal to take away the habitat of an endangered species, everyone knows that."

"See, that's your angle." Jon nodded, his eyes widening. "But you need to get proof of these critters. They haven't found those mice, Leila. If you did, somehow, that could stop, or least put off the building and construction. They will have to investigate it."

"Got it," Leila said, nodding.

"If I wasn't on their board, I'd write about this myself, or tip someone off." Jon sighed. "But I could lose my job with the papers, the magazines. It's a big conflict of interest. I can at least point you in the right direction, though, and voice my concerns to the staff at the Center for Horticulture."

A bit of silence hung in the air between the two of them as Leila looked at Jon and the front door, awkwardly wanting to leave while wanting to make up.

"Jon, look, I'm—" she started.

"Don't," Jon said, shaking his head and holding a hand up. "I shouldn't have said what I said. I want to help. I'm just frustrated, is all. Walking on eggshells around these things is difficult."

"Fair enough," Leila smiled.

"Go save the world," Jon said, waving Leila off. "Or at least part of it."

Leila opened the front door. The trees that lined the street were a shade of deep red, and patches of the grass that had pushed its way up through the sidewalk cracks had already started to brown.

Save the world?

He had no idea.

LEILA: Hey, so, you know my father, Jon?

LEILA: He knows some of the people involved in the park situation.

LEILA: And your bird place!

LEILA: He can help but we need to get all this evidence.

LEILA: I'm basically talking to myself right now aren't I?

LANDON: . . .

LEILA: I can see you debating on typing something.

LEILA: I see the dots!

LEILA: I know you want to say hi to me. I'm cute.

LEILA: Landon.

LEILA: Fine.

XIX

"Really? Nothing?" Sarika asked, as she polished one of the wooden tables in Adam's. She looked up at Leila and tossed the rag. "Sorry, can't help myself. I'm not even on the clock right now."

"It's fine. And yeah, I don't get it," Leila said. "After all we went through with the grove and the dryads. We had some real moments, you know? He's skipping the protest and won't return any of my texts."

"You could always fall back on Shawn, if you know what I mean," Sarika said with a grin. Leila snatched up the table rag and threw it at her. "Oh, gross!"

"That's what you get," Leila said, rolling her eyes. "I've got all the fliers hung up here and in the local shops, and I told the rest of the group about what Jon said. It's just going to be hard to find these mice without Landon, you know? I mean, how do you find an endangered mouse? It couldn't have been an endangered squirrel? A sparrow?"

"An endangered mole, perhaps?" Sarika continued, sitting down at the table "Maybe an ant? How about a salamander?"

"Psh, at least those we can maybe find under rocks and logs." Leila sighed.

"Whatever," Sarika said, standing up. "Let's just go *make* him help us."

"Come on, we can't—"

"He's not supposed to have that owl as, like, a pet, right?" Sarika asked, her hands on her hips. "I say we head over to where he's interning, and tell him if he doesn't help us dig around in the grove, we'll report it."

"What! No way. I'm fine with just talking to him, but I'm not gonna threaten his owl. Not Milford. That's messed up."

"Hey, ends justifying the means and all that stuff, right?" Sarika shrugged. "What's more important? His feelings and a one-winged bird, or learning the history of your family, rescuing your apparent mother, and saving a patch of woods that supposedly helps sustain the entire city of millions of people?"

"It's not that easy."

"But it kinda is."

"But it isn't."

"But it is."

Leila sighed and shook her head, pulling her phone out. She turned the screen on, stared at the last few texts with Landon, and immediately put it back in her pocket.

"We go, but only to talk to him," Leila said. "No threats like that unless . . . we have to, okay?"

"Deal," Sarika said, nodding. She grabbed her satchel off the table and swung it around her shoulder. "Let's go."

PROTESTING IN FAIRMOUNT PARK (UPDATE)
Posted by A Dash of Paprika
AUGUST 26th, 2017 | 10:02AM
Hey everyone! So far we've got an absolute legion of you on board for the big protest, and we couldn't be happier.
But! We're adjusting the message a little bit.
Turns out protesting the fact that they want to tear down something that's gorgeous and beautiful isn't quite enough, nor do they care about the history. But they *are* going to care about the endangered animals in the park.
Supposedly there's a critically endangered field mouse living in that area. We're going to head out to collect evidence and will circle back. If anyone wants to support or help out with that, give a shout, please!

RE: PROTESTING IN FAIRMOUNT PARK (UPDATE)
Posted by WithouttheY
AUGUST 26th, 2017 | 10:09AM
You are too good for this world. Too pure.

RE: PROTESTING IN FAIRMOUNT PARK (UPDATE)
Posted by LeRandelle
AUGUST 27th, 2016 | 10:17AM
What kind of mouse, specifically? I might know

someone at one of the local museums who is obsessed with small mammals. It's weird. But I guess that's her job.

RE: PROTESTING IN FAIRMOUNT PARK
(UPDATE)
Posted by WithouttheY
AUGUST 27th, 2016 | 10:39AM
Southeastern Pennsylvania common field mouse, I believe. The common in the title is pretty unfortunate, considering they really aren't common anymore.

RE: PROTESTING IN FAIRMOUNT PARK
(UPDATE)
Posted by LeRandelle
AUGUST 27th, 2016 | 11:09AM
Got it, I'll have her look into it and send you a DM.

XX

"Hello?" Leila poked around one of the massive bird habitats inside the Raptor Trust, looking for anyone working at the place. "Sarika, you see anything?"

"No!" Sarika shouted from somewhere unseen. "It's creepy, can we get outta here? Look at all the trees."

"Yeah, sure, in a minute," Leila said. Sarika was right. It was creepy. All around the Trust the trees had shed their leaves unnaturally fast, and leaves that had turned brown and crunchy far too quickly covered the ground.

What the dryads had said was happening. Whatever was in that spray paint had hurt them, and they needed to find Landon, fast.

Leila walked around the edge of the large cage in the Trust. Just a little over a week ago, a large golden-tailed eagle had sat inside the enclosure, its proud face looking about quickly and curiously, taking in everything with its sharp, wide eyes. And now? Empty, as though nothing had ever been inside in the first place. Even the water and feeders were gone. Just that large branch remained, wrapped with the same bright-yellow tape she'd spotted outside the grove and around the building.

The yellow tape was everywhere, marking the large, central building and circling the smaller enclosures. Bright red Xs marked some of the trees that surrounded the buildings, but only a handful of them. Who selected what trees were to be torn down, and what could remain?

"Landon!" Leila yelled, walking past the large enclosure toward the open fields nearby where she knew he sometimes flew Milford. "Landon, come on, if you're here we need you. I, uh, I need you."

"I heard that!" Sarika shouted, laughing.

Leila shook her head and kept walking toward the trees that bordered the field a little beyond the Trust. A handful of these, too, were marked with Xs, and yellow tape surrounded the small shed near the path that led towards the field where Landon had fished out her jacket. The trees were shedding their leaves, and the field was pocketed with brown patches of dead grass. Leila walked towards the shed. The door was slightly ajar, and a padlock hung from an open latch.

She opened it up.

Inside, a pile of leather-working tools sat scattered all over a small table, and scraps of fabric hung all over the floor and coated the walls. Scissors, needles, thread, pieces of metal and odd baubles and hinges sat everywhere: in baskets, in jars, on the ground. It looked like the lab of some kind of steampunk mad scientist from one of those fantasy novels full of brass and clocks that Sarika devoured back in the group home, with titles like *Updraft* or *Timekeeper*.

She picked up an object made of black leather and metal spokes, with little hinges connecting them and long pieces of thread dangling from it. She opened and closed it. The device flexed and moved.

It was a wing.

Landon didn't just store warm jackets in here. This was where he worked on his odd creations for Milford. She put the wing down and hurried out the door, shutting it behind her and looping the open padlock through the handle. She left it unlocked, but the latch would stop the door from swinging.

She kept walking towards the field Landon had used to help Milford fly, pushing her way down the narrow trail that led to the open expanse of grass. Here, too, more trees had been marked. Shrubs and brush had already been cut away to widen the path leading from the field to the Trust, no doubt to make room for whatever vehicles or tools would need to come through. Long patches of grass were marked with blasts of white paint, and Leila wondered what was going to go there. Roads? A parking lot? The building?

Leila stopped. She heard . . . something.

She listened.

A voice, whispering on the wind. She closed her eyes, giving it her full attention.

Hello daughter.

"Karayea," Leila said softly, her eyes shut, the breeze rustling about her and tickling her ears and neck. "We're trying to find a way to help—"

You may be too late, my sapling.

Leila's heart raced.

"Is someone there? Who is there?"

Someone was. They have rained their waters upon on our soil. It hurts. The land suffers with us.

"Rain? I don't understand—"

The boy and the bird. He will know.

"Karayea," Leila shook her head, and opened her eyes, trying not to feel silly as she spoke to nothing in front of her. "Are there mice in the grove near you?"

All creatures are welcome in our branches, the shelled and the furred—

"Right, but specifically, small, brown mice?"

Yes.

"Are they endangered? At risk or anything?"

I'm afraid I do not understand.

Leila growled with frustration. Concepts like animals being endangered, at risk or under conservation and protection, of course those were foreign to Karayea and the other dryads. Why wouldn't they be? But she was right about the boy with the bird. If anyone would know, Landon certainly would. He did know. He'd said as much.

"Hang in there," Leila said, speaking into the wind. "We're coming. I've got a plan."

Do try, and do hurry. But if you don't make it—

"Karayea, don't—"

If you don't make it, know that I am proud of how you've grown and what you've become. How you have bloomed. My sapling.

Tears started to well in Leila's eyes.

I love you, my daughter.

With a cold gust of wind, Karayea's voice and the presence that Leila felt around her whooshed away, leaving

Leila feeling chilled, her eyes wet with tears. Those were the words she'd wanted to hear her entire life.

She shook her head and pushed into the fields just ahead. As they came into view through the clearing at the end of the path, the green muddled with bits of brown, she spotted a backpack sitting near the entrance and a figure kneeling down in the grass, fussing over something. She squinted as the figure looked up from whatever it was doing.

It was Landon.

"Hey!" Leila shouted, walking quickly towards him. "Hey! Way to not answer my text messages, you—"

But before she could finish giving him the chewing out she felt he so rightly deserved, she saw the tears streaming down his eyes. His stubbly beard was slick with them.

And there, cradled in his arms, was Milford, his darling owl.

Leila ran and dropped down to her knees next to him, looking at the owl. Milford breathed in and out slowly. His eyes were closed and his single wing twitched.

"What's happening?" Leila asked.

"I don't know," Landon said, choking back a sob. He looked up and towards the path leading back to the Trust. "They came in and closed the Trust this morning. They marked trees and brush for removal, taped up the grounds. I had Milford in the shed while things wrapped up. I . . . I thought maybe I'd try to keep him."

"Keep him? Oh. Oh, Landon."

"They're going to just ship him away someplace. Lock him up in the museum's animal center or in the zoo,"

Landon said, cradling the owl. "I just can't think of him not being able to keep trying to fly." Landon sniffled and stood up with the owl. "I need to take him to an animal hospital, Leila. He's been getting worse since the other day, and now he just won't do anything. I found him on the bottom of his habitat. If I hadn't gotten there first—"

"Is this why you didn't want to talk?" Leila asked, standing with him. "The Trust shuttering? Planning to take Milford away? We need to be united on this, Landon. Everyone thinks it's just an early change of seasons, but we know better. You could have told me. I want to be there for you. I would have helped you plan something."

Landon looked at her and smiled through the tears, the flash of joy washing away just as quickly as it appeared. He grew serious.

"Look, I have something to—"

"Leila!" Sarika shouted from the path, running towards the two of them. "Landon, thank God we found you. Did you tell him? Oh." Sarika stopped in her tracks as she got closer to the two of them and saw Milford. "Oh no. What happened?"

"We have to go," Landon said, walking out of the field. Leila and Sarika followed close behind him.

"There's an animal hospital up in University City that takes care of exotics," he continued. "I've had friends at the Academy of Natural Sciences bring by chinchillas and other out-of-the-box critters." His head dipped down as he looked at Milford. "I'm thinking maybe they'll know how to fix him. People keep owls sometimes."

"Won't they ask for a permit or something?" Sarika asked as they rushed along.

"It's just a chance I'll have to take, I guess," Landon said. "If worse comes to worst, I'll say we found him. I've got my truck. I drove over today when I heard the news, basically speeding all the way here. We can drive up to University City."

They hurried silently down the trail back towards the shuttered Trust until they reached the exit, near the road that led away from the foundation and Fairmount Park along Kelly Drive. Looking at the stretch of road that moved along the Schuylkill River, Leila's mind drifted towards the day when she saw Landon trying to fly Milford and promptly crashed her bike.

Of Shawn, and that terrible first date and how he was trying to make up for things.

Of the people currently jogging up the trails that moved along the river, the kids playing in the little break areas along the walkway, the fishermen swinging lines into the raging waters just a few feet away.

None of them. Not one of them, except for Sarika next to her and Landon standing up ahead, his owl cradled in his arms, a faux leather wing attached to what remained of his natural one, had any idea what was happening in the woods right in front of them. To the world.

"Leila!" Landon shouted.

She broke out of her trance, and spotted Landon looking at her from inside his beat-up truck along the edge of the trail on the opposite side of the street. She hurried over with Sarika trailing behind.

"I'm sorry. I'm sorry I didn't message you back, but I just . . ." Landon started, fading off. "It's complicated. I'll tell you later. Hop in, I need one of you to hold Milford while I drive."

"Oh, dibs on that," Sarika said, hopping into the back seat. Leila got into the passenger side as Landon gingerly passed Milford over into Sarika's arms. The owl lay flat in her lap, breathing slowly with his eyes closed and beak open. "Oh Milly," Sarika said, running a hand over the owl's feathers. "You poor, sweet thing."

Landon gave Leila a look, and she smiled at him.

Milly. Milford would hate that.

He turned the key in the ignition, and wiped the tears away from his face.

"Let's go."

SARIKA: Leila this looks really bad.

LEILA: Shh, don't say that.

LEILA: Think positive. For Milford.

SARIKA: He isn't really moving much.

SARIKA: I'm scared.

SARIKA: Won't Landon get in a ton of trouble for having a wounded bird of prey? As a pet? Isn't that super illegal?

SARIKA: Will we get in trouble being with him?

LEILA: Something tells me that won't stop him.

LEILA: Just make sure he keeps breathing.

SARIKA: If he lives, I'll never eat owl again.

LEILA: What?

SARIKA: It was a joke.

LEILA: Oh thank God.

SARIKA: Yeah I'm not gonna stop eating owl.

LEILA: . . .

SEARCH

ALL   IMAGE   SHOPPING   NEWS   VIDEO

Search: What to do with an injured owl?

In the News:

Local birds leaving the City of Philadelphia in unusual early migration

Philadelphia Inquirer – One hour ago.

With the unusual change of weather, wildlife found throughout the city are exhibiting strange behavior that...

Early appearance of fall weather a surprise to residents and bird life through the Philadelphia region.

Philadelphia Magazine – Two days ago.

Experts at the Academy of Natural Sciences are baffled in what remains a hotly debated topic amongst the city's conservationist community...

Caring for Sick & Injured Owls

www.owlhealthcarecenter.org/sickowlswith...

If you find a baby owl on the ground, a fledgling, remember, it might not be in danger. They can climb trees with their beaks and claws, and are really great at this. Picking them up can actually...

Emergency Care: First Aid for Birds

www.birdsarepeopletoo.com

Caring for a sick parrot can be a difficult task, and ultimately, incredibly expensive. Luckily, there are some natural cure-alls for your sick friend that can be easily purchased at. . .

XXI

Landon paced the length of the waiting room at the University of Pennsylvania's Small Animal Hospital so many times that Leila lost count. Sarika fussed with her phone, gradually losing interest in the tension-filled waiting, while Leila waited for the moments when Landon looked up and locked eyes with her. Each time, his expression softened.

Seeing him in the field like that, Milford in his arms, seemed to have broken something between them down.

The door to the emergency room swung open, and a young veterinarian, tall with pale skin and light brown hair, walked through. Her features were cut with sharp lines, like she could be a model when she wasn't busy helping people's pets. She carried a clipboard and looked around the waiting room.

"Milford?" she asked. "Are Milford's, uh, owners here?"

Leila's heart sped up at the veterinarian's pause before saying "owners," and Landon looked over at her with a fraught expression.

"That's us, er, me," he muttered, walking over. Leila hopped up and went with him, with a glance over at Sarika, who was locked onto her phone. She stared down at it almost angrily. Someone was probably causing trouble on the board again.

"Dr. Saft," the vet introduced herself, shaking Landon's hand and then Leila's. "So, the good news is that Milford is stable. We've got him on an I.V. drip, just giving him fluids, as he's extremely dehydrated from what we believe is poison."

"Poison?" Landon gasped, his eyes wide.

"Yes, we managed to get him to have a bowel movement and cough up a rather uncomfortable pellet." She continued, her face turned up with concern. "There was some blood, but not his. It was a nearly complete mouse, which we believe to be the source of the poison. Its fur was practically coated in it."

"That's bizarre," Landon said.

"Well, it gets a little weirder. The mouse is a Southeastern Pennsylvania common field mouse, an incredibly endangered species," she continued, looking at the clipboard. "One of our technicians is a volunteer at the Academy of Natural Sciences' mammal's archive, and recognized it right away."

Leila's eyes widened.

"Milford will be okay. I should stress that," Dr. Saft continued. "You got him to us in time. Most owls who eat mice that have been poisoned, well, they end up with stomach hemorrhages that last a long time. Days, sometimes. But I still have some concerns. Can you explain, um," she pulled Milford's prosthetic wing out from behind her clipboard, "this?"

It unfurled and squeaked a little as it swayed back and forth, dangling from her hand.

"Oh," Landon said, his shoulders sinking. "Look, I found him as a fledgling, he lost his wing, and I've been trying for years to help him fly. That's one of his wings. I, uh, probably should have taken that off before coming here, but I wanted him to be comfortable."

"I see." Dr. Saft smiled softly, and looked back at her clipboard. "Listen, Landon, I'm going to assume you left the permit for Milford at home, yes?"

Landon's eyes went wide and he looked over at Leila, and she smiled at him in return.

"Y-yes?" Landon ventured.

"Alright," Dr. Saft said, making some notes on her clipboard. "Next time he needs an appointment, ask for me, and only me." She looked up at him, her eyes intense. "I'll make sure you're both taken care of. You obviously love this little guy quite a bit. Usually when someone comes in here with an exotic bird or mammal, and they don't have a permit, the animal is in rough shape or ends up being abandoned here. There's a reason the Academy of Natural Sciences has three fennec foxes and a capybara.

"Now, the bad news is that we will need to keep him for a few days," she said, frowning. "The poison is still in his body, it'll take a day or two before he's back in action, and even then, he's certainly going to be disoriented. He'll probably act like he's drunk." She smiled. "I'd like to keep him under observation and care until he can safely leave."

Landon nodded and then looked down at the leather wing in his hands.

He looked back up at Dr. Saft, and cleared his throat.

"Could you, uh," he cleared his throat again and sniffled. Leila reached out and put a hand on his arm, and he glanced down at her, tears welling in his eyes. "It's silly, but can you put this on him once in a while? Please?"

Dr. Saft took the wing and smiled, putting a consoling hand on Landon's shoulder.

"Don't worry. I will," she said. "Feel free to call anytime." She reached into her white coat and plucked out a business card. "And check up on him. My line is on there. I need to stress, please call only me." She looked at Leila and Landon intently. "We're clear on all of this, right? I don't have to explain anything?"

Leila nodded, and Landon followed suit.

"He's got a big heart, this one," Dr. Saft said, nodding at Landon while looking at Leila. "Hold on to him." Landon looked down at Leila and quickly glanced away, awkwardly, and Leila could feel a bloom of warmth in her face. Dr. Saft winked, and made her way back towards the E.R.

"Wait, Dr. Saft!" Leila exclaimed, taking a step forward. The vet spun around, and looked at her, eyebrows raised. "The owl pellet? With the mouse? Can we have it?"

"Why?" Dr. Saft asked, her eyebrows up.

"The section of the park where Milford ate that mouse is set to be torn down," Leila said, her heart hammering in her chest, "unless we're able to prove there's something special about that place. Supposedly there is an endangered mouse living in the park. That pellet is just what we need."

Dr. Saft's mouth twisted up.

"Sure, I guess," she said, shrugging. "It's barely recognizable. I'm not sure it'll help."

"We'll take anything. Please."

"Alright, I'll see what I can do." She disappeared into the hospital.

"I like her," Leila said, turning back to Landon. He turned and looked down at her, smiling, his eyes still shining with old tears.

"Are you okay?" Landon asked, his hand reaching out towards her face. Leila shrunk back and Landon grimaced. "Sorry, sorry. It's just . . ." His eyes focused on the side of her face, and it was as though Leila could feel his gaze burning into her cheek. She lifted a hand up to the birthmark.

"It's nothing." She exhaled. "I think," she shook her head. "No, it's crazy."

"Leila," Landon said plainly. "Come on. We are past the point where anything—"

"I think I'm changing with the dryads." Leila choked back what felt like a hard cry at revealing what she'd suspected for the past few days. "Every time something outside gets worse: the birthmark, a little bit of my hair. It's like I'm fading with the leaves."

Landon's eyes grew hard.

"We'll stop this, Leila," he said. "I promise." He softened a little as they walked back over to Sarika in the lobby. "But listen, I haven't been totally honest with you. Either of you, really. And—"

"What are these from?" Leila interrupted, taking his hand and brushing her thumb over one of the scars.

Everything was getting too real, and slipping away. The fading magic. The fading owl. She traced the calloused, bubbly, white-pink scar lines on the top of his hand, a welcome distraction.

"Ah," Landon said, taking his hand away and looking at the marks. He gave it right back to her with a soft smile. "Some are from Milford, the others are from accidents out in the park. This one is from slipping with a pocket knife while cutting some twine, this one is definitely a Milford claw, this one here is from a fall out of a tree, and cutting my hand on a saw on the way down."

"Geez," Leila gasped.

"Yeah, it's not all easy work." He grew quiet and squeezed her hand again.

"Leila, look, I have to say something–" he started.

"Oh, just tell her already," Sarika grumbled, staring at her phone.

"What is with you right now?" Leila snapped. "What's on there that's so important?"

"While you two are making kissy faces at one another," Sarika said, sounding exhausted, "I've been looking up reasons a birthmark might spread. Yes, I've noticed, even though you weren't talking about it. I've also been trying to organize the message board to come help us out, and fussing with the social media campaign to make it more about endangered animals and less about the buildings and the history."

She looked up at Landon, her eyes hard.

"But you know about some of that, don't you, Landon?" she asked. "The campaign? The board?"

"Um, how did you . . .?" Landon muttered, looking back and forth between Leila and Sarika, his eyes wide. "This isn't how I wanted to bring this up."

"Landon?" Leila asked, letting go of his hand. "What is it?"

"Look, it's not that big a deal, but–"

"Milford?" Dr. Saft returned from the E.R. and was awkwardly holding a small, plastic case, a displeased look on her face. The container was transparent, and bits of red and brown speckled with white were visible. Leila grimaced as she stood up and walked towards the vet with Landon, not eager to peek inside the plastic container full of fur and blood and bone.

"Ah, there you are." Dr. Saft smiled, holding out the bin with a grimace. "Here, please take it. I see plenty of bones and blood and other gross things every day, but owl vomit is just about my limit."

"Great, great," Landon said, nodding, the enthusiasm gone from his voice.

"Hey, would it make you feel better," Dr. Saft looked around the waiting room and then peeked back in the E.R., "if you got to see him really quick?"

Landon's eyes lit up, and Leila's heart fluttered.

"Thought so." Dr. Saft took another peek. "Let's go."

Landon grabbed Leila's hand, and they followed Dr. Saft into the animal E.R. A handful of other veterinarians were walking up and down the hallways, looking busy and harried, with clipboards or medical gadgets in their hands. They gave Leila and Landon quick glances before continuing on their way to whatever they were doing.

Surgery on iguanas? Casts on broken guinea pig legs? Exotic animal hospitals seemed like a place where odd things happened.

Dr. Saft looked around and opened the door to a small room where Milford lay, sprawled out on a small, beige table with a blanket over his little body. His good wing hung free over the edge of the table. Fluid dripped gently through an IV line.

Landon let go of Leila's hand and brought both of his hands up to his face. His eyes watered. He walked up to the table.

"Careful now," Dr. Saft said. "He needs to rest."

"You know, I . . ." He sighed and shook his head. "I almost named him Toothless," Landon said, standing next to the table.

Leila stared at him.

That name.

Realization washed over her in waves.

"You know, after *How to Train Your Dragon*? When I was little my mom would read me those stories, and I was just obsessed. Did you ever read them? Watch the movie?"

Leila shook her head, as Landon nervously kept talking.

"Well. The main character, Hiccup, he has to help this dragon learn to fly again with a prosthetic wing." Landon reached down and scratched Milford under the chin. The unconscious owl moved its head back slowly, as if in a trance. "I knew the moment I found him that I was going to try to do that, and that name stuck with me for a little bit. But, you know, when it comes to naming owls—"

291

"They should have old man names." Leila finished for him.

Landon nodded and turned away from Milford.

"Toothless. You should have told me," Leila said.

"I didn't figure it out until later," Landon said, shaking his head. "I had my suspicions, after the bicycle and all, but thought it was a coincidence. Lots of people ride bikes around the park. But when you posted on the message board about the protest, that's when it all hit me. And I bailed because I didn't want you to, like, hate me. I haven't been the nicest on there, and we'd only recently started actually talking. On the board, that is."

"I forgive you," Leila said, grabbing his hand.

They stood there quietly for a beat.

"Oooh-kay," Dr. Saft said, grinning. "Clearly something is going on here, but I need you two to get out of here before my cover is blown and I get fired or something. I like your owl, but I also like my job."

Leila and Landon hurried out of the E.R., hand in hand. Sarika sat in the waiting room, staring at her phone, and looked up to glower at the two of them.

"So he told you the deal?" Sarika asked, standing up and shoving her phone in her pocket angrily. "Imagine, our troll, here in real life."

"How did you figure it all out?" Leila asked.

"Do you have any idea how many times I've watched *How to Train Your Dragon* and cried my eyes out?" Sarika said angrily. "I know the book is different, but that movie. That is my movie, Leila. Hell, it is like, *our* movie. Our people's movie. Lonely dragon gets hurt, gets saved, last of his kind, never gets to know his fucking family."

Sarika's eyes started welling up and Leila reached out to hug her. Sarika pushed back.

"No. No, no, no," Sarika muttered, waving her hand about. "Don't do that thing parents do. I'm not that dragon. You're not the dragon. Or the owl. Or the, the . . ."

Leila pulled Sarika in for a hug.

"Nooooooo," Sarika groaned as she squirmed about.

"You know, it was really shitty seeing something that means so much to me used the way you used it, tough guy," Sarika mumbled into Leila's shoulder before looking up at Landon. "Seeing your snippy comments and having you talk down to us under that username? It made it even worse."

"I'm sorry," Landon said, shaking his head. "It's not easy being stuck at home with a family who hates what I care about. And lying about what I'm majoring in. And hiding my schedules. And books. And grades. And clearing my browser history every single time I use the computer."

He shook his head again.

"I just lash out sometimes." He sighed. "I don't mean to hurt anyone. I'm just, I dunno. There's no excuse for it."

Sarika sniffled.

"Well then." She pushed away from Leila and brushed at her jacket. "Let's channel all this rage and all these," she gritted her teeth and shook her head, "ugh, all these emotions into something a bit more practical, shall we?"

"Like what?" Leila asked.

"What else?" Sarika asked, grinning with a shrug. "Coffee."

"I fail to see how coffee is going to solve any of our problems," Leila said, crossing her arms.

"Um, I'm just going to go ahead and ignore that," Sarika said. "I believe it was Aristotle who said, 'Coffee solves all problems.'"

Leila stared at Sarika.

"Whatever, I'm tired, okay?" Sarika said. "And hungry. Let's go to Adam's for some caffeine and food before I waste away into nothingness and become useless on your mission. And that," she pointed at the plastic bin containing all the mouse bits, "that can stay in your car, Toothy."

JON: You two okay? Haven't heard from you all day, it's getting late.

JON: I might have logged onto your message board. I saw you gathering facts. Proud of you.

LEILA: We're okay! Landon the park ranger is with us. Heading to Adam's to plan next steps.

LEILA: And the message board, Jon? Again? Didn't we talk about this?

JON: Just be careful. Those unmaintained bits of park can be a little rough.

LEILA: We have proof of the endangered mouse, but it's dead. Is that okay?

JON: Uh, sure, but try not to kill the endangered animals. What happened? That's a crime, you know. It was an accident, right?

LEILA: Yes! We found it dead. In an owl. It threw it up at the hospital. It's in some Tupperware.

JON: . . .

JON: I mean, I feel like I should be concerned at this point.

JON: I'm seeing a lot of red flags here.

JON: Leila? Anything? Feel free to start with the owl, maybe build up to the hospital.

LEILA: It's a long story. I'll explain more at home.

FROM	SUBJECT	DATE
TOOTHLESS	STARTING OVER Can we maybe give that a shot? Hit reset?	8/27
WITHOUTTHEY	RE: STARTING OVER Are you seriously sending me this while we are at a red light? Also yes.	8/27
TOOTHLESS	RE: STARTING OVER Alright, good. ♥	8/27
WITHOUTTHEY	RE: STARTING OVER I feel like we discussed emoticons and what-not, and how they sometimes can mean a little too much. Careful there, Toothy . . . ;-)	8/27
TOOTHLESS	RE: STARTING OVER ;-) Indeed.	8/27
A DASH OF PAPRIKA	STOP IT BEFORE I THROW MYSELF OUT THE CAR See the above subject.	8/27

XXII

"What. The. Hell. Is. This." Sarika ripped a flier off the wall in Adam's Café and stormed over towards a table. Leila and Landon trailed behind her. She slammed the paper down on the table, her hand slapping the wood with a loud bang. Leila looked around the room. The café was mostly empty, save for a few kids working at the coffee tables, largely undisturbed by the small ruckus.

"Uh, I'll get some coffee and muffins or something," Landon started.

"No, no. This concerns you, too, Toothy," Sarika said, pushing a seat out for him.

"Can you stop—" Landon started.

"Nope. That's your name," Sarika said, sitting down angrily. Landon gave Leila a please-help-me-out look, and Leila smiled, shaking her head. He did this to himself. Sarika held up the flier and looked at them, her eyes hard and angry.

"Listen to this nonsense," she said, and started reading.

Now Accepting Donations
Coming soon to Fairmount Park, a brand-new amphi-theater! Construction is soon to be underway, but you can

help build this modern marvel in the middle of the largest urban park in the country.

For more information, contact Jessica De La Costa, president of the Students for a Progressive Fairmount club. Donations can be dropped off at the principal's office at Belford High School, or sent via PayPal to Jessica De La Costa at BITCHY McBITCHFACE DOT COM—

"Okay, that is not her email address," Landon said.

"It might as well be!" Sarika shouted, tossing the flier back on the table. "She knew this was something we cared about, and that is the only reason she is coming after it. Her and her damn friends. And look!"

She peeled a second flier out from under Jessica's, revealing the faded endangered-mouse sheet from the other day.

"Right over this. Didn't even care."

"Maybe we shouldn't have banned her from the message board," Leila said with a sigh. "She's probably only doing this to get back at Shawn, right?"

"These are some pretty extreme lengths to go to for something like that." Sarika scowled.

"I just don't get it," Leila said, as Landon picked up the flier. "What does she get out of this?"

"It makes me so angry," Sarika spat, snatching the flier out of Landon's hand with a loud smack. She stood up and marched to the register, leaning over on the countertop. "Mr. Hathaway! You in the kitchen? Where are you?"

In a flurry of pots and pans, Mr. Hathaway materialized in the kitchen door.

"Sarika!" he exclaimed. "What is it? It's a weekday, you're usually not here on . . . God, please don't tell me you tweeted you were gonna be here, we've got programs lined up for some of the kids, and–"

"No, no." Sarika shook her head. "Just taking a break from running about. Why did you let her hang these fliers up?" She handed him the sheet, and he looked at it, puzzled.

"What's wrong with Jessica?" he asked in confusion as he handed the flier back.

"What's wrong with Jessica?" Sarika looked back at Leila and Landon and threw her arms up in the air. Leila shrugged back in response. "She's the enemy!"

"No," Adam said, shaking his head. "If anything, she should be your best friend."

"What?" Sarika shouted. "Hell, no."

"Uh, yeah? Her father, Jonathan De La Costa, owns the nonprofit that helps fund us. Hell, he helps fund a bunch of things throughout the city. He works with the park service and some of the thrift stores, I think. He was with her when she dropped off that flier and even asked for you. Guy loves your coffee."

Sarika grabbed the countertop as though she was steadying herself.

Leila jumped to her feet and darted over, and Sarika leaned against her.

"I've been making drinks," Sarika started.

"Sarika–"

"For that chick's *father*?"

"Come on."

"For how long?" Sarika stormed to a nearby barstool at the countertop. "I could have been spitting in it all this time! Does he get coffee for her, too? Tea? Soda? What? Anything? Let me know so I can make sure whatever she's getting is contaminated to all hell. I will cough on everything!"

Sarika laid her head down on the countertop, her arms folded in front of her.

"Hey," Leila ventured, pulling a barstool up next to her. Sarika heaved an ugly sob, her shoulders shaking. "Hey, come on now. It's okay."

Sarika looked up at her, her eyes red and face already wet with tears.

"No, it's not okay," Sarika said, a sob in the back of her throat. "This is my thing. My one thing. And she's been a part of it the entire time, and I had no idea. I built my whole . . . my whole persona here. Me. This place is me. And her family owns it."

"Okay, first of all, I own this place," Mr. Hathaway said from behind the counter. "They help *fund* it. Remember, nonprofit? You should be happy. Hell, and . . ." he looked at Leila as though he was thinking. "And Leila's father," he paused, as if testing the waters. Clearly he'd been around enough adopted kids that he knew how to tiptoe, and Leila appreciated it no matter how awkward it got. "Leila's father must know him; doesn't he work with those people?"

Sarika's eyes went wide as she looked up at Leila.

"If Jon's on a board with Jessica's father," Sarika started, and then glanced over at Mr. Hathaway. "Thanks for listening, sorry about the meltdown."

"Don't even worry about it," he said, shrugging. He turned and walked back into the little kitchen.

Sarika looked back at Leila, and walked back over to the table where Landon still sat. Leila could practically see the gears turning in Sarika's head before she spoke.

"Okay. So. If Jon works with Jessica's dad in some sort of way, he can tell him about *this* nonsense." She shook the flier. "About how Jessica doesn't really care, it's just to get back at–"

"What will that even do? I doubt her little collection is making any kind of dent." Leila held up one of the crumpled fliers. "This isn't for her or for the cause. She made it for us. To make us angry and derail us."

"Fine!" Sarika said, standing back up. "Then we head over to the horticulture society or the park service offices, present the evidence, get the project shut down, and then we savor the sweet tears of Jessica De La Costa!"

"Hey," Leila said, angling herself to look Sarika in the eyes. "Let's not forget what this is about. If we can take her down a peg, awesome. To hell with that girl. But, you know, we have a city to save?"

"I know none of us want to say it, but," Landon cleared his throat, "some*one* to save as well."

Leila felt herself blush, and ran her hand along the pale patch of skin on her face, her expanding birthmark. Sarika exhaled, sighing.

"Okay," Sarika said, nodding. "Okay, yeah. Save the world, screw the girl."

Leila made a face.

"Not you, I mean Jessica. Look, I'll figure out a better tagline for the mission, I swear."

"So," Leila said. "Let's focus for a minute. We came here to plan, right? So let's plan."

"We've got a few more days until the protest," she continued. "Between then and now, they could still do more damage to the park. More spray paint, more shrub removal."

"And in the meantime, this could all affect Leila." Landon grimaced and shook his head, looking at Leila with an apology in his eyes.

"Well," Leila sucked air through her teeth, trying to ignore what Landon said. "We've got the mouse, or most of it. We can take it to Jon, and he can help us frame this story when we report what's going on."

Landon got up and paced, rubbing his hand over his chin. Leila could hear the scuff against his hand.

"I'm still worried," he said, turning back. "We can't prove that the mouse came from this specific patch of woods, not after going through Milford's digestive system. He's an owl. They fly around, or at least most of them do. Maybe they could examine the dirt on it or something, but I can't imagine the timing working out right."

Landon suddenly perked up.

"Shit, just how well sealed is the Tupperware in my car with that mouse in it?" he asked.

"That is not going to smell good when someone opens it," Sarika said.

"When you open it," Landon said.

"When you open it," Sarika said, looking at Leila.

"Okay, enough of that," Leila said, shaking her head. "When the poor researcher or person at the museum has to open it. How about that?"

"Deal," Landon said, smiling.

"Now, what do we need?" Leila drummed her fingers against the table. "We probably need photos or video of the mouse in that particular area. Right?"

"Three days," Landon exhaled, "to get a photo of a rare mouse in a large section of a heavily wooded area of the park when no one else could before."

"Maybe chill with the cynicism?" Sarika snapped. "Three days is a lot of time. We've all got cameras on our phones and I'm pretty sure my parents have a digital camcorder at home."

"So, do we camp out in the woods?" Leila asked.

"It's an option." Landon shrugged.

"Three days." Leila nodded, folding her arms. "I say we sleep on it tonight, visit the museum in the morning with the mouse remains, and go to the grove in the afternoon."

"And if the remains aren't good enough, trapping a mouse might not be that difficult."

"Trapping one?" Leila asked. "Landon, we need something that's alive, you know. That's the reason we're stressing over this dead mouse."

"The one currently baking in the sun in your car," Sarika grinned.

"We wouldn't kill the mouse," Landon said, after glaring at Sarika. "You can totally build a trap that catches them alive. I used to put little wooden ramps on deep, glass aquariums when I was a kid to catch chipmunks and mice in my parents' old yard. They hop in and can't get out. We'd keep them for a day or two, feed them and stuff."

Leila smiled.

"You're cute. That's cute," Leila said, and then blinked, looking over at Sarika. Sarika's mouth was a thin line and her eyes were tired.

"Gross," she said. "The two of you. Just gross."

"Sorry," Leila said, laughing. "Okay. Mouse trap."

"Mouse trap." Landon nodded.

"And what if that doesn't work?" Sarika asked. "Like, don't you think the people researching the area already tried this?"

"Well, that's what we've got." Leila shrugged. "Bring the dead mouse to the expert, try to catch a live one. I don't have much else here."

A bloom of anxiety rushed up through Leila, and panic threatened to take over. What else could they do? What else could they possibly do?

"Hey." Sarika reached out. "We'll try. Right? That's all we can do."

Leila exhaled.

"Let's go."

PROVIDING ENDANGERED ANIMAL EVIDENCE (HELP?)

Posted by A Dash of Paprika

AUGUST 27th, 2017 | 5:02PM

Hey all! One of the key things we need to do in the next few days is dig up some evidence that endangered animals exist around the mansion, the gardens, and the grove. WithouttheY and I are looking for a mouse, because that's the hardest animal to find.

Anyone have any tips? Toothless suggested building a live trap. It's a Southeastern Pennsylvania, field mouse, if that helps. We have evidence that they live in the park, but a live one will really help us prove our point, it seems.

RE: PROVIDING ENDANGERED ANIMAL EVIDENCE (HELP?)

Posted by Dr. Cordova

AUGUST 27th, 2017 | 6:09PM

Hey, Paprika. I have a Google Alert set up for that mouse, as my life is very exciting, and a friend in University City mentioned seeing evidence of one come through her vet office, but I couldn't get a comment on it from anyone. I'm sending you a DM.

RE: PROVIDING ENDANGERED ANIMAL
EVIDENCE (HELP?)
Posted by A Dash of Paprika
AUGUST 27th, 2017 | 6:17PM
OH MY GOD WHAT REALLY. I'LL MESSAGE
YOU NOW! THANK YOU!

RE: PROVIDING ENDANGERED ANIMAL EVIDENCE
(HELP?)
Posted by JessicaLa99
AUGUST 27th, 2017 | 7:00PM
Enjoy your shitty building and old-ass trees while
you can. Tick tock.

RE: PROVIDING ENDANGERED ANIMAL
EVIDENCE (HELP?)
Posted by A Dash of Paprika
AUGUST 27th, 2017 | 7:15PM
You know what, I'm not even going to ban you
this time. I've sent you a photo of a dumpster
on fire. That's you. You're a dumpster fire of a
person.

FROM	SUBJECT	DATE
DR. CORDOVA	ABOUT THAT MOUSE Hi Paprika, hi WithouttheY, When you started sounding off about the possible endangered mouse in the region, I picked up on it right away. My team of conservationists and I at the Academy of Natural Sciences have been monitoring the endangered and at-risk animals in the park for some time now, and anything posing a risk to areas that they call home is of course the subject of immediate concern. What evidence do you have that the mice are in the park?	8/27

WITHOUTTHEY	RE: ABOUT THAT MOUSE Hi Dr. Cordova! We're so happy to hear from you but, well, the evidence we have is a dead mouse, unfortunately.	8/27
A DASH OF PAPRIKA	RE: ABOUT THAT MOUSE Our friend's owl ate it and threw it up, and there was poison on it.	8/27
DR. CORDOVA	RE: ABOUT THAT MOUSE I'm less weirded out about the owl and the friend who owns one, than I am about the poison. You're sure?	8/27
WITHOUTTHEY	RE: ABOUT THAT MOUSE Positive. It almost killed his owl. He'll pull through. The owl. The friend, too.	8/27

DR. CORDOVA	RE: ABOUT THAT MOUSE	8/27
	That's good, on all accounts. The poison though, that's worrisome, especially in that area. There shouldn't be any poison anywhere near those grounds. We want to see whatever is left of that mouse, and if you find anything in the woods over the next day like you're planning, swing by immediately. I'll get a team ready to come out to investigate and see if we can halt the construction over the next few days. You can drop off the remains tonight; I'm staying here late, if you're available. It's the Thomas Mansion area, yes? Just confirming.	

WITHOUTTHEY	RE: ABOUT THAT MOUSE This is amazing news, thank you Dr. Cordova! And yes, the Thomas Mansion. There's a garden in the back, and through that, you'll find the path to the big grove with the old trees.	8/27
A DASH OF PAPRIKA	RE: ABOUT THAT MOUSE Yes, thank you! Just echo-ing what WithouttheY said. Happy to have you on our team. We'll be right over.	8/27

XXIII

"Long day," Landon said as his truck slowed down in front of Leila's house, the little blue dot on his smartphone's GPS stopping as they did. The truck still had the faint smell of decomposing, partially digested mouse, from when Sarika accidentally opened the container after hitting a bump on the drive to the museum.

"Are we really reduced to small talk already?" Leila asked, grinning.

"Ah, geez," Landon mumbled, running his hand over the back of his head. He turned the key in the ignition, and his truck's rumbling faded into the warm evening. "I'm just not the best at this, okay?" He smiled awkwardly and shrugged.

He reached over and put his hand on hers. She flinched, closing her hand, and then put it back, grabbing his. She felt a momentary push against what she wanted to do, a tension rising in her chest, and willed it to go away. Then she leaned over the middle of the car and kissed him on the cheek, his stubble scratching against her face.

She sat back, unbuckled her seatbelt, and pulled out her phone.

"Damn."

"Is it bad?"

"It's five-missed-calls bad."

"Oof." Landon opened his door, hopped out of the truck, and walked around the front. He looked at Leila through the large window, gave her a wink, and then opened the passenger-side door. "Well, after you."

"What?" Leila asked, looking at him incredulously. "What are you doing?"

"Um, walking you to the door?" He shrugged and held out a hand.

Leila blushed and took it. Her hand felt small in his large, rough grip. She hopped out of the truck, stumbled a little on something in the road, and landed pressed up against Landon with her hands on his chest. She looked up and caught him smiling down at her, his teeth bright white, his eyes playful. Her feet shifted, and the noise of something crunching caused her to look down.

Leaves were scattered everywhere, deep enough to hide her feet, twigs and small branches all around her. She looked down the street and gasped.

"Now that is bad," Landon said, his tone soft and afraid.

All the trees along the usually green street that Liz and Jon lived on were completely bare. The trees reached towards the sky, their empty branches like skeletons, empty of anything. The streets were full of leaves, all brown or faded yellow, crumbling away.

"Everything is dying," Leila said.

"Not everything," Landon said firmly. He turned to her and put his arms on her shoulders. "We've got time. We can fix this."

Leila exhaled and grabbed Landon's hand, pulling him along, tugging him toward the house.

"Hey, wait. I'm supposed to walk *you* to the front door," Landon said, pulling back a little.

"Maybe I'm taking you to meet the . . ." Leila stopped, searching. "Meet the parents." She shook her head, it still felt weird, but not as weird as it'd been. "Jon and Liz. I told Jon about you. Maybe if they see you I won't be in five-missed-calls-trouble, and will only be in late-because-you-met-a-nice-boy-that-wants-to-save-the-Earth trouble."

She was walking up the small front steps on the stoop that led into the old brownstone when Landon stopped walking.

"Landon, what—"

She turned around, and now, standing on the step, she was almost looking at Landon face-to-face. He smiled, lowering his head a little, and looked up at her with his deep-brown eyes. He bit his lip before he spoke.

"It's nice to see you," he grinned. "You know, up here."

"Shut up," Leila laughed, pushing him a little.

And then his arm reached out, and his hand found the back of her neck, his fingers slipping through her thick, black curls. She gasped, fighting the urge to stiffen up, to push away, and he quickly let go and stepped back.

"I'm . . . I'm sorry," Landon said, his eyes wide. "I just thought, you know, the moment felt right, and—"

Leila jumped off the stoop and grabbed Landon's jacket, pulling him back towards the stairs.

"Wha—" he started, as Leila stepped back up on the

step. Now face-to-face again, she pulled him towards her, tugging on the thick leather of his jacket. Her mouth found his, and he kissed her back, his hand finding its way to her neck again, his fingers inching their way up through her hair.

Landon gasped, pulling away from the kiss, and stumbled back once more.

"What?" Leila asked, stepping off the stoop. "It's okay, I'm sorry, I—"

Landon held up his hand, his eyes wide.

In the fading dusk, Leila saw a large patch of hair in his hands.

Black, wild, full of curls.

Leila moved her hand up along the back of her head. Where she normally had hair, she now felt a missing patch, the hair gone and her skin smooth. A few odd splotches of hair remained, like someone had shaved her head with a dull blade. She ran her fingers toward the top of her head, and when she pulled away, a hefty part of her hair came with it.

"Leila?" Landon ventured, taking a step forward.

She screamed, the hair tumbling from her hands, as Landon reached the stairs. The lights in her home lit up and the front door quickly swung back.

"Wh-what's happening to me?" Leila screamed, looking at Landon frantically. Landon looked up, his eyes connecting with someone in back of her, and before she could turn to see who it was, Jon bounded down the stairs.

"Get off of her!" Jon shouted, shoving Landon, who

stumbled and fell back on the sidewalk leading to the house.

"Jon! No!" Leila shouted, her sobs still stuck in her throat.

"Leila, get inside!" Lisabeth's voice exclaimed. Her hands appeared suddenly on Leila's shoulders, tugging her inside the home.

Landon got to his feet and held out his hand, his palms up. He stepped back, clearly trying to calm Jon down. Leila could see the thin, white scars on his palms, the puffy lines along his forearms, as his jacket shifted up.

"Who are you? What did you do to my daughter?" Jon shouted, taking another step toward Landon.

"Liz, let me go! Jon!" Leila shouted, wrestling free from Lisabeth. "Jon, stop it!" She grabbed Jon's arm, tugging back at him. "That's Landon, that's the guy I was talking about."

Jon looked at Leila, and her heart felt like it was going to stop. Instead of fury in his eyes, instead of a red-faced, rage-filled man, she saw him full of . . . terror. He looked terrified. His eyes glassed over and his mouth quivered as though he were about to cry. He softened, and threw his arms around Leila, hugging her in tightly, his face burying itself against her neck.

"Jon, careful, I—" Leila started.

"I'm sorry, oh God, I'm sorry, I was so worried, you hadn't called us back today, and I . . ." he drifted off and looked up at Landon. "Oh, oh my, I don't even know what to say right now. I'm so embarrassed. Can I hug you, too? Is that weird?"

Landon looked over at Leila, and she urged him on with a look, nodding her head towards Jon. Landon made a face and walked over towards them, and Jon awkwardly hugged the two of them at once.

Landon stepped away.

"It's okay, I'm fine," Landon said, nodding at Jon. He walked back to Leila. "Are you okay?"

"What happened?" Liz asked, stepping down the front steps.

"Yes, why the screaming?" Jon pressed, moving closer to them. Leila gently pushed away from Landon, her breath quick, her heart pounding.

"I . . . I don't know what's happening," Leila said, the rush of the confrontation fading into the back of her mind, replaced with the fact that her hair had just fallen out in Landon's hands. "One moment we were," she looked up at Landon, who promptly stared down at his feet. "It just fell out." She looked up at Jon, who stared at her with worry. "Oh, God."

She reached up and wiped long strands of hair off of Jon's face, her curls stuck on his cheek and chin and neck from hugging her.

"Come on, let's get inside," Jon, hugging Leila from the side. "Whatever it is, it'll be okay. It'll be—"

Jon's eyes went wide.

Leila felt it.

The odd feeling of movement on top of her head, of something not quite being rooted the way it was supposed to, like a loose tooth coming undone or an old fingernail falling off. Of something there, and then suddenly completely gone.

With a terrible, heart-wrenching, slick sound, Leila felt the curls slide off the top of her head and fall in a pile around her feet. She took a step back and lifted a hand to her head, running her palm over the smooth surface. Bits of hair still clung here and there, but for the most part, it was utterly gone.

Leila looked up at Jon, her heart racing, panic surging through her.

"D-Dad?" she muttered. She lost her footing, feeling woozy, and Jon quickly grabbed her and held her up.

"Liz!" Jon shouted, the sound of a sob in the back of his throat forced down as he yelled.

"Hospital! Now!" Liz yelled.

"Come on, my keys are still in the truck," Landon said. "Plus, I've got some emergency lights for the roof."

Leila felt Jon rushing her forward, and she clumsily pressed her feet against the ground, trying to walk. Lisabeth came up behind them and wrapped an arm around her waist. Jon placed her in the passenger seat of Landon's truck and closed the door behind her.

"No, don't, Dad, don't leave," Leila said, watching Jon move away from the window. Jon bolted back to her, and reached in, grabbing her hands.

"We'll be right behind you. Right behind you," Jon said, his eyes hard and focused. Intense. He looked to Landon. "Drive safe, that's my daughter you've got in there."

He let go of Leila's hand, and she leaned back in the car seat and closed her eyes.

She wondered if this was how the trees felt.

XXIV

"Honestly, we'll have to do a few more tests," the nurse said, standing at the side of Leila's hospital bed with a clipboard in her hand. She looked a lot like the veterinarian, Dr. Saft, only with lighter hair and wrinkles along the edges of her eyes, like someone who spent a lot of time wincing at things and hearing bad news. "But we're having a hard time finding anything really wrong that would have led to the hair loss."

"Kids don't just lose a full head of hair when they are perfectly healthy," Lisabeth said, sitting in a teal, cushioned chair next to the bed. Jon stood next to her, his arms crossed, leaning against the wall. Leila turned to Liz and noticed her red eyes and tired face. She'd clearly been there all night. "It has to be something."

"We're going to run some more tests. The first blood sample came back contaminated with . . ." she flipped through pages on her clipboard and shook her head. "Well, there was an error. But right now we see no reason why she can't go home later this afternoon while we review her lab results."

"Home?" Lisabeth stood up so quickly the chair squeaked across the floor. "Are you fucking kidding me? Something is wrong here."

"Liz," Jon said, his tone quiet and comforting. "Come on, now—"

"Don't," Lisabeth said, turning to him, one finger up to shush him.

"Listen, Mrs. Kline, we genuinely see no reason to keep her here right now. We're going to wrap up some tests, and we can likely discharge her later in the day. It could be a late-stage advancement of what might be vitiligo, if that's what the birthmark on her face is. Late color loss and alopecia is a possibility. Or it could be exposure to some kind of chemical. We'll figure this all out in the lab work, but right now, the best thing for her is a lot of rest."

"Is there a mirror? Can one of you show me a mirror?" Leila asked, stretching. She looked around, and scowled. "Did Landon leave?"

"He *just* left, darling," Lisabeth said, fishing in her purse and handing Leila a small compact mirror.

Leila flipped open the mirror. She gasped at her reflection. She was bald. At least, practically bald. Bits of hair still clung here and there, but they were just little wisps. The birthmark on her cheek seemed to have grown even more. It looked like it pushed up from her cheek and moved up along her scalp above her ear. Had it always been this big, just hidden under her hair?

"Fuck," Leila said, snapping the mirror shut, tears welling up in her eyes. "What the hell is going on?"

"That's what we're trying to find out," the nurse said. "But like I said, head home. Get some rest. And drink lots of fluids. You were terribly dehydrated when you came in."

"I was?" Leila asked, looking to Lisabeth, who nodded.

"That's why you fainted, they think," Liz said, shrugging. Something buzzed and Liz pulled her phone out of her pocket. A smile crept over her face. She looked up at Leila, warmly, and showed the phone to Jon, who smiled.

"You have really good friends, you know that?" He grinned.

"What is it?" Leila asked.

"Sarika. Asking for you." Liz pointed at the table next to Leila's hospital bed. "Your phone died while we were in here, and she's been texting me for updates like every other hour."

She texted something back, and the phone immediately buzzed. She looked back at it and sighed.

"Alright," Liz said, nodding. "I guess let's get you home. Sarika and Landon are planning to meet us at the house."

Leila stretched and pushed her legs over the side of the bed, preparing to stand up, when she stopped and looked at the nurse, who stood there keeping a watchful eye on the whole scene.

"Question," Leila said, as Liz handed her some clothes to replace the old ones from yesterday.

"Hm? What is it?" the nurse asked. Her warm, practiced smile returned.

"What was the weird thing that came up in the blood work?" Leila asked, nodding at the clipboard, her heart hammering in her chest. "What was so weird about it?"

The nurse let out a laugh and shook her head.

"I'm sorry, I shouldn't laugh, but it's pretty bizarre. Have a look." She flipped to a page towards the back, and handed the clipboard to Leila. Liz quickly walked around to the side of the bed to peer down at it.

"There," the nurse pointed at the bottom of the sheet.

"Wow. Yeah, that is weird," Liz said, shaking her head.

Leila's heart beat madly as she stared at the word, written large in looping, sloppy handwriting, the sign of a doctor in a rush.

Chlorophyll.

SEARCH

ALL   IMAGE   SHOPPING   NEWS   VIDEO

Search: Weather in Philadelphia

In the News:

CDC Investigating Massive Fish Die-Off in Philadelphia Water System

GRID Philadelphia – One day ago

After massive numbers of dead fish appeared in the Schuylkill River, resulting in halted water traffic and panic from Philadelphia residents over drinking water, the CDC has. . .

Philadelphia Horticulture Society Baffled by Tree Sickness

Philadelphia Magazine – Two hours ago.

As the trees in Philadelphia continue to shed their leaves far earlier than expected, it's become less of a surprise shift to fall weather and more of a sign of a potential environmental crisis . . .

Audubon Society Expresses Concern Over Sudden Bird Migration

Philly.com – 20 minutes ago.

"Birds are leaving the city in droves in surprise migrations that don't match any natural patterns,"

a representative of the Audubon Society said.
"Something is wrong, and we. . .

Philadelphia, PA
Thursday, 10:15AM
Partly Cloudy
78 F | C

Philadelphia, PA Weather
https://weather.com/weather/today/.../
Philadelphia. . .
Weather Around the Area. . .

XXV

"I am not happy about any of this," Leila said, staring at the selection on the kitchen table.

"Come on, try one," Sarika said, nudging Leila playfully. "You might like it."

"I'm going to throw up," Leila sighed, "but okay."

The wigs sat neatly in a row on the small kitchen table inside Jon and Lisabeth's home. It looked like four little animals had broken into the kitchen, eaten their fill, and were now napping on the wooden surface, snuggled together in the sun that peeked through the window. One was black and curly, a small afro, and looked strikingly similar to the hair Leila had just a day ago. Two looked the way her hair did when it was straightened, long and thick, the hair pressed together tightly. And the last was a horrible-looking thing, full of different colors. Red and blonde streaks weaved in and out of each strand.

"I can guess who picked that one out," Lisabeth said, crossing her arms.

"I thought it looked fun!" Jon exclaimed defensively.

Leila let out a soft laugh, and moved to pick up the natural, curly wig.

"Try one of the other ones, for me?" Sarika begged.

"Who knows, Landon might like you with straight, pressed hair." She winked.

"I'll be lucky if he's into me at all anymore," Leila sighed, grabbing the curly wig. She pushed it down on her head. It was itchy against her now-bald head. She fussed with it, picked up a mirror sitting on the table, and looked at her reflection.

"You look great," Sarika said, smiling.

"Sure," Leila scoffed, and pulled out one of the kitchen seats. She sat down and laid her head on the table, trying to hold back the sobs that threatened to come out.

"Hey," Sarika said, rubbing her back. Other hands joined in, and Leila looked off to the side to spot Jon and Liz, their eyes full of worry. "Will it make you feel better if I said we were gonna save the park?"

Leila sat back up.

"Oh?" Leila asked, a smile on her face. "I was worried. We lost like, an entire day."

"Well, that's not quite what we told you, Sarika," Jon said, pulling out a chair from the table. "This morning, while your moth—" he stopped, and shook his head. Leila's heart hammered at the change of word, and she thought about speaking up. It had felt . . . okay. It felt right. She stopped herself from saying anything.

"While Liz was out with you at the hospital, Landon and I went down to the Academy of Natural Sciences to get some more information on the mouse remains and check up on his super-illegal, but still very cute, owl at the animal hospital." Jon laughed softly. "And, you know, so I could apologize profusely and beg his forgiveness again."

"And?" Leila asked, warmth returning to her.

"Well, it's complicated. He's at least forgiven me, though," Jon said, nodding and looking up at Lisabeth. "They can't really be sure the mouse is from the park. It's far too, well, eaten. It'll take too long to analyze the soil, and even *that* is contaminated because of the poison in the fur. Your best bet is to head back to the grove and try to catch one of the mice or find some droppings. But even then . . ."

Jon shook his head.

"Leila, construction and demolition of that mansion is set to happen on Friday," Jon said solemnly. "Today is Wednesday. Even with this additional push from you and the club to turn up that endangered mouse, even with the backing of the museum and scientists, it'll take weeks to prove anything unless the evidence is right in front of the developers' faces. Or, even better, in the press."

"So nothing we do matters," Leila said bluntly, adjusting her itchy wig.

"Well, no, that's not really what I said," Jon continued. "If you can find evidence of the mice in the park, we can save it. People from the academy were there all day today, though, as were a few people from Mr. De La Costa's office—"

"What!" Sarika shouted.

"Okay. The two of you need to understand something about him and his people," Jon said calmly. "They aren't the enemy in all of this. They really aren't. There's no proof of that mouse. They have been searching for months and haven't turned up a thing. With this renewed interest, especially with the museum jumping in, they're back at it, but it's only going to go on for so long. If they don't find anything, well, there isn't much we can do, and they'll tear it all down to make room for the amphitheater construction.

"But it isn't all bad!" Jon exclaimed. "I heard they are going to have a greenhouse by the theater, which is going to harbor rare, native plants that need to be reintroduced to Pennsylvania and the countryside. Trees that have died out or plants that are in danger, like wildflowers. You'd be surprised how many plants are in danger. It might be good for the city, considering what's going on."

Leila resisted the urge to roll her eyes.

The irony of it all was so thick, it was almost painful.

Destroying a grove with magical creatures that sustained the entire region to build a greenhouse to save a few rare plants and animals who would end up dying anyway.

Leila stood up and pushed her chair in. Her head still pounded with a dull ache from her bike accident, and she still felt a bit woozy from all the drugs at the hospital. She held her balance, pressing against the chair.

"So," Leila said, exhaling. "Two days to find the animals."

"Yes, but remember—" Jon started.

"No guarantees," Leila finished flatly. "You don't have to tell me that, Jon." She laughed. "I've been dealing with a whole life of *no guarantees* since I was born." She turned to Sarika. "To the grove? Call up Landon?"

"Yeah, I guess." Sarika shrugged. "I mean, if we're going to help them find any proof, it'll have to be—"

A soft sob echoed through the kitchen. Sarika's eyes went wide for a moment, and then she caught Leila's eye and bit her lip. She moved her chin slightly to tell Leila to turn around.

Lisabeth had her head in her hands, her elbows on the kitchen table and her face buried in her palms. Jon reached over and took one of her hands and she looked up at him, her face glistening with tears and her eyes already red. When she looked at Leila, her face turned up in pain and she closed her eyes. Liz turned her face back down at the table.

"Liz, what—" Leila started.

Lisabeth held up a hand at her, shaking it dismissively.

"I'm fine, it's fine," she muttered. She wiped at her face and sniffled loudly, clearing her throat. "Just, you know, happy you're okay." Jon cocked his head to the side and looked at Lisabeth with a warm expression, his smile soft and his eyes glistening. He wiped another tear off her face, and turned to Leila, his eyebrows up.

His expression said You know what this is really about. You know.

"I'm . . . no," Leila said, taking a step towards Lisabeth and Jon. "No, I'm sorry. I didn't mean that. The 'no guarantees' stuff."

"Oh, no, darling it's not about that," Lisabeth started, sniffling. Jon still had that look.

"But it is . . . you don't have to, you know, be all careful with what you say around me, when most of the time I'm not careful about what I say around you. It's just been a hard few days, is all. I mean, I have a wig on right now, you guys."

"I just . . ." Lisabeth looked up at Jon, and Leila could see her squeezing his hands, their hands shaking together. "I just try so hard. I do." She pressed her face into her hands again, and Jon reached across the table to rub her shoulder.

"I just want to be a good mom," Lisabeth choked out.

"Oh, Liz . . ." Jon said. He wrapped his arms around her from behind her chair, and she snuggled her head into his forearms.

Leila could feel the anxiety rushing through her, the pressure in her chest.

"Do something," Sarika whispered.

Leila took a careful step towards Jon and Liz, and then another.

The urge to turn and run out of the room, to escape through the house and out the door, to hide someplace, any place other than here, was almost overwhelming.

The voice.

The dryad's voice in the woods.

It didn't come. She didn't speak. Karayea didn't insert herself into the moment, or insist that she was her mother. If there was ever a moment to dispute this, to chime in, to actually say something that wasn't just her asking for something from Leila, this would be the time. The time to say no. It's me. I'm your mother.

But she wasn't.

And she hadn't been for a long time.

Leila took another step and opened her arms. She could feel them shaking as she reached out, and gingerly wrapped them around Liz, wedging her right arm between her and Jon. Liz turned away from her husband's arms and wrapped her arms around Leila, pulling her tightly.

"I just love you so much," Lisabeth said. "When your hair fell out, and the bike accident, my heart, my heart stopped."

Leila's heart raced, her breath came in quick bursts. "I . . ."

And the wall broke. For the woman who wouldn't stop trying, no matter how much Leila pushed back. No matter what passive aggressive remarks she made, or how many dinners she blew off to go out with her friends, to hide in the coffee shop or sulk in the gardens. No matter how often these past few weeks she closed her eyes, listening to the whispers of the woman who called her daughter on the wind, the woman who gave birth to her was most certainly not her mother.

"I love you, too," Leila whispered.

Lisabeth looked up at Leila and a smile beamed over her face, still slick with tears. Leila's lip quivered. She glanced out the kitchen window at Major Willow in the yard. Not all the leaves had fallen yet. She wasn't willing to give up. She was still fighting.

Leila looked back to Lisabeth, and exhaled.

"Mom."

XXVI

"Mouse trap?"

"Check."

"Bait for the trap?"

"Also check."

"A kiss for me, a literally magical creature?"

"Che–"

"I swear to God, I am not hanging out with you two anymore!" Sarika shouted as Leila walked down the long, wooden path towards the mansion with Landon. He carried two glass aquariums under his arms, with small planks of wood inside that clattered about as they walked, perfect for making simple ramps into the tanks. A jar of peanut butter rolled back and forth with each step, making soft *thunk* sounds against the glass panes.

Leila walked next to him, her hands feeling strangely empty without his. He leaned over, despite the crazy amount of materials in his arms, and kissed her on the cheek.

"Check."

"Has the world ended yet?" Sarika asked as they continued forward. "Maybe let's stop this quest. Let it all just fade away. I've done what I need to do in this life."

Leila slowed down and walked next to Sarika, letting

Landon taking the lead with his arms wrapped around all the materials. He'd insisted he carry it all solo, leaving Leila and Sarika to casually stroll their way along the path.

A soft breeze picked up and the trees that lined the path towards the mansion and the grove rustled, a gentle *swoosh* through empty branches and the leaves that laid all along the ground. Leila closed her eyes as the rush of cool air tickled her skin, then sighed. The way the wind tickled her hair, the way it flowed through her thick curls . . . it was gone. She adjusted her wig with her free hand.

She stopped and shut her eyes tightly.

Waiting.

"Anything?" Sarika asked, letting go. Leila could feel her taking a step ahead, and listened as the jostling of Landon's tanks and materials stopped.

"Leila?" Landon called from a little bit away.

"It's fine, I'm fine," Leila said, breathing in and out slowly. She shook her head and opened her eyes, rejoining Sarika, looping her arm through hers as they continued towards the end of the trail. "It's just weird, you know? All the trees are empty. The birds are quiet. And the whispering? Nothing. I thought I'd hear at least something." She sighed loudly. "God, I hope they didn't—"

"Don't even think it," Sarika said firmly. "Come on."

They moved faster, hurrying towards the end of the trail. Soon they caught up with Landon, who had kept up a pretty quick pace despite all he carried. The developers had clearly been through the area again. The pathway that was once so narrow, and that had been lightly trimmed and marked before, was now several feet wide, large enough for a car to rumble down.

A twinge of pain hit Leila somewhere inside her chest and she stopped walking and placed her hand over her sternum. She breathed in slowly, feeling woozy again, the way she had when her hair fell out.

"What is it?" Sarika asked. They had reached the end of the trail, and the large, broken-down mansion came into view. In the late afternoon (or "golden hour" as Shawn had called it on that awkward, poorly planned first date) it looked far more beautiful than ever. The sun cast a faint glow on the stone face, illuminating the small details that were crumbling, but still holding on tight. More of the plants and shrubbery in the area had been cleared out. The ones that remained were brown, dying, and something else was . . . off.

Leila shook her head and looked down at the ground. The patches of dirt visible through littering of leaves looked strangely lighter, paler almost.

"I don't know," Leila said. She felt nauseous, the discomfort flowing over her and nestling itself in the pit of her stomach like a rock.

Landon stopped abruptly and turned to Leila and Sarika.

"Someone's still here!" he whisper-shouted, his eyes wide. He looked around, set the aquariums down, then darted towards the mansion. He motioned to Leila and Sarika.

"Come on!"

Sarika grabbed Leila's hand and they hurried into the

crumbling building. The inside was full of dirt and over-grown plants tucked into cracks and bursting through the shattered windows. Even the leaves in here had faded to brown, but their stems and small branches were white with death, like bleached bones. Each step left Leila feeling short of breath, and as she pressed herself against the mansion's old, crumbling stone walls, she winced, feeling sore all over.

"Something—something isn't right," Leila said, start-ing to feel breathless. "The plants . . . everything around here . . ." Landon and Sarika hurried to her side. A pain shot through Leila's stomach and she doubled over with a grimace. "I think . . . we are too late. . . ."

Landon peered over her shoulder to look at some-thing past her, and his eyes went wide, his expression turned furious.

He practically snarled at Sarika, "Keep an eye on her, I'll be right back." And then he looked right into Leila's eyes. "You hear me? I'll be right back. I'm not going anywhere."

Leila waved him off, letting herself slide down the wall and onto the floor. Sarika knelt down and wrapped her arms around her.

"Hey! What do you think you're doing? I'm talking to you!" Landon shouted from somewhere outside the crumbling mansion, his voice fading as he moved farther away. Leila tried to push herself to her feet to look out the shattered window at what was happening outside, but the movement made her cover her own mouth to stop herself from shrieking.

"Don't, don't," Sarika said softly. She stood up slowly

and looked out the window, standing on her tiptoes and leaning against the wall. "He's chasing someone."

"Get back here!" Landon yelled from farther away. A few additional unintelligible shouts carried on the wind as Sarika sunk back down and nuzzled Leila. Leila's head was still throbbing with pain, and now her stomach was, too. It radiated throughout her body.

Leila closed her eyes, breathing in slowly, and listened. Nothing.

Silence.

They were gone. The voices of the dryads. Of her birth mother, and the two creatures who were essentially her biological aunts. What had happened to them? Had the developers cleared out the grove? Was everything dying around her because they were gone?

Was she next?

She squeezed her eyes shut until her head started to throb again.

Footsteps.

Leila opened her eyes and spotted Sarika jumping to her feet and peering back out the window. She squatted back down at her side and took her hand. Landon bounded into the mansion with his fists balled up, his eyes hard. He looked down at Leila with a mixture of fury and concern.

"Sarika, help me out." He bent down and put his arms under Leila's legs.

"Wha-what are you doing?" Leila muttered.

"Getting you off the ground," he said, as Leila looped her arms around his neck. He hoisted her up, and the pain in her chest and head boomed. "It's okay," he said softly.

"It's going to be okay." He turned quickly to Sarika. "We have to get Leila the hell out of here."

"Why?" Sarika asked, as they started walking out of the mansion. "Who were you chasing? What is going on?"

"Some kind of poison. Maybe weed killer? I'm not sure what it is," Landon said firmly. "It's everywhere. We're not going to find *any* animals here."

"What?" Sarika exclaimed. "Why? Why would they . . ." she faded off, and Leila looked down at her from Landon's arms. Sarika's expression went cold, and she shook her head.

"They know," she said, softly. "Whoever it is, someone told them what's going on here. They know what our people are looking for." She stopped and stooped down to run her hand over the ground.

"Sarika, don't!" Landon cried.

She lifted her hand up to her nose and squinted. She immediately whipped her hand back and forth, and wiped it on her jeans.

"The poor mice. The other animals around here, your owl. What do we do?" Sarika asked.

"We keep Leila away from it. It's clearly hurting her," Landon said resolutely. "Let's get out of here." He turned to walk away from the mansion, and Leila could feel the world around her spinning as he moved back and forth. She swayed in his arms.

"N-no." Leila muttered, trying to move out of Landon's arms.

"What?" Landon asked, stopping. "What's wrong?"

Leila pointed back towards the mansion.

"We can't leave," she said, feeling like she had to force her voice out. "The, the dryads. We need to see if they're . . . if they made it." She coughed out the last few words and Landon held her tighter.

"Leila, I don't think—" he started.

"We're not discussing it," she said as sternly as she could. "I'll crawl there if I have to. If you take me home, I'll find a way back."

Landon looked over at Sarika, who shrugged in response.

"She's stubborn," she said, and Leila could hear the smile in her voice. "Let's go."

"Karayea!" Leila gasped as they walked into the grove. It took so much energy to even raise her voice. Landon took slow steps, each cautious and careful, muttering about how slippery and slick the soil around them was. He slid on the dead leaves a few times, and each time his foot made a quick, squishy sound against the earth Leila felt his hands grip her tightly, his strong arms flex around her as he cradled her against his chest. She pushed her head against him and took a deep breath, but the smell of sandalwood and sawdust had been replaced with a raw, harsh chemical smell that seemed to permeate the air around them.

"Do you . . . do you smell that?" Leila asked, pressing a hand against Landon's chest.

Landon looked at her and then at Sarika with a worried expression on his face.

The dark soil that they could see under the leaves that surrounded the grove was tinted an off, pale-blue color, and specks of the liquid stained the stone ring around the dryad's trees. They all still bore the red Xs from the developers. The dryads' trees were barren, their leaves gone.

"Tifola! Shorea!" Leila shouted as loud as she could. She coughed and shook her head against the pounding in the back of her skull. Sarika darted ahead of Landon, and they walked into the grove.

The trees were silent.

The woods were quiet.

The sounds of wildlife that normally scampered about most of Fairmount Park were simply gone. Leila looked around, moving her head slowly. No squirrels, no birds singing in the nearby trees. No insects lazily buzzing by her face.

Nothing.

"Let's get closer," Leila muttered.

Landon walked towards the three oak trees, which stood tall and quiet in the middle of the stone ring. He held Leila close as they approached the trees, and she stretched out from his arms to run her hand over the surface of the middle one, where Karayea dwelled.

"I wonder how long they've been poisoning the ground here," Leila said, her fingers caressing the hard bark on the tree's surface. "She wasn't acting the same the last time we were here, and the others . . ." She looked at the two trees, neither of which had awoken even the last time they had come to the grove. "What . . . what if they're gone?"

"I don't know," Landon said, shaking his head. "Will the park really wither up?" He looked up at the sky, towards the canopy, and then around, taking Leila with him for the spin. "I just, I can't imagine it. The city with no trees. No breathable air. No people."

And no me, Leila thought.

A rustling.

A soft breeze shook the empty branches in the trees, and the center tree split open.

Landon stumbled back a little at the resounding *crack* from the tree, and Leila could hear his feet sliding against the slick earth. She winced, preparing for the inevitable impact against the ground, when Sarika darted over, grabbing and steadying him.

"Whew. Thanks," Landon muttered as he regained his footing. Leila smiled at Sarika, who then gawked at something behind her. Leila turned around to spot Karayea watching them from inside the split oak tree.

"Hello, children," she said, her voice old and haunting. A soft smile appeared on her weathered, bark-like face.

"You're alive!" Leila exclaimed, despite the pain that pounded in her head at the effort. "I thought, I thought that was it. All of this." She waved at the poison on the ground from Landon's arms.

"The soil," Karayea said, the power gone from her voice. "It's in the soil, spilled upon the earth. Our power is fading, I feel the life in your city draining away."

"I know," Leila said. "All the trees, the leaves are falling off everywhere. Birds are leaving. It's all over the news. But no one understands why it is happening. But we're . . .

we're going to take care of it. We're going to tell the right people, and they'll clean it up. We . . ." she faded off.

Would anyone clean it up?

They'd come to the woods to get evidence of the endangered mouse. They'd brought the traps here to capture them and show people. They would tell the press, present their proof to the board and Dr. Cordova's team.

Leila looked around at the blue-ish earth, at the soil covered in poison. It glimmered on the ground like weed killer. She closed her eyes, shaking her head, but couldn't hear a thing. The silence of the woods, barren of life, of animals. It was the loudest of noises.

"It is fine, my sapling," Karayea said, reaching out a hand, her arm made of brambles and branches, her fingers small twigs with tiny leaves bursting from them. Her leaves had gone from bright green to a dull brown, and as she ran her fingers over Leila's face the leaves crumbled off her hands, breaking and dissipating into the wind. Leila looked at Karayea's once bright-green eyes, which had faded to brown.

"Why . . . why is this happening to you? Why now? After all this time, to find you and now to lose you. It isn't fair! It isn't right."

"We had some time. It is likely more than most," Karayea said, her incredibly human eyes sad and wet.

"What about Leila?" Landon choked out, holding her close. "What will happen to her? With all of this?"

Leila stared into Karayea's fading brown eyes.

The dryad didn't have to say it.

She knew. With that look, she knew.

"She's one of us," Karayea said, lowering her arm. "Just like all the trees surrounding these woods. Tall and bordering the rivers, thin and struggling in the human's cities . . . all of them . . . this whole park, as you and your friends have called it. As we fade," she gazed at Leila with a pained expression, "so, my dear, do you."

Leila's heart hammered in her chest as she glanced up at Landon, whose eyes were already watering.

"No," Sarika said, taking a step forward. "No. No. No. We will clean everything up here ourselves if we have to, chain ourselves to you and the other two. No bulldozer is going to come in here and tear you from your home. There are three of us, three of you—"

"Two," Karayea barely whispered.

A pause, full of silence.

"What?" Sarika asked.

"There are . . . two of us." The dryad walked over to the two trees that stood behind hers, her limbs creaking and groaning, and ran her hand over the one that had held Tifola. "I'm afraid my sister did not survive. I felt her leaving this world, returning to the Earth, just days ago."

Karayea turned and looked to Leila.

"You should know," Karayea said, walking towards her oak tree, her movements slowed and measured. "I have valued this time we have had, short as it may have been." She stepped inside her tree, and with loud cracks and snaps, it began sealing up but stopped halfway, leaving her exposed from her torso up.

"My sapling." She reached out from the tree, and again, ran her hand over Leila's face as Landon held her out towards the dryad. "I wanted so much more for you. A real life, among the humans. I never wanted you to know of this. I should have never called you here. But I watched you. I listened. Through the trees and the wind, as you grew and blossomed, and I knew you would want to help those other than yourself. This is who you are."

Leila sniffled back, closing her eyes, tears streaming down her face.

"It was always about more than just you and me . . ." Karayea said, pulling her arm back. "But at the same time, it never was."

"What do I do?" Leila asked.

"I'm not sure how long I have," Karayea said. "This ground, this soil . . ." she sighed, and the wind rustled around them. "I'm stronger than my sisters. My sister," she corrected herself, her eyes closed and pained. "If these woods aren't mended . . ." She looked at Leila, her eyes hard and worried, washed with concern and fear.

"If you only had a few days left in this world," Karayea said, her voice gone quiet, "how would you spend them?"

Sarika stared forward intently, fire brewing in her eyes. Landon's mouth was turned up into a forced line, as though he was holding back something, and his eyes were watering. Just like that, it was the old him again, trying to hide who he really was, only this time it was so easy to see through it all. Leila felt his arms around her, holding her tighter and tighter with each line of conversation with Karayea, as though she might float away and up into the sky without his grasp. She glanced down at Sarika, who stared forward intently, fire brewing in her eyes. Her thoughts wandered off to Jon and Liz, back at home.

How she'd called Jon her dad, and how he'd never asked for it.

How Liz desperately wanted to be called Mom, and how she'd struggled with the word for the person who deserved it most.

Her heart felt as though it was trying to wrench itself from her chest.

"I think I'd spend them just like this," she said, nodding. "Maybe say the right things to the right people. As often as possible."

"Then go," Karayea said, the tree starting to seal up around her. "Say those things. Don't leave one word unsaid, one word forgotten."

Leila glanced up at Landon, then to Sarika, her thoughts again wandering.

"I won't," Leila said, reaching out to Karayea. The dryad held her hand, giving it a soft squeeze, before vanishing inside the tree. "I promise."

"What do we do?" Sarika asked, tears welling up in her eyes as Leila settled into the passenger seat of Landon's truck. "I can't lose you. I won't lose you."

"I don't know," Leila said as Landon closed the door and made his way around the truck. "I don't know what to do."

"I think I know where we can start," Landon said, as he got into the truck and fastened his seatbelt, his movements quick and precise. "We need to figure out who this is." He pulled out his cell phone to show a photo to Leila and Sarika. "This is the person who was in the grounds earlier, with the bottles of poison. I managed to get one somewhat clear photo before . . . what is it?"

Leila glared at the phone, and when she looked up she saw a similar fury washing over Sarika's face.

"What?" Landon insisted.

"We know that person," Sarika snarled, as she kicked the back seat of the truck. "Hell, I can't believe this."

"Who?" Landon asked, taking his phone and staring at the photo. "Who is it?"

"Just drive," Sarika said. "We'll explain on the way. Looks like we don't need that mouse. We just caught ourselves a rat."

PROTEST CANCELED, DANGER (PLEASE READ!)
Posted by A Dash of Paprika
AUGUST 28th, 2017 | 6:02PM
The protest this weekend by the Thomas Mansion in Fairmount Park is canceled.

We'll post more updates when we have them, but please, PLEASE do not go there. Construction is starting soon, and poison has been sprayed on the ground to presumably eliminate any "pests" and overgrown plants in the area. We don't want any of you getting sick, so please, stay home.

WithouttheY and I will be sending out DMs to everyone who planned to attend, and if any of you know each other IRL, please reach out and let one another know.

RE: PROTEST CANCELED, DANGER (PLEASE READ!)
Posted by Dr. Cordova
AUGUST 28th, 2017 | 7:15PM
My God. I hope you're all okay! Be sure to clean up and take a seriously long shower. Any sign of the field mice?

> RE: PROTEST CANCELED, DANGER (PLEASE READ!)
> *Posted by WithouttheY*

AUGUST 28th, 2017 | 7:17PM
No, we tried. I'm afraid there's not much else we can do.

RE: PROTEST CANCELED, DANGER (PLEASE READ!)
Posted by Dr. Cordova
AUGUST 28th, 2017 | 7:25PM
That is tragic. Just tragic.

> RE: PROTEST CANCELED, DANGER (PLEASE READ!)
> *Posted by WithouttheY*
> AUGUST 28th, 2017 | 8:02PM
> It's okay, Dr. Cordova, check your DMs and emails. We'll be in touch regarding some other projects.

RE: PROTEST CANCELED, DANGER (PLEASE READ!)
Posted by DeLaJessica
AUGUST 28th, 2017 | 9:02PM
LOL.

> RE: PROTEST CANCELED, DANGER (PLEASE READ!)
> *Posted by A Dash of Paprika*
> AUGUST 28th, 2017 | 9:12PM
> Karma is a bitch, Jessica. Remember that. Banned.

XXVII

"Is this the one?" Leila asked, leaning against the cold metal of the lockers that lined the hall. Today was the day. The last day. Her body ached with every movement.

"Yeah," Gwen muttered, staring at her feet.

"Are you . . . are you sure you want to be here?" Shawn asked, looking up and down the hallway.

"Yes," Gwen said, her tone a little more resolute. "I'm sure."

Leila and Shawn leaned against the lockers as Gwen fidgeted awkwardly, her eyes fixed on the cold, hard floor for what felt like an hour. She resisted the urge to pull out her phone and check the time, making quick glances at Shawn and Gwen to pass the time, small nods between the three of them, as the clock ticked down. Everything hinged on the moment being just right.

Jessica and Rebekah pushed through the pair of double doors at the end of the relatively empty hall, their conversation unintelligible but clearly interesting, their tone sarcastic and smooth.

"Here they come," Shawn said softly, speaking out of the side of his mouth.

"You ready?" Leila asked.

"Hell, yeah," Shawn said resolutely.

"Gwen?" Leila glanced over, but received no response. The girl stared at her shoes, breathing quickly. "Hey, Gwen." She looked up. "You're doing the right thing, you know that, right?"

Gwen nodded softly.

Jessica and Rebekah drew closer, laughing at whatever was glowing back at them on those screens. When they were just a few feet away they stopped abruptly and glared at the three of them.

"Uh, what is this?" Jessica spat, gesturing at them and then glaring at Gwen. "What are you doing with them? And why are you two at my locker?" Jessica covered her mouth and sputtered a laugh. "Wow. You look terrible."

Leila stepped forward and ignored the flash of rage that brewed in her chest and the ache in her legs at just taking that one step. She pulled her phone out of her pocket, ignoring the small burst of pain that nudged at her with every move.

"Recognize this?" Leila asked, pushing the screen towards Jessica with gritted teeth.

Jessica staggered back and looked at Rebekah, her eyes wide with panic, then turned back to the girls and at Shawn.

"Where did you get that?" Jessica said, the confidence gone from her voice despite the anger in her words.

"We know what you've been doing," Leila said, putting her phone back in her pocket. She coughed, and took a deep breath before continuing. "And you're going to tell us why."

"The hell I am," Jessica spat. "You *three*," she emphasized, glaring at Gwen, who promptly shrunk back, "can go fuck yourselves. You and your stupid trees."

"Why?" Leila asked, taking a step forward and wincing. "Why destroy that patch of woods? What's any of it have to do with you? Any of it at all? Why would you even be out there in the first place?"

"What's it even matter?" Jessica replied. "It's just a bunch of trees and whatever it was that you and that friend of yours were freaking out about over on your dumb message board. A rat or something."

"A mouse, and you have no idea what you've just done!" Leila shouted. She moved to rush at her but stopped when a wave of weakness washed over her. Her legs buckled a little, and Shawn grabbed her, steadying her.

"What I've done?" Jessica asked, laughing. "Who the hell cares? It's all coming down tonight anyway. And now your precious little animals or whatever won't get in the way of actual progress. My dad works hard, and all your nonsense was slowing him down."

"Your dad cares about the environment just as much as we do!" Shawn shouted. "You keep painting him to be some villain but he isn't. You can't hide this from him. There are going to be consequences."

"Please, like what? He *owns* people like your family, Shawn. He might care more about his little projects than he does about me, but whatever. After this, that'll change. The only thing that could have stopped this project were those stupid mice of yours, and now they are gone for sure. Just, you know, a little early."

"He'll think you're a monster, which is exactly what you are," Shawn shouted.

With a resounding crack, Jessica slapped Shawn across the face.

"Shawn!" Leila shouted.

"What the hell, Jessica?" Shawn yelled, glaring at her. "You can't—"

"I can do whatever I want," Jessica spat. "You don't get to talk to me like that."

"People are going to look into it all," Leila said, pointing at finger at Jessica. "You cheated."

"So?" Jessica scoffed. "No one's gonna know. Yes, I killed your little mice and probably everything else in that forest, but my dad's project gets to move forward. Maybe one day I'll tell him, and he'll actually appreciate me for once."

Leila sighed, her chest grew heavy, and she shook her head.

"What?" Jessica snarled.

"It's just sad, is all." Leila shrugged. "I actually feel kind of sorry for you. I . . . I know what it's like to have questions about your family, to feel a little different. You know?"

"No, I don't know, and I don't need people like you feeling sorry for me," Jessica said. "I have everything, and you have—"

Leila banged on the locker by Gwen.

"Did you get all that, Sarika?"

The locker squeaked open, and Sarika squeezed out of the space sideways. Her phone was in her hand, and she pressed a button on it.

"Sure did." She waved the phone in Jessica's face. "You're going down."

Jessica reached out and swatted the phone out of her hand, sending it crashing to the ground in a shattering of glass and plastic, bits splintering all along the cold, hard hallway.

"Aw, what the—" Sarika started.

"It was a nice try," Jessica said, walking over to the phone. She stomped on it and promptly kicked the broken pieces down the hallway. "I swear, every time some idiot tries to trap somebody in movies with a recording, I always think they should have just broken the thing. But—"

"What kind of idiot do you think I am?" Sarika shouted. She glared at Rebekah. "You should really get out of here." She turned back to Jessica as Rebekah bolted down the hall. "I had that recording saving to my Dropbox and my cloud drive. You really thinking breaking my phone is going to stop me? Please. I'm not some dumb supervillain in a cartoon."

Jessica stared.

"But you are," Sarika said coldly.

"What are . . . what are you even going to do with that?" Jessica groaned, leaning against the row of lockers. "Construction starts tonight. *Tonight.* No one's going to stop everything from getting torn down. Your precious little park belongs to my family. My dad controls the rights to—"

"Well that's just it, isn't it?" Leila asked, breathing hard and trying to smile at Jessica. "It would be terribly easy to stop the construction and demolition if the rights to develop there no longer belonged to him."

"What are you even talking about?" Jessica asked, her eyes full of panic.

"Here's the thing," Leila continued. "What you did, poisoning public land in a city park? That's a serious crime. Killing an endangered species? That's a federal crime. Double the time, no doubt. And poisoning them maliciously and on purpose, contaminating, what, *acres* of land? What do you think, Sarika?"

"Sounds like serious jail time to me, never mind the fines." Sarika crossed her arms, and Leila fought the urge to smile. She made an excellent bad cop in this situation. "Any scholarships you were hoping to get this year? Bye."

"Colleges in general?" Leila added. "Forget it. Who wants the girl that was splattered all over the news for murdering endangered animals in an historic section of a national park?"

"No one?" Sarika asked.

"No one," Leila said, staring at Jessica hard. "And a powerful man like your father will be really disappointed. I mean, incredibly disappointed. How would he recover? People might even think he had something to do with all of it. Might shut him out."

"Maybe he did have something to do with it!" Sarika exclaimed. "Who says he didn't?"

"Okay!" Jessica shouted, tears streaming down her face. Her pale skin had turned bright red. "Okay. What can I do? What do you want me to do?"

"Oh, we just want you to squirm and be miserable,"

Sarika replied. "Leila's dad, who sits on that board with your dad, already has the photo of you poisoning the park and running away. He should also have the recording we just made, so . . ."

Sarika shrugged.

Jessica took a step forward. She balled her fists and shook them at Leila and Sarika.

"This isn't over," she snarled. "And you!" She pointed at Gwen. "How could you? I *made* you in this school. People only know you because of me."

"Maybe I don't want them to anymore," Gwen said, crossing her arms. "You're a bad person."

"Shawn?" Jessica said, her voice weak and sad.

"I've got nothing to say to you," he said, staring at her hard. "You manipulated me. Threatened me. Made it seem like your family would shut mine down if . . . I broke up with you. I'm my own person."

"Whatever. Fuck all you." Jessica turned on her heel and stormed away, her shoes smacking hard against the floor as she disappeared down the empty hall. "This isn't over!" she shouted, her voice echoing in the hallway.

"Yeah, it is," Leila said. She leaned back against the lockers, the metal surface cold against her back, and slid down to the floor. Sarika knelt down and threw her arms around her, hugging her tightly. Shawn edged up cautiously to join in, his embrace soft and barely noticeable.

"Hey," Leila said to Gwen while Sarika and Shawn hugged her. Gwen looked pensively at them, offering a small smile. "Get in here."

They hugged in the hallway until the bell rang.

CLEAN UP DAY AT THE THOMAS MANSION (SATURDAY!)

Posted by WithouttheY

SEPTEMBER 1st, 2017 | 1:02PM

Hey everyone!

After the accidental poisoning of the grounds around the Thomas Mansion, Philadelphia's *GRID Magazine*, that local mag that talks about the environment and sustainability and all that, is organizing a clean-up crew to fix what's happened in the now-preserved and donated area.

If you're coming, please bring protective gloves that won't absorb too much liquid. Those weird yellow ones your grandparents have under their kitchen sinks will work just fine. You know the kind.

Also, if you have buckets, brushes, and tear-free shampoo, that would be very welcome. While we haven't found too many poisoned animals in the area, we will be expanding the search beyond the grounds to look for sick animals that wandered away from the area after being poisoned.

So protective gloves are key, because as cute as squirrels and chipmunks and rabbits might be, when they are delusional and poisoned they're mad and will bite. Wouldn't you?

We'll meet at the grounds at noon on Saturday, and bagged lunches will be provided as well as snacks, thanks to *GRID*. We'll be cleaning until dark, and into the weekend. Questions? You can DM me for my cell number.

Thanks so much!

RE: CLEAN UP DAY AT THE THOMAS MANSION
Posted by DontCallMeGwenifer
SEPTEMBER 1st, 2017 | 1:16PM
See you soon!

RE: CLEAN UP DAY AT THE THOMAS MANSION
Posted by Dr. Cordova
SEPTEMBER 1st, 2017 | 2:02PM
Check your DMs / texts. I'll be by with a crew from the Academy of Natural Sciences this afternoon, as well as through the weekend with whoever we can spare.
We're all very proud of you girls.

> RE: CLEAN UP DAY AT THE THOMAS MANSION
> *Posted by Toothless*
> SEPTEMBER 1st, 2017 | 2:17PM
> HEY.

> RE: CLEAN UP DAY AT THE THOMAS MANSION
> *Posted by A Dash of Paprika*
> SEPTEMBER 1st, 2017 | 2:23PM
> LOL.

RE: CLEAN UP DAY AT THE THOMAS MANSION
Posted by *Shawn Jawn*
SEPTEMBER 1st, 2017 | 6:02PM
I am so in. I got my father to donate some materials too. I'll be there with the rest of B.E.A.C.! Or, you know, who we've got left and all.

RE: CLEAN UP DAY AT THE THOMAS MANSION
Posted by *A Dash of Paprika*
SEPTEMBER 1st, 2017 | 7:15PM
Well, well. Look who it is. Just kidding, glad to have you, Captain Planet.

RE: CLEAN UP DAY AT THE THOMAS MANSION
Posted by *WithouttheY*
SEPTEMBER 1st, 2017 | 7:18PM
Come on, Paprika.

XXVIII

"I need some cleaner over here!"

"Someone toss me a sponge?"

"Hey! I need a bathing basin, I found a sick rabbit."

"What do we do with empty bottles?"

The voices around the grove were loud and frantic as people walked through the area excitedly, passing materials back and forth to one another, bags wrapped around their shoes as they made their way over the poison-sprayed earth. Leila knew most of the poison was gone, but she couldn't tell the others how she knew. Walking on the ground didn't leave her with the massive pains it had earlier, just a dull ache. And her hair was starting to grow back, in a way that felt strange and unnatural, oddly fast. She could almost feel it happening. Leila smiled and nodded at people as they walked by, each with that familiar look in their eyes, the sort you gave to someone who you kind of know because of the Internet, but not really. She'd never posted photos on the board, and neither did many of the people on the site, but somehow, she could just tell.

"How's it going over here?" Leila asked.

Sarika, who was busy scrubbing out some of the blue poison from the rocks surrounding the dryads' trees, wiped her forehead with the back of her arm and wrung out a rag into a bucket next to her.

"Slow, but I'm making some dents. Look." She pointed at some of the nearby stones, which all shone with the clean, slick reflection of water, as if it had just rained an hour ago. "But of course, there's still all that. Stay away from there." In the opposite direction the stones still glimmered with the blue color, like a filmy slime. "But hey, we've got time, right? We do have time?"

"We do. I feel better," Leila said, nodding with a smile. "Have you seen Landon?"

"He was over doing some repairs at the Trust earlier, but I think he's helping your, um," Sarika stopped, looking over at the dryads' trees in the circle. Landon, Jon, and Mr. De La Costa were standing there talking to one another, hands on their hips, heads nodding in excitement.

"I think you can say it," Leila said, warmth coursing through her chest.

Sarika smiled.

"He's over there with your dad."

Leila stepped over the ring of stones and walked into the circle just as Landon dipped a rag into a bucket of cleanser. He looked up at her and smiled.

"I just don't understand how a tree can wither up and die that fast from that cocktail of, what was it? Weed killer and—" Jon had started.

"We don't have to dig into it, Jon, really." Mr. De La Costa said. "I feel bad enough as it is, you know."

"I know, I know," Jon said, nodding. "Sorry. It's just, you know, interesting."

"Right." Mr. De La Costa said, and grabbed a sponge. Lisabeth walked up behind Jon and wrapped her arms around his waist.

"Hey darling," Jon said, giving her a kiss on the cheek and turning back to the trees. "These two look fine, but damn. That's such a tragedy. I can't even imagine how old this girl was." Jon ran his fingers over the bark of one of the dryads' trees.

"It really is sad," Lisabeth said, her head tucked over Jon's shoulder. "I'll get started cleaning around the roots here. Leila, you need anything?"

"No, I'm good. Thanks, Mom," Leila said. Liz smiled and hurried off as Leila stared at the tree.

It was Tifola.

Leila smiled sadly. Jon had wondered how old the tree might have been.

He really had no idea.

And really, Leila had no idea either. The dryads had left so many questions unanswered, and she wondered if they'd ever awaken and talk to her again. While life seemed to be returning slowly to Philadelphia, flowers re-blooming, trees sprouting buds, scientists scrambling madly around town, there was no sign of the two remaining dryads in the grove.

"Leila, you have any more of that paint remover?" Jon asked. He picked up a small bucket with a rag in it near the stones, a spray bottle dangling off the edge.

"Sure, Dad," Leila said, a blast of warmth coursing through her chest. Jon smiled and then spritzed the large oak, scrubbing at the large red X on the bark. Bits of bark flaked off as he scrubbed. Leila winced.

"Careful there," Leila said, as pieces of the bark fall off the tree.

"Don't worry, it's made of an orange and citrus solvent. It won't hurt these any further. You were right about this place, Leila," Jon said, taking a step away from the dryads' trees and setting his hands on his hips. "It does have this magical feel to it."

"I agree," Mr. De La Costa chimed in, stepping towards them and nodding. "I've apologized for my daughter already, yes?"

"Hah!" Jon smiled and patted Mr. De La Costa on the back. "Seriously, Patrick, relax. As far as anyone is concerned, we found the mice. I mean, technically we did. Your secret is safe with us. Isn't it?"

He looked at Leila expectantly, and she nodded, offering a soft smile.

"As long as this place stays safe," Leila said, shrugging.

"Good, good." Mr. De La Costa said, wringing his hands. "It will. You can rest assured of that. I've already put in some proposals for a restoration project for the mansion. And some of the Academy staff will be around to work on the mice habitats." His eyes looked beyond Leila, towards the entrance to the grove, where Jessica was angrily spraying water over the dried-up shrubs and bushes. Leila scowled.

"Gentle, Jessica!" shouted Mr. De La Costa, shaking his head. Jessica glared at him and sprayed the water about wildly.

"God damn it," Mr. De La Costa muttered. "Excuse me. Jessica!" He stormed off towards her.

Leila looked over at Landon, who grinned at her. Shawn, Britt, and Mikey were closer to the mansion, working on the stones around the grounds there, but she could hear Britt's distinctive loud laugh echoing through the bare trees. She grabbed a rag out of the bucket, and approached the center tree.

Karayea.

She removed the bottle of cleanser from her belt, and sprayed the red X at the front of the tree. She scrubbed gently.

"Leila, come on, you really need to push into it," Jon said.

"It's okay," Leila said. She gently brushed the red paint away, watching the X fade into a pinkish color as it came off the tree, even if the bark around it lost a bit of its color with it. "I've got time."

Leila closed her eyes, and pressed her bare hand against the tree, listening.

She sighed.

And the wind rustled.

♥ 102 Likes

WithouttheY Major Willow, two months old.

sarikathepaprika ♥

Acknowledgments

The Girl and the Grove was a novel I'd been wanting to write for a few years. My darling wife, Nena, had been pushing me to write a novel about adoption and identity, to write about something so deeply personal to me.

"Write the tree book!" she would say. I thank her endlessly for giving me the courage to try. This book is here first and foremost because of her, and due to the following amazing people.

My rockstar agent Dawn Frederick and my amazing editor Mari Kesselring, for pushing me and this novel and for never giving up. And to the whole team at Flux, for believing in this book.

To Adi Alsaid and Zoraida Cordova for that retreat in Mexico. You are keepers of magic.

My Philadelphia writing group: Randy Ribay, Julie Leung, Lauren Saft, and Katherine Locke. Thank you for challenging me every step of the way while I fought with this story.

Good friends Blair Thornburgh, Preeti Chhibber, Swapna Lovin, Ashley Poston, Chris Urie, Mikey Ilagan, and Lauren Gibaldi for the constant pep talks. My P.S. Literary colleagues, whom I adore to pieces.

A huge thank you to McCormick Templeman, Melissa

Albert, Heidi Schulz, Shveta Thakrar, Elizabeth Keenan, Laurel Amberdine, Alisa Hathaway, Rebecca Enzor, Brenna Ehrlich, Thomas Torre, Willa Smith, Natasha Razi, Leah Rhyne, Amber Hart, McKelle George, Jenny Kaczorowski, Nic Stone, Samira Ahmed, Kim Liggett, Sangu Mandanna, Hannah Siddiqui, Naseem Jamnia, Phillip Hilliker, and Bill Blume.

And to my amazing parents and my sister Lauren, thank you for giving me a story.

About the Author

Eric Smith is a young adult author and literary agent who grew up in the wilds of New Jersey. When he isn't working on books (his and other people's) he can be found writing about books for places like *Book Riot* and *Paste Magazine*. He lives with his wife, Nena, and their legion of small furry animals. Find him online at www.ericsmithrocks.com or on Twitter at @ericsmithrocks.